The Three Behind the Psychologist

By Courtland O.K. Smith

Table of Contents

A Thank You to Bill

[Two weeks later]

Bill,

First things first: I have decided to begin by thanking you. But let me be clear, this was a difficult decision made after much deliberation; I considered a spectrum of options ranging from profanity-laced belligerence to... well, thanking you. After much thought I have decided on this particular extreme because, despite your apparent and repeated attempts to infuriate me, you are still helping me and this is help that I unfortunately and desperately need. This is something that I have to remind myself of over and over so that I do not lock into my mind the certainty of your strangulation upon our next meeting. Rest assured, any homicidal impulses I might have harbored have been checked.

But, as I said, I have had to and will continue to have to remind myself that, after my arrest, followed by the abysmal performance from my court-appointed lawyer during the sham hearing, and then my resulting imprisonment, it was you who came when I called, you who assembled a new team of lawyers, and you who have been working with them so that the pending trial might at least approximate justice.

You asked me to spend some of my abundant idle prison time writing down my account of the week leading to my "situation" so the process of my exoneration might be sped up and you and the people you are working with would be able to quickly familiarize yourselves with every detail of the time period in question and thus devise an appropriate way forward and away from the wrath of my in-laws as they attempt to avenge Julie after everything that happened. This account you requested is nearly complete.

I would have preferred it if you had read what I had written before our previous meetings, but I am hopeful that you will, as you state, "read through thoroughly then make an appointment to meet with" me, after I send to you the final sections.

For the sake of clarification, your selflessness needs to be reiterated over and over as I sit here in my prison cell—*Bill is trying to help me, Bill is trying to help me*—because your tone consistently falls deep into the well-defined category of condescension and far below the bounds of professional courtesy. Not only that, but you keep adding instructions to the initial "write your account of the week," as if I were a trained monkey with a typewriter. I, here and now, politely refuse all your additional instructions. I will not "put additional thought into what has happened beyond a 'straight recounting of the week' so we can discuss [my] perspective and perception when we meet." Additionally, I will not "pay closer attention to Courtland's connection to everything; to [me], to [my] sessions, to [my] demeanor." He was a patient who committed suicide; he has no bearing on what happened with Julie. End of story. I will continue my account of the week. Plain and simple.

I have said it before and in closing I will say it again: Bill, I am not one of your patients.

I remain,

-Nick

P.S. It will be up to you to place this note into the report when you receive it. I'm done keeping your files for you.

Friday Morning

From a sharp fleeting glimpse of the ceiling piercing through the blurry pinkish mist inside my eyelids to an overwhelming black and back to the quick stab of focus on the ceiling; cycling through, back and forth, black and white, from waking to sleeping, eyes opened and closed. The morning felt overcast and thick with a shivering cold humidity as I huddled under the one thin sheet that remained atop my contorted body.

My phone was beeping every two minutes for some unknown reason, maybe a message, maybe a low battery. The beep, normally enduring less than a countable second, now occupied several seconds in my head, ever increasing in annoyance and length, but I had not the energy to end it.

Julie unintentionally broke the cycle, entering the bedroom and crouching down to retrieve an item from the floor in front of the bed. Pulled from the cyclical daze, I rolled over to inspect the phone's screen. 8:45 a.m.

"Hello, Nicholas." She spoke quietly, softly, as her seemingly disembodied head floated above the foot of the bed. The tone of her voice solidified an unspoken understanding that the previous day had been nothing more than the previous day.

My mind briefly went back to the abrupt ending of the cocktail party at the Martins' Townhouse as Edward, the host and a close friend to Julie's family, became inebriated beyond any discernible sign of control over faculties. It had been clear that Julie was shaken by the incident, her nerve lacerated, her psyche agitated.

For those few last minutes at the Martins' Townhouse, Julie, and everyone there, had had to endure Edward's very public misconduct as he acted out in his belligerent state. This was a man she grew up with and frequently called "Uncle Ed" so she was justified in being afraid of what would come of the incident, how she would inform her parents or even if she should be the one to tell them. It had disturbed her to a hush for the remainder of the previous night, but, come morning, she was putting it behind her and was, with her tone, informing me of that fact.

I confirmed with, "Good morning, Julie." Then, seeing a glass in her hand, I asked, "What do you have there?"

"Glass of water. Must have been here for a couple days; I completely forgot it. Teeming with living creatures now."

Before I could respond, we were inundated with the sound of the birds chirping, but for only a moment. They halted quite suddenly, quite uncharacteristically. Julie and I looked at one another, expressions of inquisitive confusion. "They must have flown away across the heavens," I said to her whimsically.

"I'm sure they're being fruitful and multiplying," she responded. Then she stood up, displaying a colorful summer dress with a myriad of pastels, blue being the overarching theme. It flowed lazily after her, mimicking her movements, but a second after she had made them, as she began to walk toward the doorway.

"Looks like rain…" Her voice faded away as she turned down the hall on her way to the living room, leaving me with my impossible dream of returning to unconsciousness.

Knowing myself incapable of returning to a comfortable consistent slumber, I swung my legs to the hardwood floor and held my head in my hands, elbows on knees.

"I really don't want to go..." I shouted, forcing my voice out from my throat through the bedroom and down the hallway to the living room.

"We're only visiting for three days," Julie shouted back.

"Three days is a long time with your family."

Julie then tried to soften the blow. "When we get there, the day will almost be over. And we're leaving on Sunday. So it's really only Saturday that we'll be there, one day. Factor in sleeping; it's just a couple hours really."

"Right..." I agreed sarcastically as I lifted myself from the bed then stumbled across the hall to the bathroom.

The shower was warm for just long enough to become comfortable, relaxed, unguarded. Then the water went ice cold for three jarring, freezing seconds before returning to warm again, as if nothing had happened. The shock my mind and body went through was too traumatizing to fall back into the hypnotic state of relaxation I had previously attained. I toweled myself off, still shaking, tense, angry. The aroma of cooking bacon wafted down the hallway, the scent further frustrating me for some unexplained reason.

Quickly I threw on a pair of loose gray sweatpants accompanied by an equally baggy brown T-shirt. Both fit incorrectly; the left leg of the pants was noticeably shorter than the right and the left side of the shirt stretched just far enough from the correct size and shape to be noticeable at a glance. I did not care in the least. I was comfortable.

I took my old duffel bag from the back of the closet and placed it on the bed.

Julie barged in, instantly complaining. "Why do you always do this?"

"Do what?"

"Wait until the last minute to pack! We need to leave soon."

"It takes five seconds to pack," I insisted as I walked to the closet and grabbed a pair of pants, a collared shirt, and my rarely worn but old and dirty sneakers, the aglets brittle and broken, releasing the fraying ends of the shoelaces in every direction. I shoved the clothes into the bag, zipped it to a close, and announced triumphantly, "Look, I'm all packed!"

Unamused, Julie snapped back, "You need more than that: toothbrush, socks, underwear, and swim trunks, don't forget swim trunks."

"What can I say, Julie? I like to fly by the seat of my pants." Knowing Julie hated that expression because it made absolutely no sense, I used it in an attempt to frustrate her into walking out of the bedroom, thus allowing me a last bit of alone time before the weekend.

"Fine," she grumbled, falling prey to my ploy and exiting the room, but my time of solitude was but a fleeting moment, broken again by Julie's voice as she reentered.

"Are you going to wear that?" she asked with a needlessly degrading tone; I had not questioned her choice of attire.

"Yes, I am," I said as I attempted to shove my left foot into my right sneaker.

"Great, so you'll be wearing your discount irregular merchandise to my parents' house? They'll love that."

"We're going to be in the car for hours. Every New Yorker is driving in the same direction on the same highway at the same time. I want to be comfortable. Okay?" I persisted in pushing my left foot into the wrong shoe without realizing the problem.

"Everyone is going to ask you if you just finished jogging or something. Some joke like that to mock you."

"What do I care what they think?" I said as convincingly as possible.

"Fine, suit yourself," she allowed.

"That's what I'm trying to do!" I said, angry at my inability to fit into my old shoes.

"Come on, Nick... They're my family." Her tone softened.

"I'll change when I get there, alright?" I said, hoping the hollow offer would pacify her.

"Fine, that's fine," she responded, visibly relieved. "The shoe is on the wrong foot, by the way," she added.

I looked down, embarrassed; then tried the correct foot in the right shoe. Perfect fit.

Julie stopped laughing at my confusion long enough to ask, "How do I look?"

Knowing that anything less than "you look great," would be treated as an insult, I simply responded, "You look great."

Julie smiled, turned, then left the room, her dress flowing behind her.

Both feet finally in the correct shoes, I said to myself, "They fit as comfortably as I remember." Then I shouted to Julie, "You know, maybe you can go without me? I'll just be a bother to you while you're visiting with your family."

"No, you're coming! And we're going to have a wonderful time!" she shouted back.

"It's just that your family really doesn't like me. And they have absolutely no trouble showing it."

"That's simply not true, Nick," she insisted.

"Uh… yes, it is. Do you remember the first time we visited there… right after we got married? Your mother took me outside and said, 'Nicholas, every member of this family really doesn't like you and we have absolutely no trouble showing it.' "

"I don't think that ever happened. I don't even remember that trip," Julie responded.

"It was our honeymoon, Julie. We didn't have any money so we couldn't go anywhere. You convinced your parents to host us. How do you not remember this?"

"I don't remember it happening like that... Are you done packing?" she asked.

"You honestly don't remember? We spent the better part of the summer there. And by 'better' I certainly mean 'longer' because there was nothing *better* about that portion of the summer, other than its duration."

As I spoke I finished filling the duffel bag with another set of clothes, reluctantly adding underwear and socks.

"You know who will be there?" Julie spoke loudly and with forced pleasantness, changing the subject. "Adrianne. She's the writer. She wrote that book."

"Who?" I asked.

"Adrianne. I saw her on Monday with Kathy and Abigail. And Tuesday also."

"What kind of person is she?" I asked, hoping Julie would paint a fair picture to jog my memory.

"Oh, she's wonderful. I love her. She's big in the art world. You wouldn't like her though."

"What a condescending thing to say. Like I am incapable of seeing what you see in her?" I was indignant.

"It's just that... you don't like anybody," she responded.

I said nothing, knowing well that she had me there. My phone slid comfortably into my pants pocket before I grabbed the duffel bag and walked across the narrow hall to the bathroom to retrieve my still slightly wet toothbrush.

"Moist," I said aloud, then cringed at the oddly upsetting word.

The duffel bag hit the couch with a soft thud, absorbing the impact by shifting its shape to a flatter stance. I readied my back for the uncomfortable wooden chair as I approached the small wooden table in anticipation of my breakfast.

Julie saw that I was waiting expectantly; so she slowly removed the single piece of cold bacon that was languishing in one of the pans on the stove and the remaining half of an egg's worth of scrambled eggs in the other and slid them onto a small plate. She then walked slowly, dramatically over to the wooden table and delicately dropped the plate in front of me. Most of the eggs bounced off and fell onto the table. Unfazed, I ate every bite, even those from the table, which would have disgusted me more had I not been ravenous.

After ingesting the cold scraps, then lingering on the small wooden chair for another fifteen minutes, I became bored then anxious that we were still in the apartment. But Julie was nowhere to be seen.

"What are you doing?" I finally shouted. "Let's go! What are we waiting for? You said we had to leave soon!"

"I'm in the bathroom." Her muffled voice came through the bathroom door.

"Fine then. I'll go get the car and meet you out front."

I grabbed my duffel bag and keys before taking one last look at the apartment, then suddenly decided to leave the door open behind me. I knew exiting the bathroom to discover the door ajar would twist into Julie, but its open position mollified my anger so the decision was upheld.

I further justified my pettiness by reflecting that at least I was consistent in my churlishness. Julie, on the other hand, had been jumping back and forth between sad and angry and complacent. It became impossible to guess, impossible to gauge the temperature of an appropriate response, so I had stopped trying. Her actions felt like constant attacks, her tactics guerilla style. Leaving the door ajar was a defensive proactive retaliative offensive move, reminding her that I was still there, still kicking, despite my own complacency.

The downward spiral of the staircase felt uncharacteristically bright for a windowless hole to the dungeon that is the ground level city. I descended quickly in an attempt to burn off some of the excess energy that had built up when I misjudged our time of departure.

Reaching the lobby and holding the duffel bag in my right hand, I half jogged to the large iron and glass door of our Brownstone. I shook my head, disgusted at my ongoing lie, claiming the building on several occasions. But the lie had become not just my own, but Julie's too. Never did I witness her claim the building as our own, but she never stopped me. On occasion, when I argued in favor of our *choice* to rent the building's apartments to our low-income "tenants," she would nod or verbally agree. It was curious really; Julie prided herself on her honesty, never telling a lie in her life. But still she maintained this mistruth.

The day was truly bright, not like the fictitious bright that fluorescently illuminated the stairwell. The sky was clear, no hint of rain in the near future, and the ground was only slightly moist. Again, I cringed at the word as it squished between my toes.

Must have been cloudy earlier, I mused as I thought of Julie's incorrect morning forecast, "Looks like rain."

Cars passed in both directions, up and down the sloped street, as shadows cut their paths into a thousand separate but fluid pieces.

As I strolled into the garage, I waved to the rude parking attendant who always pressured me for a tip despite the fact that I parked and drove out my own car. He smiled obnoxiously and waved while saying something to another parking attendant I did not recognize.

Down to the second floor belowground, I turned the corner to see the rolling monument to my fear and selfishness shining out from its shadowy place of rest. The lights flashed at the touch of a button on the key remote followed by the driver door rising to greet me. I tossed my duffel bag through the opening and onto the passenger seat before strenuously lowering myself into the hip hugging soft seat. The door came down, sealing me in solitude. I placed the key in its slot and pressed the start button before taking my phone out of my pocket and plugging it in.

The dark green car crept quietly out of its space. I felt powerful. I felt untouchable, unquestionably better than the parking attendants. The new one's bottom jaw dropped down two inches as I passed. The one I recognized was sure to look away, ignoring the absurdly abysmal gap between the have and the have-nots.

" 'Blessed are the poor'?" I obnoxiously questioned aloud, disregarding the quote's real meaning of being blessed when one recognizes that they are poor in spirituality.

The car moved slowly around the block, dodging potholes, people. I stopped in front of the Brownstone expecting Julie to be standing in front, but she was nowhere in sight so I sat and waited impatiently. My fears began to multiply about spending the weekend with Julie's family, all of whom despised not only my status as a legal member but my very existence. I knew there was no action I could take to insulate myself from their jibes, so I did nothing but wait and occasionally rev the engine.

———

To the Hamptons

After ten minutes, I pressed the off button and opened the driver's door to bring my duffel bag around to the trunk. I stood waiting outside of the car for another ten minutes before Julie finally emerged from the building, struggling with two large suitcases. Slowly I walked up the steps to assist her. No words were exchanged before or after she turned and disappeared back into the building.

Why would she need this much stuff? I asked myself as I placed the luggage gently in the trunk. Then I stood for ten more minutes, waiting and staring up at our purported Brownstone.

Again, struggling, Julie stumbled with her second set of two suitcases to the door of the building. Slowly, I walked to help her, but this time I broke the silence.

"How could you possibly need this much luggage?"

"I'm taking some things for the cousins," she responded flippantly. "I'll be back down in a minute, okay?"

"Where are you going?"

"I have one more bag, maybe two," she said with her back turned.

"This isn't all going to fit, you know," I informed her.

"Maybe we should drive my car then? Take yours back to the garage and unplug mine."

"No!" I shouted. "Cars shouldn't have to be *unplugged* when you want to drive them! Just hurry up!"

"Okay, Grandpa," Julie shouted back before disappearing again into the building and up the stairs.

After some thought, I shouted my retort. "Calling your packing practices sluggish would be an insult to gastropods." I then shrugged to myself and nodded in agreement with the statement.

After I had exhausted my spatial reasoning skills arranging and rearranging the bags in the trunk of the car, I then waited an additional twenty-six minutes for her to return. Each minute after the tenth, I convinced myself she would be right down during the next, that there was no reason to leave the street level.

When she finally appeared in the doorway, I shouted, "Where the hell were you?"

"Mom called. We were just chatting."

"Are you kidding me?" I yelled.

Julie, smiling, bounced her way to the trunk, dropped in one of her remaining two bags, opened the passenger door, hopped in effortlessly, and dropped the other bag by her feet.

I watched her, seemingly rejuvenated by the conversation with her mother; either because her mother brought her joy or because making me wait needlessly did. I closed the trunk then slid myself into the driver's seat and brought the door down to a close. 10:29 a.m. read my phone's screen.

We picked up speed effortlessly as we left the island of Manhattan behind, stalled only by the aggravatingly timed red lights.

Slowing for the toll, I dropped my hand down onto the middle console, my probing fingers rewarded with nothingness.

"Where's my money? I keep ample money for the tolls right here! Those valet parking kids probably stole it at the restaurant!"

"Oh, I borrowed some money a couple days ago. I was out of cash so I opened your car and got it. I wanted to tip the parking attendant."

"What? Why would you tip them? They don't do anything! We drive in and park our own cars. And we're renting the spaces. We're not supposed to tip them."

"Don't be cheap, Nicholas…"

Disgusted, but concentrating on the problem at hand, I shouted, "We're coming up on a tollbooth! Get me some money."

"How much is it?" she asked as she slowly reached for her bag.

Because I was unsure of the current amount for the rapidly increasing toll, I searched the outdoors and then pointed at the "PAY

TOLL" sign with the absurd toll cost stated below before huffing at Julie.

On my direction, she saw the sign and then began to slowly search her bag for cash. Frantic at her inefficiency, I shouted, "We can't pull up with nothing in hand. I'll hold up everything! Don't make me be that guy! Don't make me be that guy! Just give me some money!"

Seconds before we reached the window, Julie handed me a crushed wad of bills which I blindly thrust at the tollbooth worker. The sum covered the exorbitant charge exactly; no change exchanged hands.

Shortly after the averted disaster, we were zipping along at a smooth high speed, skipping the boring chapters of the speedometer with ease and grace. The silky smooth ride quickly dismissed the posted notions of an acceptable cruising speed as compliant yet stiff shock-absorbers churned the potholed pavement into butter while eliminating any potential for body roll.

Not a handful of minutes ticked by before traffic came to an abrupt halt.

"I hate this drive…" I muttered.

"What?" Julie asked as she opened her eyes, having already fallen asleep.

"Nothing," I replied angrily.

"Getting there is half the fun, Nick," she chirped annoyingly.

"Is it?" I asked, fully ready to answer my own question. "How can driving to a vacation home be half the fun especially when you're leaving New York City at the same exact time as every other idiot who assumed no one else in the entire city would attempt to avoid traffic by leaving at 10:30 a.m. on a Friday during the summer?"

She responded with a silent stare.

"On second thought," I began, "you're completely right! If you take into account that I hate sitting in traffic all day and I equally hate spending time with your family, getting there is, indeed, half the fun! Right again, Julie. Right again."

This time she forwent the stare, reached into the bag she kept at her feet, pulled out a pair of small earphones, and silently plugged her head with sound.

"I don't want to hear your negativity," she said as she pulled her knees up by her chest, the supple hand-stitched seats supporting her sandals.

Suddenly I was alone in a sea of traffic moving slowly toward our destination, still at least one hundred miles away. I turned on the radio to a classical music station, hoping it would help to both calm me and maintain that calm.

After an hour of creeping along, staring at a flutter of countless brake lights, my anxious frustration overcame my awareness. "Can you believe this?" I asked Julie, forgetting that her ears were plugged with the sounds of her choice.

I waved my hand in front of her face to get her attention only to learn that she was fast asleep. She looked as if she had been sleeping for a long time, mouth slightly open and hair a bit disheveled.

"Unfair," I said, leaning back to my side of the car.

The hour following was spent attempting to locate something of interest outside the car. Trees, leaves, signs, other vehicles; nothing was worthy. I tried spying on neighboring motorists, but found that none were entertaining enough. Most read from books or tablets or were fiddling with their phones; another sadly unchangeable and painfully boring program on the TV of modern life.

One car, in a lane moving slightly quicker than mine, was filled with what I determined to be a dysfunctional family. The mother had long greasy clumpy curly dirty-blond hair, worn in an unappealing manner that moved about unnaturally. Her body type, from what I could see as I scrunched low in the car to get a better view, was as unappealing as her dented and misshapen car. I judged her quickly by her mannerisms and her facial demeanor, allowing her size to define her in a negative way rather than allowing it to be a meaningless footnote.

I inferred her upbringing and that she suffered from diabetes because of her excess of calories combined with the absence of a nutritional diet. I knew she had a crass and rough voice from years of smoking and that her temper was something it would be prudent to stay on the correct side of. Her driving style, erratic despite the slow moving traffic, only solidified my assumptions; pulling forward hard when space opened up, then slamming on the brakes when she neared the car ahead. Targeted stereotyping, I knew her type...

What appeared to be the father of the family had the same hairstyle, but with a more masculine hairline (receding), and a significantly skinnier build. He was as asleep as my passenger, but looked much less dignified in his repose. His arms were dead at his sides and his head was craned back, facing straight up; the vehicle offered no headrest upon which to rest his head. Mouth open wide, he appeared in great danger of swallowing a piece of the car's ceiling which was itself peeling off in chunks.

Their two children, a boy and a girl, covered the entire rear window on the left side with their flat squashed faces. With vulgarity in their hearts, both were waving their central digits by way of commentary in my automobile's direction with nothing more than their own reflections on the darkly tinted windows as a response. The mother appeared to be encouraging the behavior, smiling and nodding at her children's inspired gesticulating before throwing up her own disrespectful right hand.

I feared for the future of those children. They, trained to judge with jealously and express their warped opinions in the most inappropriate of manners, would likely not go far in life. I was certain they were capable of being better people, but they were sadly cursed with terrible parenting. I hoped nothing more for them than to see themselves as they were in the reflection on my tinted windows. I knew, however, that they would never find the right path. Their slightly quicker lane placed my car out of sight and likely out of mind after their disrespectful display.

An hour later, the road turned slowly toward the unfortunate direction of the sun. Or the sun found its way in the line of the road. My fleeting attention found it difficult to determine which one was the aggressor. I pulled the sun visor down, but its lowest would not suffice. My head began to ache from my squinting eyes.

I dropped my hand to where my sunglasses normally resided, but never located them. Leaning over, my hand searched beneath my seat, then beneath Julie's. The sun, directly ahead and straining my eyes, provided no illumination inside the car making locating any concealed objects impossible. The dark plush floor mats and tinted windows only aided the hiding sunglasses.

"This is the one time that glow-in-the-dark sunglasses would make sense," I said to myself. I smiled and chuckled arrogantly at how humorous I was even in times of frustration, but humor never found my sunglasses.

Almost thirty minutes of searching abruptly ended when I decided that Julie had probably borrowed the sunglasses when she could not find her own. I looked at her, angry at her incessant borrowing and jealous of her deep slumber.

Half an hour later, traffic started the hour long process of returning to a normal highway pace; from a crawl to a walk to a jog to a run, then back to a crawl as the cars funneled into the left lane to accommodate the construction (inactive at the time we passed) which was taking up all the right lanes.

Suddenly, the lackadaisical feel of the trip switched to a frantic explosion of pent-up anger, frustration, and energy as all lanes reopened simultaneously and thousands of motorists were given a venue for release. Each car accelerated as hard as it could from the crawl, most to a reasonable speed, some to an inappropriate one.

I watched a magnificent sounding red sports car— exotic at closer look—pull off faster than the rest, weaving through traffic effortlessly as its driver proved, in his mind, that he was better than the rest of us. Never one to allow another to feel superior, I applied the appropriate amount of pressure on my own accelerator, raising the rpm of the engine by several thousand.

As our battling cars sped to a dangerously illegal pace, we passed others with ease, the landscape resembling a surrealist painting. I pulled ahead of him on the right then he took up chase, following as closely as possible. We passed what felt like hundreds of stray cars as they crawled within the legal limit.

Weaving in and out, left and right then right then left, modulating the accelerator appropriately, the challenger stuck close behind me, pulling to within a foot of my bumper to show he had the power and speed to be granted the pole position.

Feeling threatened and near to emasculation, I made a series of erratic maneuvers to evade; from the left lane, driving hard between two cars, splitting them in their adjacent lanes, then pulling around and in front of the previously split car on the right and then, continuing the weaving, around and in front of another in the same lane only to then swerve back into the left before crossing all lanes and ending in the farthest one to the right, sliding in front of a truck, just missing his front with my rear. The challenger, much less insane, was left behind as I held the accelerator down hard. Seconds later he found a hole in the traffic, his engine howling behind in an attempt to regain his pride, but to no avail.

Unfortunately, my last unsafe and rather jarring maneuver, plus the accompanying soundtrack of the truck horn, woke Julie from her deep sleep.

"What are you doing?" she shouted, scared and startled. "What's going on?"

"Nothing," I said calmly.

"How fast are you going?" She leaned over to see the speedometer.

"Not too fast," I said, again calmly.

"You're going over 160? What are you doing? Slow down! What are you doing?"

"Haha… boys will be boys?" I offered.

"Slow down!" Julie's voice had a tone of desperation, as if she was pleading for her life.

"Getting there is half the fun, right?" I quipped.

"Nick, this is dangerous! You're going to kill us! Please!"

"A little danger never hurt anybody," I joked, still well over the 160 mark.

"I'm not kidding," she said as she reached over and grabbed the steering wheel, wrongly assuming that to be a safe or good idea.

"Let go," I yelled out. I looked in the rearview mirror. My depth perception determined that the challenger had decided to admit defeat and decrease his pace down toward a more appropriate speed.

"I'm slowing down, okay?" I said as I lifted my heavy foot from the accelerator sending Julie's head bobbing toward the windshield, car slowing quickly from the intense wind resistance. My foot returned to the pedal when we had reached what I determined to be an appropriate speed.

"You're still going 80, Nick. There're police everywhere. You need to slow down."

"Just focus your eyes on the horizon if we get pulled over and we'll be fine," I responded.

"Slow it down, Nick. The speed limit is 65."

"That's '65 mph, conditions permitting.' These conditions permit a much higher speed."

"Slow down," she shouted with a tone that indicated it would be the final time she would speak those words.

Again, I released my smothering my right foot from the accelerator, this time until the car slowed to the posted speed limit, a speed that felt as slow as the pace we had been traveling for the previous handful of hours.

Content, Julie pulled herself to a more relaxed position abandoning the tense one she had adopted when contesting our speed. I expected a companion with which to converse for the remainder of the trip, but Julie's eyes had already begun to close.

"I knew you were going to make me slow down," I said defiantly. "You're predictable like that."

"You don't know anything about me," she responded.

"Really? Ask me anything."

"What am I going to do next?" she asked.

"Probably passive-aggressively destroy my seats by dragging your dirty feet across them."

For a moment, she said nothing. I felt that I had won.

"What color are my eyes?" she asked quietly.

Immediately, I opened my mouth to answer, ready to put her in her place, but somehow the color of her eyes, still closed, eluded me despite the fact that I spent years staring into them seeing first joy then, more recently, the tears of sadness.

"Eh... is beautiful a color?" I finally said.

She scoffed at me then put on a pair of sunglasses that looked suspiciously like my own, plugged her ears, and no longer allowed my ignorance in.

A minute later, a motorcycle darted past at maximum acceleration, the speed pushing the rider to a short squat at the back of his seat under the windscreen, almost sliding to the ground, front tire fighting to stay grounded. The flamboyant coloration of his bike and the high-pitched squeal of the engine suggested it to be quicker than my own machine, but I still wanted to try; unfortunately Julie was there, killing the fun even after she had checked out mentally.

The snail's pace cruising that followed was excruciating. Mile after mile of cringing at the consistent low hum of the engine, no fluctuations at all. I followed Julie's instructions of caution because glancing at her told me nothing about her level of awareness; sunglasses hid the clues. Fast asleep or wide awake, her mere presence kept the speed at a consistent boring 65 mph.

After slightly more than an hour, I noticed movement in my peripheral; Julie was stretching.

"Where are we?" She yawned.

"Long Island," I snapped, bitter that she had slept comfortably while I dealt with the idiocy of the outlandishly low speed limits and my fellow motorists.

Her voice was still heavy with sleep. "I'm starving. Let's stop for some food. Which exit are we at?"

"At which exit are we?" I corrected, not allowing the sentence to end with a preposition.

"Oh, you don't know either," she said. Then she adjusted to sit up straight and look around, removing my sunglasses from her face in the process. "I know where we are," she announced. "Get off at the next exit. There's a little place to eat. And you can fill up the car."

"As you command," I responded.

That this was the poorer part of town was easily distinguishable by the small cabins and cottages, pulled close to the ground by an absence of wealth, scattered along the roadside. Minuscule unmanicured yards showcased unkempt plants, overgrown in the absence of landscapers.

"We're not there yet," I said. "Not even close..."

"Turn here," Julie said, pointing into a parking lot with a refueling station and a building with the letters "D-I-N-E-R" floating above.

The Diner

The car glided softly through the parking lot.

"You can get a table while I fill up the tank," I said as the car stopped in front of the building.

Julie's door ascended skyward slightly before she did, then dropped down behind her. I pulled off to refuel then parked the sated vehicle across two spaces toward the back of the lot to avoid door dings from careless adjacent motorists.

After a short car-side stretch, I rubbed my left shoulder and frowned. To divert attention from the still lingering soreness, I began counting each car that my eyes could find as I walked through the parking lot. My mind was thus distracted so, unbeknownst to me, my hand-to-phone distance increased with every step I took. I felt a phantom phone with me, ready to alert me to an impending message, ready to connect me to the world, ready to allow me access to the Internet, but in my pocket, right beside me, it was not. It was, in fact, resting comfortably in its place in the car.

After I counted sixteen cars in the parking lot and refueling station, the door of the small, quaint-feeling, brightly sunlit restaurant shrieked a haunting scream which plagued my ears for seconds after I opened it. Julie sat at a booth, alone; no one and nothing accompanying her at or on the table.

I slipped in across from her and smiled. She smiled then looked away, out the window for three minutes before I asked, "Have you ordered yet?"

"Ordered? No. No one's come over yet."

26

"Oh," I said, looking around the restaurant. I touched the arm of a woman passing by our booth wearing a medium length light blue short-sleeved dress with a white and black apron design on the front.

"Can you get us some menus, please?" I asked politely.

"Go to hell," she barked back angrily.

"Alright," I said, turning to Julie. "I don't think she works here."

Giving up on harassing customers, I adopted Julie's approach of staring out the window at the parking lot and adjacent field of long grass.

"Hey, guys," a waitress slowly said, pulling Julie and me back into the booth. "Here're yur menus. Can I get youse anything to drink?"

"I'll have a cup of coffee," Julie responded.

"Nothing for me, thanks," I said.

"Sure you don't want anything, honey?" asked the waitress.

"No, I'm fine, thank you," I insisted.

"I think you should order something," Julie chimed in.

"Okay, fine!" I said, feeling rather frustrated and coerced. "I'll have some scrambled eggs and bacon. And a glass of orange juice."

"There now," said the waitress, hazel eyes smiling. "That wasn't too hard, now was it?"

I smiled a fake squinting quick smile, scrunching my mouth as if it was experiencing a bad taste. The simple looking but pretty dark-haired waitress took this as genuine gratitude and replied with a wink of her left eye before shifting her attention to the other side of the booth.

Julie, seemingly questioning her choice as she spoke, said, "May I please have your Eggs Benedict, but I'm trying to eat better… Um, can you do the egg without the yoke? Maybe Eggs Benedict with egg whites? Yes, I think that sounds good. Do you think they can do that?"

I smirked and asked Julie condescendingly, "Do you even know how they make hollandaise sauce?"

"What's *hollandaise sauce?*" the waitress said slowly.

I rolled my eyes and said nothing.

Embarrassed, Julie then awkwardly said, "I'll have a piece of pie, apple pie please."

"Coming right up, guys," the waitress sang as she slowly moved off.

After some silence, Julie asked me, "Why don't you try something else? You always order the same thing."

"I wasn't going to order anything. Then you two pressured me into it. And I didn't even have time to look at the menu. She only even asked if she could get us something to drink. Don't turn this around on me. You're the one forcing me into things I don't want!"

"Calm down, Nick. I was just saying that I thought you could benefit from trying something new."

"I guess I'm just boring then…" I said sarcastically.

"Remember the story about the guy who kept saying he didn't like green eggs and ham?" she began. "At the end of the story, he actually tried it and he loved it. Now it's all he eats. The moral: try new things because you might end up loving them."

"That was a Dr. Seuss book. This is reality, Julie."

She just looked at me and frowned so I added, "And, technically, other than the color inconsistency, I am essentially having green eggs and ham so there really isn't anything you can complain about."

Again she just looked at me and frowned, then looked out the window, saying nothing but letting out a low sigh, so I again adopted her method of "wait and see," admiring the long grass dancing with the constant cool breeze from the nearby ocean.

Despite her slow pace of speaking and what I assumed to be an accompanying slow mental processing ability, after only about three minutes of staring, our waitress slid onto the table Julie's pie then my eggs and bacon followed by my orange juice, large with a straw, and Julie's coffee.

"Oh, thank you!" Julie and I said, she thanking one second before I.

"Enjoy," the waitress said as she slipped away.

"Oh, Nick, can I have a sip of your orange juice?"

"Absolutely not!" I said with honest intent. "I don't want your germs."

Julie frowned at me before suggesting, "What if I get my own straw?"

I responded in no way except to slide my papered straw into my hand, flip it around, then break the paper in the middle with both hands before undressing it, dropping it into the juice, and taking a long enjoyably obnoxious sip.

"Excuse me," Julie said, raising her voice toward the waitress.

"Yes, dear?"

"Can we have one more straw please?"

The waitress patted her apron, then looked behind the counter for a moment before saying, "Sorry, dear, he got our last one." She pointed to me sipping gleefully.

I smiled as I sipped, looking straight at Julie. The defeat on her face almost made my smile dip, but I managed to hold it up, strong and proud.

Julie looked down at the pie on her plate and ate slowly, never taking her eyes off of it. She did not add sugar or milk to her coffee like she used to. Years of marriage had made her tough; I had made her tough. Sweeteners and softeners were unnecessary. Again, I felt strong and proud.

As I admired what had been created by my years of harsh treatment, I noticed Julie's hands, her bare hands, smooth and light.

Her ring... I thought, realizing that her left hand held no metal other than the fork.

Julie had always worn her wedding ring, since the day we said our vows. It only left her finger to rest briefly in the shower's soap dish. She had known it was fake the second I handed it to her, a consequence of having a wife who grew up rich, but she said nothing back then and never did.

The ring was at the same time worthless and priceless and its absence spoke volumes, but I said nothing. I merely looked away from her hand and back to my eggs and bacon suddenly rendered unappetizing by the state of our marriage. The bacon was crispy. The eggs were firm. Despite adding salt, nothing but texture came through. Even the orange juice was nothing more than a thick liquid

30

with dots of pulp clogging the straw. So I joylessly ate, drank, and tried to avert my eyes from what had been created by my years of harsh treatment.

I noticed a lone man at a booth across the way, ten or fifteen feet off. The waitress slid a plate with French fries and a large bacon cheeseburger to him. Next to it was a tall glass of root beer, the empty brown bottle off to the side. He thanked her then picked up the burger with both hands, rotating it until the end of a strip of bacon was sticking out toward his mouth. That was where he started.

"Anything else for youse?" the waitress asked some minutes later.

"No, thank you. Just the check," I responded.

She pulled it, already printed up, out of her apron and set it on the table next to me.

Without looking at it, I handed her my credit card from my pocket.

"Thank youse," she said, leaving then quickly returning with a signature pad and a line for the tip.

"I'm workin' my way through school," she said. "Expensive these days. I'm hopin' it'll get back to me; you know, the investment, some of it anyway. You look like a professor. On their days off, they dress like you're dressed. Are you a professor?"

"No, Ma'am," I said as I scribbled on the tip line.

"Oh, you look like you'd be a good professor. Smart and such; educated. But me, I'm just working my way through it. Waiting for change but taking tips…"

I stopped adding for a moment and thought about the words she had just used. I added a zero to the total I had come to and handed back the filled out credit card receipt.

I then told her, "Hard work will get you anywhere you dream as long as you try your absolute hardest and never give up."

She smiled and thanked me with a nod as Julie, assuming I was trying to flirt, huffed then looked out the window as she had done earlier.

"I'll get the car," I said to Julie. She kept her head facing toward the window which I took as acknowledgment. I tried smiling at her as I left the booth, but she never allowed the smile to meet its mark, continuing to direct her gaze elsewhere.

As I exited the diner, but before my hand found the door, the waitress caught me by the left arm, turned me, then exclaimed in a heartfelt tone, "Oh, thank you so much, Sir!"

"No problem, Ma'am. Good luck to you," I replied, smiling into her teary hazel eyes.

She released and smiled as she held her hands, together, to her chest, watching me leave.

The squeal of the door lingered in my head, down the steps, and past each of the eleven cars in the lot and the refueling station. Eight vehicles had left and three were new since I had walked into the diner. Slowly, the remnants of the sound dissipated, but my ears felt as though they had lost the ability to detect a wide range of frequencies. Sounds felt flat and one dimensional for several minutes of my zig-zagging illogical route of reading and memorizing license plates until I reached the back of the lot.

Then I saw her, the most beautiful thing in the parking lot, admiring my car from a safe distance near her light blue convertible with true roadster proportions, long hood, short overhangs, and a small rear deck behind the seats. Her left hand was on her left hip as she stood at a magnificent slant with her feet touching at the bottom of her perfectly tailored blue jeans.

I fumbled for the keys and pressed the unlock button as quickly as possible. The lights flashed and she swung around to reveal her beautiful round face. Her long brown hair followed her head, delayed and cascading farther and farther down.

"Is this *your* car?" the aqua-eyed natural beauty inquired.

"Why, yes it is," I said handsomely.

"Well, I *do* believe this is the most beautiful car I *ever* have seen." Her adorable Southern drawl pulled me in effortlessly.

"Well, thank you, Ma'am," I responded. "You know a little something about cars?"

"Oh no. Cars, well, I don't know the first thing about cars. They go fast; that's all I really know!"

"Oh, I see," I said as I leaned in slightly. "Nicholas," I said, extending my right hand.

"Alexandria," she said beautifully. "But you can call me A."

"A? Like the letter?" I asked.

"That's the one," she confirmed.

I leaned against the car, smiling as she sweetly asked, "You live around here or just going to your summer house on this beautiful summer weekend?"

Before I could answer, before I could lie, Julie broke between us, stomping her feet and looking straight at her destination, the passenger seat, which she reached after pulling the door up then attempting with some degree of success to slam it down. Her hand then came to rest squarely on the horn which I had never heard from outside the car before.

"Looks like I have to go… T'was nice to meet you, Alexandria."

"Charmed, I'm sure," she said rather uncomfortably before turning and gliding on her heels toward her small light blue convertible, blue jeans accentuating her movements which I studied until Julie leaned aggressively on the horn for a second time.

"Okay," I shouted before opening the door and sliding in. "What's the problem?"

"Who was that? I was waiting in there for fifteen minutes! I walked around the whole parking lot looking for you."

"It wasn't fifteen minutes," I responded.

"Yes, it was. Let's just go. I don't want to talk about it anymore."

Frustrated that she had started a fight then abruptly cut it off before it could progress, absorbing all the power in the situation by acting like a child, I started the car and pulled off violently.

Then I looked down to notice my phone, plugged in, but not blinking with messages. Surprise jolted through me that I had forgotten it in the car, but the emotion left quickly, replaced with anger directed toward Julie. However, before I could do anything, she put in her earphones; alone again.

Back on the highway, cars were moving briskly. I decided to hold pace with those moving the quickest in the left lane, passing when they moved over, then repeating the process when I came upon another. Julie's discomfort and anger with my smooth maneuvering were apparent. She assumed that I was either oblivious to her discomfort and anger or that I was ignoring them. But they were, in fact, my motivation.

After exiting the highway, south of Route 27, in the more desirable area, we sat in traffic for more than thirty minutes on local roads. Julie was enjoying it. Not only did the sights and sounds bring her back to the days of her youth, but she knew that I very much disdained both traffic and witnessing an excess of wealth with which I was not connected.

Mostly wooded land lined the streets. The chimneys of the mammoth mansions which lay within were all I could glimpse. Properties were large and private. Landscaping company trucks were more prevalent than luxury automobiles, but both still plentiful. There are parts of the world in which excessive displays of power and wealth are considered to be in poor taste. Not so in The Hamptons.

We passed wind turbines, hundreds of feet above sea level, turning slowly and providing energy and an unnerving low hum; audible only when I opened the windows, one of which Julie was leaning against at the time. I did not apologize.

The rhythmic whooshing of the large white blades echoed through the air and created unnaturally long spindly shadows which tormented the long dancing grass. Left turns and right, Julie never attempted to direct me. She wanted me to lose my way so that she could capitalize on my weakened state, but I stayed on track, stayed strong. I knew the route from my few previous trips, all of which had been disasters.

The Douglas Estate

The tall twisted cast-iron gate stood open at the beginning of the absurdly long cobblestone driveway. A quarter mile of slim trees—menacingly hunched over the path, leaning at grotesque angles, branches swinging and swaying about—were meticulously spaced along the drive. As we passed, all were illuminated at once; the landscaping lights flickered to life seemingly early given the sun's position far above the horizon. I looked down at my phone. 4:19 p.m.

"Traffic..." I muttered to myself, shaking my head in disgust.

The driveway opened to a field filled with old respected luxury brand vehicles: Range Rovers, Rolls Royces, Maseratis, Porches, Aston Martins, and Jaguars; the sports models eclipsed in size by the bulbous big bodied Bentleys, BMWs, and Benzes. All breeds were represented by their newest, most expensive models and trim levels. The family's money was displayed prominently, proudly, provocatively.

For miles, I had felt as though I were driving into a movie in which all the characters were much much richer than was believable. The millions of dollars in automobiles immediately made me feel inadequate despite the fact that my car fit in just fine. But, behind theirs, truth and wealth. Behind mine, lies and debt.

"Drive around to the front," Julie said excitedly.

"Your father yelled at me last time for not parking with the rest of the cars..."

"Don't worry about it," she assured me as she slipped out of her sandals and into high-heels from her bag.

I continued around the bend to the largest private house I had ever seen. Breath taken away each time I saw it, I was again stunned by its sheer magnitude. I had used the word "palatial" prior to visiting this home, but I never had a real-life reference to the true meaning. Magnificent and gigantic, dwarfed only by the ego and arrogance that lived within, it was architecturally unremarkable; a large rectangle to my untrained eye; but the labyrinth of rooms and halls and walls and windows inside were challenging to comprehend. I searched for an inscription that read "Gatsby," but found none. Had one turned up, it was more likely to have read "Buchanan" anyway.

Detached was another rectangle, this one much smaller and with six large doors for the cars. Parked next to the smaller of the structures were three golf-cart-sized electric cars, one red, one white, and one blue. Julie's father had informed me several years before that they were "the estate cars." He and Julie's mother used them to get from the pool to the house to the tennis courts to the stables to the beach. They were legal for road use, but Julie's parents preferred to be driven in one of their larger more luxurious automobiles when they exited the grounds.

As I pulled to the side of the driveway in front of the house, Julie's door slid up and she climbed out then started up the walkway.

"Wait!" I shouted. "Wait for me!"

She stopped, motionless until I quickly stretched and then made it to her side.

First heard before seen, four or five children raced by with Julie's older cousin Rufus. Rufus had always struck me as a strange awkward fellow and I could not help but bring my concern to Julie's attention as we moved toward the house together.

"What's your cousin doing with those children?"

"I don't know. Playing, I assume," she responded.

"I'm a little uncomfortable with that."

"What? Why?"

"Well, he doesn't seem like he would... well..." I trailed off as I tried to choose my words carefully.

"What?" Julie asked.

"...act appropriately around them," I finally said.

"Nick, he's good with children. His psychologist says that he relates better to them than to adults or something."

"Isn't he a priest for Halloween like every year? If that isn't saying something, I don't know what is," I joked.

"Yes, that will hold up in any court," she said sarcastically.

"All I'm saying is I wouldn't let my children line up behind the Pied Piper over there."

"You were Charlie Brown for Halloween; what does that say about you?" she asked.

"Maybe he should just go climb a tree and leave those children alone," I suggested.

"This really is not a subject to be joking about, Nick," she scolded before increasing the speed of her stride as we passed a magnificent granite fountain.

Despite her response, I decided to continue my thought process aloud. "And Rufus; that's not a human's name. It's more of a dog's name. It's like being named Rover or Fido or Spot."

"I know you think you're being funny—" Julie began.

I cut her off to continue my rant. "Being named Rufus and not being a dog is like being named Kermit and not being a little green frog."

She shook her head at me. "No one here will find your jokes to be funny, okay? Do you understand what I'm telling you?"

"I'm hilarious," I declared to Julie's stern face. "Okay," I admitted after a few seconds of thought. "I'm a little nervous so I'm making jokes. That's what I do!"

She ignored my attempt at a meaningful dialogue and kept walking. We stopped in front of the front door; ten feet in height, two in quantity, mahogany in material. My arm stopped, left hand on the doorbell, but not yet depressed.

"It's not too late," I told her. "We can still go back to the city…"

Julie looked at me, leaned over, and pushed my left hand into the button.

"Your mother is terrible to me," I pleaded. "And your father despises me."

All Julie could respond with was, "Like my father says, my mother is 'an angel that fell from heaven.' "

"So was Lucifer," I pleaded again.

The intimidating door slowly opened and behind it was Julie's mother wearing a long loose green dress and far more gaudy jewelry than was necessary to express her wealth while in her gargantuan abode.

She took two steps outside and greeted Julie with a long loving hug and a kiss to her left cheek. No words were exchanged, but tears appeared to be not far from falling. After they released one another, Julie's mother looked at me in a way that only a mother could; immediately I felt shame though she used no words, displayed no change in her stern facial expression.

"Hello, Marry-Anne," I said as I extended the white flag of my right hand.

"I would appreciate being addressed as 'Mrs. Douglas,'" she snapped back.

I smiled a quick fake smile and scrunched my face as I placed my flag back into my pocket.

Mrs. Douglas then angrily demanded, "Who do you think you are to look at me in that manner? Do you think it's appropriate to speak to me like that? Must I refuse entry to a man who persists with this rude behavior?"

"Must I answer your riddles three before passing through without a key?" I said, already challenging her, showing her I would not back down.

After staring me down for several seconds, she turned to Julie and said, "Come in, my dear." They entered arm in arm through the gateway of hell, leaving me outside as I contemplated the consequences of entering and those of returning to the car and driving back to the city.

"Close this," Mrs. Douglas ordered me over her shoulder, gesturing at the door with her chin.

I closed it behind us as Mrs. Douglas released her daughter and pulled a pair of small rectangular glasses from a pocket then unfolded them before placing them upon her nose. She held Julie's cheeks, inspecting her face, and said, "You're sad. What has he done to you?"

I, having forgotten how blunt and obnoxious the old woman could be, gasped out of shock. Mrs. Douglas turned toward me, still holding Julie's cheeks, tilted her head down, and glared at me over her frames.

After an inappropriately long staring contest, she turned back to Julie who had remained silent.

"A mother is only as happy as her least happy child, my Julie. Now don't you sadden me! What is the problem here? What has this man done to you?"

Julie looked down and said quietly, "Nothing different than normal, Mother."

"Excuse me. I'm standing right here…" I chimed in.

Mrs. Douglas looked at me again with anger, let go of her child's cheeks, and approached me menacingly. I quickly and silently questioned whether a jury would consider self-defense as a viable plea.

She pulled my head down close to her own, her right palm on the back of my neck, and leaned in. The cross on her thin gold necklace dangled away from her body.

Cross, I thought. *Right…*

"Now you listen here," she hissed. "You hurt my daughter and you will regret it more than you regret any of the numerous unsavory acts you've committed in your life." Then she pushed my head away and whisked Julie down the hall.

The dynamic of Julie's family was slowly coming back into my mind; they protect their own and adopt a strong offense as a defense against outsiders. As I followed six steps behind them, I readied myself for what I knew was to come.

The choppy hum of dozens of people's chatter increased in volume until it plateaued on entering through the open French doors into a large room with couches lining three long walls and arranged into three separate rectangular sitting areas at the corners.

"My little girl!" yelped Julie's father. "Come here, my little girl!" he said while he shuffled his way across the room to meet the three of us just outside the doors.

As hard as I had tried over the years to win his acceptance on even the most minuscule level, I continuously failed. He believed that I was viciously after an inheritance and that I saw Julie as merely an ATM; the portal through which his money would reach me. The man disdained me, but he tolerated my presence with slightly more civility than his wife did.

His tan suit was bright, almost glowing atop a white collared shirt. Family and friends called him "Captain," but I only dared attempt that once. He had humiliated me by requesting "a more formal label from a man whose connection to me is merely a legal technicality." From then on, he was to me "Mr. Douglas."

"Captain's Log, 16 hundred 23 hours," he said, glancing at his old-fashioned wristwatch. My Julie Alicia Douglas arrives at The Hamptons Estate." He hugged her as tightly as his old arms would allow.

Feeling it absolutely necessary to remind his audience that he owned several boats, the old man frequently began stories with "Captain's Log" as if dictating to an unfortunate member of the crew.

42

I reached into my pocket and pulled out my phone to check his temporal accuracy. 4:23 p.m. "Darn it," I whispered.

He then turned to me and extended his right hand to my left hand, forcing me to turn to the left and twist my hand to catch his. He squeezed the tips of my fingers in the resulting awkward handshake as he looked me up and down then let go abruptly.

"Nicholas," he said without expression.

"Hello, Sir. I see you're still alive," I said, patting him on the back with my open left hand.

His mouth opened out of shock.

"I'm just joking, Mr. Douglas!" I said, laughing and putting my left hand on his right shoulder. "Just trying to keep the mood light."

His face held a smile as much as did his wife's and Julie's— not at all. He was a man who would never laugh at my jokes, but was always the first to laugh at his own.

"This is not funny at all, Nicholas. You know I've been having heart difficulties recently," he said very seriously.

"You seem pretty serious there, Mr. Douglas," I said. "As serious as a heart attack!"

"Nick!" Julie exclaimed. "What are you doing?"

"We're just kidding around," I explained.

Mrs. Douglas merely shook her head and led Julie through the open French doors and into the loving arms of her large extended family. Mr. Douglas stood there looking at me for a while longer before leaning to the left, away from the party, then walking in that direction. Apparently he needed the help of momentum to get his locomotion started.

"Come, Nicholas," he said.

I followed without question despite the fact that he could have easily led me to a room to be murdered by one of his butlers.

It took very little thought for me to decide to apologize, but in the form of allowing him to drone on about sailing. "Mr. Douglas, I notice that you leaned left before you walked in that direction. Did you pick that up during your sailing days? There is a rule of thumb, if I'm not mistaken, that you lean toward the side of the boat that you want to sail in."

"Nicholas, a rule of thumb is just one finger when trying to get a grasp on a concept." His response was smug and condescending and disregarded my inquiry completely.

"The thumb isn't a finger," I said, retaliating with correction.

"Yes, it is, Nicholas. How then do we have ten fingers if the thumb is not one of them?"

"Wouldn't the thumb be two of them?" I said, pointing out his flawed arithmetic.

He appeared frustrated for a moment before continuing. "Nicholas, I would like to speak with you about appearances. Clothing, Nicholas; it is very important. It says who you are, where you come from, where you're going. A man's clothing; it is the best way to see into a man's life, a man's world. And, I am sorry to say, you are not quite up to par, to say the least."

"Do you golf?" I asked.

"Yes, Nicholas, but that is irrelevant. Try to focus."

"Well, I only asked so that I could be sure you would understand why your statement was flawed. If I were 'not up to par' or 'below par,' I would be doing better than the average. One who plays golf should know this."

"Nicholas," he said leaning in and speaking quietly. "Do you understand what I am trying to say to you? I do not think you are dressed appropriately to be in my home. If I might draw your attention to the solid Japanese tamo ash wood plank flooring beneath you and, when I say 'beneath you,' I only mean physically beneath you."

"Well, I apologize," I said out of respect for his Japanese tamo ash wood plank floors. "I wore comfortable clothes for the long drive from the city. The traffic was—"

"That is no excuse, Nicholas," he interrupted. "My little Julie, she is dressed impeccably. She too took this 'long drive from the city' with you, did she not?"

At that moment and out of frustration from the effort of restraining my mounting anger, I may or may not have begun to roll my eyes, but stopped the roll as quickly as possible. Unfortunately, I caught my eye roll a fraction of a second after Julie's father noticed it.

"Now I know this is difficult for you, Nicholas," Mr. Douglas began. "But I'm going to have to ask you to try, really try. You're going to have to give 110 percent."

"Sir, one cannot try more than 100 percent. It is physically impossible to do anything to more than 100 percent of one's ability."

Stoic, but with a slight anger beneath, Mr. Douglas stared at me before raising his left hand and motioning with his index finger straight up in a semi-circular swing. The swirling digit summoned a man dressed similarly to the butler from the previous night's cocktail party, wearing a black suit with the bottom corners of the jacket elongated in the back, an impeccable white collared shirt underneath, white bow tie, and equally white gloves.

"Nicholas, this is Eliot," Mr. Douglas said, pointing with his right hand at the butler. "He will help you with some clothes."

"Oh, I really don't think that's necessary," I said.

Completely ignoring me, he spoke freely. "You see, Nicholas, a man lives his life in his clothing. Clothes, they are a work of art when done correctly, when executed in the correct manner. The designers; artists. Some would say better than Van Gogh. Do you know the artist Vincent van Gogh, Nicholas?"

"Yes, I do," I responded sharply, insulted at the condescending inquiry.

Again ignoring my response, Mr. Douglas answered his own question. "He is one of the greats. If you are fortunate enough to own one of his works, as I do, maybe you can touch it once a year, but even that is not recommended. The oils on your hands will eat right through, destroying it. But, your clothes… your clothes are to be worn daily. You feel them against your body, your skin. Soft, firm, the cut of the pants, the jacket, the shirt, the knot of the tie, the endless array of colors with as much depth and breadth as any of the pallets of the classic artists. Nicholas, understand this if you understand anything in life. It's power of example, not example of power." He took a step back and pointed at himself with an open hand raising and lowering on each side.

I looked at the butler and rolled my eyes slightly. His facial expression did not change in the least.

"Mr. Douglas, I do not intend on changing my clothes. I have already apologized to you and that is all that I offer. Unless you intend on having this man drag me to the back room, tear off my clothes, then dress me in a way that you deem appropriate, I believe this conversation is over."

The butler's facial expression remained impassive, but Mr. Douglas's morphed into a powerful intimidating stare. After ten seconds, he blinked first, turning and moving back into the room with his family.

"Come, Eliot!" he shouted, to which Eliot hurried after his employer.

————

The Douglas Family

The Douglas family had a reunion each year around the same time, toward the middle of the summer. During my two decades as husband to Julie, I showed up only a few times. The first time I had actually been looking forward to some time at the beach, but was instead forced to painfully mingle with the plethora of in-laws. Sadly, they had all been informed by Mr. and Mrs. Douglas prior to my arrival that adherence to the anti-Nicholas family policy was mandatory. I would have preferred for them to have ignored me or not invited me or even treated me like I was nothing, but they did something far worse; they treated me as though I was trying to harm Julie and thus harm them. They treated me as an enemy.

The family was an unwavering stubborn force of rejection. Once I had been deemed an enemy, winning them over was impossible. At the second summer's reunion, I managed to convince Julie we should stay in a hotel then fake an illness effectively enough for Julie to allow me to remain there watching TV. Thus I relaxed for the weekend and was only later forced to hear all about how wonderful everyone in the family was doing.

For years after, I managed to avoid joining Julie on her joyous summer reunion. I used work as the primary excuse, but she knew I was merely disinterred. When the family met in the city during the colder seasons, I rarely was able to find a viable way out. "Excruciating" never began to explain the interactions with each member of the large well-connected and well-dressed Douglas family. The vast majority would merely glance in my direction, showing their dissatisfaction with a look or some choice words, while the others would ignore me for the entirety of the event.

Remembering all the names over the years began as a fun game, but had ended in an angry rebellion about ten years ago when my brain flat-out refused to allocate additional space in my long-term memory for the venture. Still the elder family members remained firmly lodged in my remembrance. Mr. Douglas had two brothers, Otis and Thomas, and one sister, Jillian. All were his senior, by three, six, and eight years respectively, yet all were present in a semi-active state.

Otis and Jillian had three children each with their spouses, Edith and Perry respectively. Otis and Edith had two sons, Stewart and Isaac, and one daughter, Abigail. Jillian and Perry had two daughters, Emma and Sophia, and one son, Joseph. Thomas and his first wife, Olivia, had two children, Thomas Jr. and Penelope. Later Thomas had another child, Anthony, with his second wife, Michelle.

Each of all of Mr. Douglas's siblings' children had between two and four children of their own, biological or step, with between one to three spouses, who usually had previous spouses of their own. That set began to be born and integrated after I stopped keeping track of names, but many of their labels managed to slip their way into my memory indirectly as Julie would shove a screen with pictures in front of my disinterested face after she saw them.

Mr. and Mrs. Douglas had one child, Julie, who was the only one of the children of that generation without children of her own.

Additionally, Mrs. Douglas was an only child herself and her family lives in California and very rarely make it out to the East Coast so none of them were in attendance on that fine warm, but breezy, summer afternoon. Despite Julie's absence of siblings, she referred to the younger generation as her nieces and nephews; I suppose because they all called her "Aunt Julie."

I stood in the wide doorway to the room, in the middle of the open French doors, and watched most of the members of the family show me their sour faces while giving Julie their happy or concerned ones and affectionate greetings. Five identically dressed butlers roamed around with trays; some took orders while others offered hors d'oeuvre or sliced fruit.

"Oh no, you can't wear those in here," I heard Mrs. Douglas shout with a palpable distress. Her left index finger was pointed directly at me.

Assuming she was referring to my tattered clothing, I responded, "I've already discussed this with your husband. Thank you for your concern, Mrs. Douglas."

"No, no. Just take them off," she insisted.

"Excuse me?" I asked, fully intending on keeping my clothes on my body.

Again she pointed in my direction, but toward the floor in front of me. The rest of the room did the same with their eyes. I too looked down.

"Oh, my shoes?" I asked.

"Yes! No shoes in the house," she demanded.

I looked around the bottom quarter of the room to notice a sea of socks and bare feet. Even Julie had slipped out of her heels without informing me of the requirement to succumb to the mandatory formality. I knew not when they came up with this atavistic policy, but I mentally questioned if forks would be outlawed next. All members of the family, cousins, aunts, uncles, nephews, nieces, and siblings were shoeless. All except Preston, Julie's Cousin Joseph and his wife Elisha's middle son.

"Well, he's wearing his shoes," I said defensively, pointing to young Preston.

"These are orthopedics," Preston said in a sadly nasal voice.

"Damn it," I muttered, quietly slipping off my shoes and taking them in hand back down the hall to the front door where dozens of shoes occupied a large space on the floor.

How did I miss this? I thought.

Upon reentering the sitting area, I found myself out of the loop once again, this time an inch and a half lower. The only open spaces were between groups already in conversations. The couches and seats were all filled, mostly by the children and the elderly, so I stood in the doorway between the wide open French doors, touching the side of the opening with my right shoulder as I allowed my balance to adjust and body to lean.

I noticed the pale red woven fiber wallpaper with swirls of dark blue intertwined covering the entire room's walls above the high light blue wainscoting. I paid close attention to the décor in the different rooms of the Douglas estate because, on my previous visit, I had found myself in a room with the most exquisite and odd wall covering that I had ever experienced. I had to confirm with three different family members to be fully convinced that it was indeed what it appeared to be: flawless light brown leather walls with hand-hammered floral designs highlighted with brushed gold. Other rooms, I learned, had walls of Venetian velvet and gold threaded Thai silk. The Douglas estate was like nothing I had ever seen before; once I would have given anything to be invited inside.

As I stared into nothingness, I noticed that the family was indeed dressed much better than I. Men wore white or tan linen suits of a tailored fit. Many jackets had been casually shed, exposing mostly short-sleeved collared shirts. All colors of the pastel rainbow were present. Women were in mostly summer dresses, soft, silky, and saturated with beautiful bright colors and understated patterns. The room was vibrant.

It did not take more than five minutes of me standing helplessly and Julie catching up with her family, smiling, and laughing, for her to absorb the right amount of confidence to start shouting directions at me.

"Come in here, Nick. Sit down."

"I'm fine here," I responded quietly, smiling and pointing at my space in the doorway.

"Nick, sit down," she insisted, waving me in.

"Nowhere to sit," I said, palms and shoulders rising simultaneously.

"Oh." Julie then looked to her mother for guidance; her mother turned away and continued her conversation with her niece Sophia.

Julie excused herself from her two cousins, Emma and Michelle, and walked halfway to me.

"Maybe take a chair from the dining room across the foyer?" she said above a dozen conversations in the room. She then turned and walked away, taking with her my chance to protest.

I slumped my shoulders and walked back down the hall, past the foyer, and into what appeared to be a dining room with a large wooden table and sixteen ornate wooden chairs covered with plush purple and red cushions.

"No!" Mr. Douglas exclaimed as I put my hand on one of the chairs without armrests. "Those chairs stay in that room. They were made in France in the twelfth century and belonged to..." He trailed off in my mind, but I'm sure he continued explaining for an inordinate duration.

"Pardon me, Mr. Douglas," I said, interrupting him. "Might I have a chance to apologize?"

He looked back at me then shuffled his way back down the hall. I counted fifteen seconds before following.

"What was he doing there?" I questioned aloud before I found my place between the French doors looking into the room filled with people who hated me. For a moment, I began to feel almost comfortable, almost.

Maybe they'll just ignore me the entire weekend. That would be nice, I thought.

"Where is your chair?" Julie said loudly in my direction, over the dozen different conversations, all of which halted to listen for my answer.

"No seats available, Julie. But, I'm fine. Don't worry about me."

"Sit somewhere," she said, gesturing around the room rather aimlessly. "Sit."

No one spoke for ten seconds while they watched me awkwardly step through the room to find an open space. Finally on my third trip around, a small unfamiliar boy who I assumed to be a nephew moved over to make room on one of the couches. He likely forgot that no one was to acknowledge my presence.

I looked down at the space, questioning if it would be a better idea to just keep searching until dinner started.

Julie noticed me contemplating so instructed loudly, "Sit!" Her gesturing left hand finally found some direction thanks to the unfamiliar nephew.

All of those who were on the couch rolled their eyes when I made myself as small as possible and squeezed on. They were mostly young teenagers, my least favorite group of human beings; the age at which each sentence is spoken with an upward inflection, as if it ends in a question mark.

They pretentiously and precociously wore collared dress shirts, sleeves rolled up, and one too many buttons unbuttoned, both male and female. The boys' khaki pants were rolled up three or four rolls while the girls' summer dresses were far too short. One of the boys, Cameron, was clearly in the middle of a rebellious phase, evidenced by his Mohawk; a look with which I was certain his parents found issue given that it is a hairstyle that has no chance whatsoever of transcending its designated social status.

"So, how is everyone?" I asked, somewhat interested.

All blatantly ignored me and continued their conversation that appeared to have something to do with someone's ex dating someone else's ex, a topic I found unfathomable for such an age group.

"Is everyone here still in school? What grades are you in?"

Again no answer, so I addressed one by name.

"Danielle, you ride horses, right? I had a friend who rode in college. Do you all know what *Jinba ittai* means?"

This time I expected nothing in response so I could answer my self-posed question.

"It means rider and horse as one," I said happily.

They all turned away and continued their conversation about Chloe's ex-boyfriend.

"Oh, you already like boys, Chloe?" I asked.

Chloe then turned and gave me a very angry look, an ability that ran in the family apparently. "Please don't trivialize my maturational process by suggesting it to be on some normalized scale. I'm a unique individual. I ask that you recognize and respect that fact." She then turned away from me and continued her conversation.

I stared for a moment at the back of her thirteen-year-old head before the voice of a young boy directed a question toward me.

"Why are you dressed like that?"

"Well, hello, Brendan," I said to the boy.

"Why are you dressed like that?" he asked again, too young to mean any harm.

"These are my driving clothes. I knew I would be driving on the road for a while, so I put them on before I left the city. Thank you for pointing them out."

"You look like a homeless person," said Malinda, who had always been an obnoxious little girl, but had matured into an obnoxious fourteen-year-old.

"Well, hello, Malinda. What grade are you in now?" I asked pleasantly.

"Don't you care I just said you look homeless?" she asked, shortsightedly trying to provoke an altercation during which she would inevitably be made to cry.

"Well, I'm not homeless, thank you," I responded.

"My mother says if it wasn't for our family, you would be," she replied in quite the matter-of-fact manner.

"Well, that's not true, but if we're splitting hairs, you would be in the same position without your family, now wouldn't you?" I informed her.

"Pul-leeze," she sassed as she tossed her blond bangs. "I have a trust fund. What do you have?"

I said nothing and smiled, content to allow the conversation to end so that I could go back to being ignored by the spoiled rich children with whom I sat.

After some time relaxing, I felt as though I was being watched. I knew the feeling well when I was around Julie's family and I had come to expect it, but it was different this time. I looked down and to my left to see a young boy staring up at me, the same young boy who had moved to allow me to sit.

"And what is your name, young man?" I asked him.

"Archie," he said quietly; too young to ignore an adult, but old enough to know he was probably not supposed to talk to this adult.

"Oh, like Archimedes the mathematician or Archimedes the owl of Merlin the wizard? Do you like wizards?"

"I dunno," he said quietly.

"Good answer, good answer. Not wanting to commit. I got it. I'm with you," I said, extending my fist to him so he might reciprocate with his own.

His facial expression of confusion turned to discomfort as I watched him for several seconds, fist still hovering, waiting for his. I had become far too accustomed to watching patients during their time of thought; apparently the behavior had followed me out of the office without my knowledge.

"Who are you anyway?" Malinda's younger sister Alexandra inquired as obnoxiously as her older sibling.

Despite my assumption that she knew well who I was and was only asking to be obnoxious, I told her, "I'm your Uncle Nick! I'm married to your Aunt Julie."

"No, you're not. She would never marry someone with clothes like that," the snooty little girl responded.

"Well, I have other clothes."

She paused for five seconds before looking up at me and saying, "Oh my God, I'm so bored of you."

There had been several prior indications that I would be best served by relaxing and enjoying the fact that no one, including the children, had a desire to converse with me in any kind of civil way, but having an eleven-year-old tell me that she was "so bored" with me was just what I needed to gently lean back into the couch and remove myself from the surroundings, drifting away to another place.

Not a half hour passed before someone whom I did not recognize, I assumed that he was a new husband of one of the cousins, felt it completely necessary to attempt to make me feel even more uncomfortable than I already was. Perhaps this was some Douglas rite of passage.

"Aren't you a little old to be playing with kids?" the man asked with a tone of joshing obnoxiousness.

"No, actually I'm fourteen years old. Benjamin Button," I said, introducing myself and extending my hand upward to shake his.

The man clearly had trouble recalling where he had heard the name, but he knew it was familiar somehow.

"Ahh, Kipp Marshall Moore. Nice to meet you, Benjamin," he said, still failing to remember F. Scott Fitzgerald's novel. "Glad you could make it."

The man then smiled and walked away, rubbing his chin in continued contemplation.

After another thirty minutes of attempting to pay no attention to the nieces' and nephews' juvenile discussion of mature topics, my legs and back began to ache. The hours in the car had lowered my threshold for the duration I was comfortable sitting.

I stood up slowly, making cracking sounds from every joint. Stepping over legs and arms with my white tube socks, I moved slowly away from the children then through the older members of Julie's family. Most ignored me; some acknowledged me, but in a way that made me wish they too had ignored me.

"Nick," Julie's voice sang behind me.

"Bathroom," I said without turning around. In that moment, I decided that, although I was not normally permitted to wander freely in the Douglas home, a search for the bathroom would likely prove an exception.

Either Julie said nothing more or I did not hear the rest of the conversation. It was difficult to determine which one was the reality.

Long Search for the Lavatory

One would assume that finding a bathroom in a very large house would be no more difficult than finding one in a smaller house because the number of bathrooms increases proportionally with the size of the house; but I spent almost fifteen minutes wandering around and opening doors before I gave up and stood in the middle of a grand double staircase, both sides curling upward, one the mirror image of the other; huge crystal chandelier between them and above the polished wooden floors upon which I stood, lost and confounded. The room had a feeling of centrality, as though I was directly in the center of the mansion. I hoped this was the best place to be found by someone willing to assist in the search.

After several minutes spent pondering my next move, Julie's father's brother Thomas found me, but Uncle Tommy appeared more lost than I, wandering around muttering to himself; then he, apparently too old to realize that I was the one with whom no one was permitted to converse, started telling me about his early days working at the stock exchange before it went "all computers."

He began a tale of the founding of his business, taking as partners two friends, both of whom had passed away four or fourteen or forty years earlier. He was too confused to remember. A story during which more time is spent trying to remember details than telling the story is never something I am interested in standing through.

Something, however, was learned during story time. Uncle Tommy took yet another step closer after countless attempts at recollection to where he was literally standing between my two white tube socks. I learned, from his breath, that Uncle Tommy's confusion was perhaps not entirely age induced. It was clear the man loved his whiskey. I feared that I would reek of his choice of beverage if the conversation went on too much longer, so I interrupted him during an inhale pause.

"Thank you, old friend," I said, shaking his left hand with both of mine. "We'll catch up over there." I pointed off down a hall.

He looked down the hall, smiled, wobbled a bit, then shuffled off. I increased his speed of departure by moving swiftly in the opposite direction, but I had been up and down so many halls, into and out of so many rooms, and through countless doors to the point of complete loss of any sense of direction so the likelihood of reaching my destination was unknown, presumably slim.

In a miraculous fit of luck, I managed to stumble into a very dark room which contained a door that somehow opened up into the room that held the family.

"Ahh!" I said aloud upon entering the room, squinting a bit in the transition from dark to bright. I was almost happy to see Julie's family, all ignoring me. The joy was surely attributed to the perception that *I* had found them, not that I had found *them*.

My sliver of space on the couch with the handful of teenagers had been absorbed by their readjusted positions, which did not trouble me in the least. I had little desire to squeeze back into their lives, so I found my way over and around children and adults to a spot on the pale red woven fibers with swirls of dark blue that covered the walls. I felt that there I could just lean and be ignored, overshadowed by the wallpaper.

Julie caught my eye as I watched the group enjoy one another's company. She was laughing and smiling and talking with family, mannerisms animated with joy. Her whole being was glowing, and she actually seemed taller. Seeing her like that, something that had been missing in her for so long, made me want to join the conversation, but I feared my presence would push her joy away; the Julie I wanted to see would be lost yet again. I debated for a moment, but, in the end, I found I lacked the courage to jump into frame. Instead, I leaned back into the wall.

Shortly after settling into my space, I noticed a butler glide toward Mrs. Douglas then attempt to politely attract her attention. She looked at him, but ignored his presence, continuing her conversation with Penelope and Michelle, Mr. Douglas's nephew Thomas's first and current wives, and a man whom I did not recognize.

Almost ten minutes of standing idle while being blatantly ignored appeared to be the humiliation limit for the butler. He backed away from Mrs. Douglas and then made his way toward Mr. Douglas, who was speaking with his brother Otis, probably about getting together a search party for their other brother, Uncle Tommy.

Mr. Douglas acknowledged the butler immediately. They exchanged a few words before Mr. Douglas made an announcement.

"Excuse me, everyone, excuse me."

The crowd of happily mingling family members all quieted at the command of their patriarch.

"Captain's Log, 20 hundred 13 hours. Dinner will be served in ten minutes in the dining room at the far east corner of the house," he said smiling, butler behind him backing up the validity of his statement with a slight nod. "Maybe we could all make our way outside for some refreshing fresh air before we eat? The children can catch some fireflies? That's what we used to do when we had the youth, the energy." He put his arm around Otis.

There was a hazy hum of response from the group so Mr. Douglas asked them to "Raise your hands if you would like to go outside. Let's see if we can get a head count."

"That would be a hand count," I remarked quietly.

At that point, before hands or heads could be counted, Mr. Douglas attempted to arouse interest by requesting a more acoustic response.

"What say ye, Family? Yea or nay?" he posed.

An unenthusiastic "uuaahhyyy" sound permeated the room. Unfortunately the words "yea" and "nay" not only rhyme, but sound remarkably similar. Determining an overwhelming consensus was impossible so Mr. Douglas made an executive decision.

"Outside we go!" he shouted.

The youngest male members of the family jumped off the couches and raced out the open French doors and away. They were soon followed by their young female counterparts, then the adults slowly filed out behind them; this time with the oldest members leading the way. Next were the lingering teenagers who moved slowly as they gossiped. I followed after all had exited to avoid being mistaken for part of the family.

Three sets of French doors later, the setting sun amazed us all. Tall skinny cast-iron incandescent bulb lamps, like old-fashioned street lamps found in a small early twentieth-century European town, illuminated the outdoors directly behind the house with the cooperation of lights imbedded in the cobblestone patio.

Everyone's socks will get dirty, I thought before realizing that none of these people did their own laundry. Many of them probably never even wore the same pair of socks more than once.

The air was as described; fresh and refreshing. A hand came to rest on my left shoulder after some seconds of breathing in deeply. The hand and the resulting tingling of pain upon my sorest of body parts startled me, swinging me around into a somewhat defensive pose.

"Everything okay?" Julie asked, pulling her hand away quickly.

"Sure, sure. Oh, but how do I go about finding a bathroom without having to go through her highness the queen or his arrogance the king?"

Some cousins in the immediate vicinity overheard my joke and scoffed loudly. Julie looked at them embarrassed, then looked back at me infuriated.

"Why do you do that?" she asked.

Rather embarrassed of my behavior and rightly so, I muttered, "Sorry."

"Maybe my family would like you more if you acted more respectfully."

"Maybe they'd like me more if I had a prestigious last name which had clout in society."

"I told you to take my name when we got married," she said rather obnoxiously before walking away with confidence in her step.

The fresh air was beginning to lose its appeal and the family's appeal had been lost long before so I decided to go back into the house and again attempt to locate the bathroom before dinner started.

Cavernous and confusingly laid out and with more rooms than I could comfortably count, finding the bathroom without guidance amounted to an impossible task. I started down a wide hall then another narrower one, then through two sets of French doors on either side of a large room with dark bluish gray walls and a fireplace twice my height. I was unsure where I was going and was ready to again give in to the labyrinth when I noticed a man dart past a doorway. At first glance, it was Courtland and I was shocked to a halt in my pace. Then the thought of my recently deceased patient wandering around my in-laws' mansion and the resulting realization of definitive impossibility directed me to follow.

So I took up chase, following the mystery man's every move twelve steps behind and increasing. The combination of him moving so quickly and changing direction so frequently and the accompanying low level of light produced by the multitude of antique lighting fixtures made it difficult to determine any discernible features of the figure as he seemingly attempted to evade. We moved through three halls, then into a room, then through a door which swung both ways, then through another. Then, before I could get through the third door, he locked it.

Why would he do that? I thought. *Did he think I was going to hurt him or rob him or something?*

I almost knocked so I could confront whatever was on the other side, then my deductive reasoning skills overcame my impulse and stopped my hand. I had determined that the man was very likely to be in the lavatory. The quaint beaten old painted wooden sign that read "Lavatory" hanging on the door was my easily decipherable clue.

"Found the bathroom," I whispered to myself triumphantly.

I did the only appropriate thing at that moment and waited two minutes by the door until one of the butlers emerged, clearly not expecting to see anyone standing in the doorway.

"Sorry, Sir," he said, apologizing for some transgression of which I was unaware.

"Hi, I'm Nicholas; Mr. Douglas's daughter's husband." I extended my hand toward him.

He then nodded at my hand uncomfortably and asked, "Is there anything that I can do for you, Sir?"

"No, no… I was just looking for a bathroom. I've been walking around forever looking for one. You would think there would be a hundred of them in this huge house, you know?"

"Yes, Sir. The Douglas estate is quite expansive. Is there anything else?"

He appeared anxious to get back to what he was doing and extremely uncomfortable with me in that remote corner of the house, blocking his exit from the bathroom.

"No, nothing else. Have a good one," I said, stepping aside to allow his passage.

He nodded and backed away, turning quickly, then darting off.

The light yellow tiled bathroom was minuscule. It felt as if it had been fashioned out of an old closet too small to house more than six or seven jackets. Dangling from the center of the ceiling by a wire was a single lightbulb with a string attached, dangling down further.

On and off, I mused insightfully and, with a slight tug upon the string, was proven to be correct.

I bumped into three of the walls just turning around. Washing my hands was a chore in such tight quarters, but a necessary one given that dinner was next on the agenda. At that moment, I questioned whether the butler had a similar level of hygiene to my own, then I hoped it was not he who had helped prepare the meal.

On the uncertain journey back to the patio, I passed through two rooms, then came upon the kitchen. It was a scene right out of a five-star restaurant. Everything was shiny stainless steel, countertops, drawers, stools, refrigerators, doors, ovens, shelves, stoves, backsplash, cabinets, compartments, walls. A line of six stood at a stainless steel counter cutting and massaging and cleaning and seasoning all kinds of food. The stoves occupied one entire wall of the room, probably twenty burners in all, most of them in use; several hosted flat cooking skillets, others large pots or wide pans bubbling and flaming. Above the stove wall was a wide air vent to suck out the multiplying aromas. I counted six large refrigerators; half must have been freezers. Desserts were being prepared on the countertop on the wall across from the food preparation. Every kind of pastry and chocolate and fruit that I knew of were accounted for.

A butler appeared inches from my face. "Can I help you, Sir?" he asked.

"Uh, yes. Can I have a glass of water please?" I said, unable to think of anything else with which to respond.

"Of course, Sir." He glided away, grabbed a glass from a shelf, opened a refrigerator, took out a carafe of water, then poured while another butler dropped a straw into the mix. I lost sight of the glass when the first butler spun around as he glided back toward me. With a very deliberate and dramatic motion, his quickly moving hands halted right in front of me; I was presented with the physical response to my request. To my great surprise, a wedge of lemon had been added to the order, dangling off the edge of the glass.

I thanked him and he nodded before exiting the magnificent kitchen.

How it must be to live with these people granting your every wish and desire... I thought a little resentfully.

The lemon made my face and body pucker and recoil in a bitter fit. The water itself was refreshing, rejuvenating. Not until the glass was emptied seconds later did I realize how dehydrated I previously had been. The hydration and resulting feeling of ease were accompanied by a confidence that I lacked earlier. I felt far better equipped to attempt to be a part of the family or, at minimum, a more respectful guest than previously.

Finding my way back to the patio proved to be troublesome. Slowly and smoothly I walked in and out of rooms, through archways and doorways. I was completely lost when I opened a door to find an extremely small room, closet sized, with walls covered in red cushy satin and the floor with cherrywood. Accents of gold and a railing around my dangling hands confused me further.

"This is either a large jewelry box or a coffin," I said aloud. Then I turned to see buttons on the wall with the numbers 1, 2, 3 and the letter B at the bottom, referring to their walk-out basement.

"Elevator," I said definitively.

Three hallways, four turns, and two rooms later, I found myself in the dining room where the members of the family were just finding their seats at the extremely long table. Uncle Tommy shuffled in from another door just as I popped through mine, both different from the arched opening the rest of the family was pouring through. We gave one another a surprised look, then continued on our ways.

"Made it," I said to myself. "And just on time."

———

Douglas Family Dinner

Mr. Douglas was standing at the head of the table alone, surveying all that was his. I approached him quickly. "Mr. Douglas," I said, addressing him as he had requested.

He sighed. "Yes, Nicholas?"

"Was that an elevator I saw over in another part of the house?"

"What were you doing over there? Who was with you?" He spoke quickly and chopped his words off at their ends.

"I was just looking for the bathroom…"

"Hmm," he said, contemplating a call to the authorities. "Yes. That is an elevator. We added it recently. Scrappy was beginning to have trouble getting up the stairs. She's elderly and arthritic."

"Aw, that's nice. Is 'Scrappy' your nickname for Mrs. Douglas?"

His lips pursed up and the ends dropped. "Scrappy is our dog, Nicholas. Our dog."

At that, I knew the conversation had no place else to go. I smiled and walked toward Julie.

"I'm sitting next to you, right?" I asked rather desperately.

"You can sit wherever you want to, Nick. There aren't assigned seats."

"Okay, great! Let's sit here." I pointed to the seats in front of where we stood about in the center of the length of the table.

"Fine," she said, pulling out the chair and sitting.

I did the same and we said nothing more to one another, she to my right and no one to my left. Having finally found the room, I marveled at the oversized Chinese onyx tiles beneath our feet and the mahogany marquetry table hidden, at the moment, beneath a lavish white tablecloth. I pulled it up a bit to examine the opulence before Julie slapped my hand down frowning.

Preston, the boy wearing his orthopedic shoes, sat across the table from us. He was arguing with his mother, Elisha, as he squirmed in his seat. "But, I'm not hungry. I ate like a hundred hamburgers for lunch."

Elisha then chastised him with, "If I've told you once, I've told you a million times: Don't exaggerate!"

I laughed aloud at the clichéd hypocrisy; no one else seemed to notice.

"Good parenting," I said to myself as Elisha found her seat. One side of the table appeared to be for adults while the other was for children. And I had, this time, chosen correctly.

The room quieted down after two or three minutes of children and adults and elders settling into their places. Julie's brash, perpetually inebriated, fictitiously red-haired, and recently divorced cousin then fell into the seat to my left.

"Hello, Kathy," I said without looking.

"Nicholas," she slurred. "You…"

"Yes, it is I."

"Not tonight… not tonight," she said before attempting to intimidate me with a wobbly stare. She then stumbled to her feet, spun around, and fell into the seat next to the one in which she had previously been sitting.

"Thank you," I said obnoxiously, referring to her move away from me.

"You're welcome," she responded, just as obnoxiously.

I was comfortably happy to see everyone sitting, putting their napkins on their laps, and exchanging smiles, small words, and short bouts of laughter with their neighbors. The fact that my only neighbor was Julie helped grow the joy within me. And, since all were seated, I would not be forced to be cordial to a random family member other than Julie.

Then, unexpectedly, Julie's insufferable and late-to-the-party Cousin Abigail exploded into the room with a boisterous roar, hugging each member of the family seated around the table beginning with Julie. Abigail sped her circumnavigation by using her large manly hands to rub a head or squeeze a shoulder of the children who all sat on the opposite side of the table. When she made it to Kathy, she shook Kathy awake, out of her drunken stupor, red hair a mess, then sat in the vacant seat directly to my left between Kathy and myself. She frowned at me. I frowned back. We had a mutual disdain for one another.

"Good talk, good talk…" I said to her.

I knew from before I ever met them that Julie's family would not accept me, but I never imagined that they would treat me in the dismissive way they did. Throughout our years of marriage, I never mistook any behavior or misinterpreted any gesture to represent any level of acceptance.

But, had I been confused or in need of an indication of how the family felt about me at any point, I would, as I inadvertently did at that moment, sneeze. When not one person responded to that sneeze with a "bless you" in any of the many languages it is appropriate to deliver that blessing, I definitely received the message that I was unequivocally hated by all. Not even Julie had spoken.

After the ignored sneeze, I looked around the table angrily, hoping to attract eye contact with someone from whom I could draw guilt. No eyes met my own.

"Really?" I asked aloud. "Really?"

Mrs. Douglas started the festivities by addressing the group. "I know I've been snacking all day, but my stomach is telling me that I'm starving!"

A few laughs were scattered over a smattering of yeses, others smiled, while others agreed with a nod.

"Your stomach can't talk," I bellowed. "But, if it could, it would probably speak Hungarian!"

Shocked faces turned to me. Disdainful stares injected "how dare you" under my skin.

"Ha!" I exclaimed, hoping the laugh would be infectious. It was not.

"Nick," Julie whispered to me loudly, "nobody thinks you're funny."

"Yes, Julie... This fact is painfully obvious, but thank you for letting me know."

Then Kathy leaned back in her chair, around Abigail, and chimed in. "Nice try, Outcast."

Abigail, sitting far too close to me, leaned in and laughed loudly in my left ear at this witticism.

I showed my appreciation of Kathy's kind words and Abigail's encouraging laughter with a nod and a dramatically insincere pursed smile in their direction. Then I turned back to Julie.

"Sorry," I whispered to Julie's left ear, though she in no way acknowledged my apology.

All eyes remained on me for a very quiet interval until Mr. Douglas began to speak. "Are all the glasses filled?" he asked, directing this not to his guests but to the butlers, who had multiplied in quantity. "I'd like to make a toast."

Mine were the only eyes that rolled. I allowed my head to slightly follow my eyes' example.

"Don't be an idiot," Abigail demanded aloud.

I ignored her crass voice despite her rather intimidating manly stature as I stared ahead and held back any semblance of acknowledgment.

While Mr. Douglas stood up in several stages, aided by a butler on each side, the remaining butlers hurried around the room, filling wineglasses for the old and young, with wine and grape juice respectively. Many previously filled glasses were emptied by *thirsty* guests and required a second and, in some cases, third visit from the bottle. The recipients' smiles grew with each sip or gulp they took.

Finally standing with a glass of red wine in his right hand, raised to shoulder level, Mr. Douglas spoke.

"Captain's Log…" He paused, looking down. The glass lowered to his waistline. He continued, "My old mind is having trouble recalling exactly when this story took place."

His "old mind" received several laughs. I resisted rolling my eyes again to avoid reprimand.

"Well, so then... Captain's Log, when I first set off on an impressively lengthy trip... It was likely four years into my life as a sailing man. I had been at sea for nearly a week, far far off the coast, with little intention of returning in the near future. Provisions would last for another week, but then, the unthinkable happened...a storm.

"It unexpectedly changed course, was headed right for me. Nothing I could do but buckle down for the thrashing. Two days it battered the vessel. When the winds and waves finally died down, we were a mess. The food? It had all been soaked by the seawater or washed overboard; door to the fridge had bumped open somehow, someway. The sails were in tatters, rendering them useless. The fuel tanks had been damaged, rendering the backup engine useless. And I was shaken, bruised, and fatigued... rendering me useless.

"Days were spent floating aimlessly. I had no knowledge of where I was. I had no knowledge of how to get home. I turned my head to the west and there was nobody, nothing in sight; just a vast sea of undrinkable water. I turned my head to the east and, again, nobody, nothing but a vast sea of undrinkable water. The same was true for dead ahead and directly behind me. Then, I turned to the north, not true north but to the sky, straight up and I prayed. I prayed that I be brought home safely to my family. It was at that moment that I realized what mattered most in life. It was my family who I thought of in my desperation. It was my family that I prayed for.

"The sea guided me back to shore miraculously with no sails, no fuel. I thought it was a mirage; a result of my dehydration, my fatigue and hunger. But it was not; it was land, real land; a miracle! Where I landed, I bought that land. I knew it would mean more to me than I could easily articulate at the time. I built a house on that land, this house, and it has served me... it has served us well ever since.

"This house is the heart of our family. We have spread to all corners of the country, all corners of the world, but this is our home base. This is where we converge for our annual reunion. This is where we meet to remind ourselves of what it is in life that we love; family. This house, this property; they are family. It's about togetherness. It's about love. It's about celebrating the new," he said as he pointed to the youngest members of the family. "And respecting the old," he said, pointing to his siblings. "Long after I am gone, this will be where we continue to gather to celebrate what it is in life that matters; family.

"To family!" he roared, raising his wineglass to the level of his high held head.

"To family!" everyone shouted in unison before drinking generously from their wineglasses, children and adults alike.

Remembering the speech from the other times I sat through it, I almost struggled not to mouth along. It was the same, almost word for word, every time. That no one had ever commented on that fact was astonishing to me. Not even a glance from one person to the next to acknowledge the self-plagiarism passed off as some level of novel toast-making. I allowed my eyes to roll, the action relieving my built-up frustration over the situation.

After most of his red wine was enjoyed, Mr. Douglas, still standing, continued. "I was hoping to make it down to the Caribbean on that trip. I wanted to purchase some exotic jewelry for Marry-Anne. Instead I returned with nothing but a battered ship, a better understanding and appreciation for life, and my soul. All duty free, of course."

A light laugh wafted over the table, as it always did.

"Ha, 'duty,' " young Preston across the table said.

My resulting laughter was cut short by Julie's left elbow to my right ribs. She then scolded the boy with a sharp look.

"Sorry, Auntie Julie," he said.

Mr. Douglas lifted his right hand and twirled it around. Six butlers went to work, holding baskets of bread and bowls of salad as he lowered himself into his seat unassisted.

"Wait!" he shouted when he finally hit the chair. "Please serve Nicholas first."

My mind skipped the possibility that the gesture was a white flag and went directly to the certainty that the food was poisoned.

"Thank you?" I said slowly, suspicious of Mr. Douglas's motives.

His next words, though, explained away any of the possibilities that had multiplied in my mind by that point. " 'The first shall be the last and the last shall be the first,' " he said, quoting the Bible.

I squinted and thought about his words before asking Julie in a whisper, "How should I feel about this?"

"Just smile," she said under her breath.

From his seated position at the head of the table, Julie's father explained that all of the food that we were to eat that night was from his favorite restaurant. The restaurant had sent the food accompanied by part of their waitstaff and kitchen crew so that the experience was, as they put it, "an accurate representation of their high standards, from the taste to the service."

Mr. Douglas knew them all by name, probably a trick he worked quite a while on so that he could convince people he was a supporter of the common man. He introduced them one by one.

"Say hello to Mark, Jeff, and Ivan, everyone. They are serving the bread while Luke and Troy are serving salad. And John is refilling your glasses."

"Seriously?" I asked aloud.

Julie shushed me, but to no avail.

"Excuse me, Nicholas?" Mr. Douglas inquired.

"You have someone named Mark serving bread and someone named John pouring wine?" I asked with a smile on my face.

"That's right, Nicholas. Is there a problem?" Mr. Douglas persisted.

"No, no problem," I responded quietly, giving no more information.

As Mark lowered a roll onto my bread plate, I asked him loudly and for all to hear, "What are you? About 6 foot 4 or so? Pretty tall guy we got here."

"Yes, Sir. That sounds about right," he responded politely.

"You have a big family, Mark?" I asked. "Maybe four siblings, something like that?"

"Yes! And I'm the fourth born!" he said, astonished. "How did you know that?"

"Oh, just a lucky guess," I said before unveiling the holy meaning loudly to the table, "Mark 6-44! Bam!" I shouted as I hit the table with my right hand.

Most members of the family ignored my antics and line of questioning while the others, those who had tried to attend to the conversation, just looked at me confused.

"What are you doing?" Julie demanded, embarrassed.

"Really? You don't get it? Mark 6-44. Body into bread. This is hilarious. Hold on, hold on," I said as I searched for John.

"Hey, John," I shouted, not knowing which one he was because another butler began to assist in filling glasses with wine.

John poked his head up from the far end of the table. "Yes, Sir?" he asked slowly.

"You look like you're from a smaller family than Mark. You have maybe one other sibling, am I right?" I asked knowingly.

"Well, I have two half-sisters."

"So that's one full sister then," I joked, fuzzy familial mathematics at work as I maneuvered toward the punch line. My parlor trick had become more of a spectacle and was increasing its audience by the word.

"We'll count them as two," I continued. "Is one of them, by chance, eleven years old?"

"Fourteen and seventeen," he responded before saying, "but I do have a cousin who's eleven, if that helps."

I then unveiled, "John 2-11. Blood into wine!"

Expecting applause, I was surprised to hear only sounds of disgust, scoffs, and to see the shaking of heads. I heard more than one "oh my" and several instances of "well I would never..."

Abigail, sitting still far too close to my left side, said, "There is not one person in the room who thinks you're funny."

I shrank into my seat, hoping to become as invisible to the family as I had been before I had attempted to impress with humor.

After some time passed, small conversation began to emerge and my attempts at wit passed from consciousness.

"Who wants to say grace?" Mr. Douglas asked, knowing that the privilege would rest solely on his shoulders. "Okay then," he said after a short pause. "I'll do it. I suppose that I'm running this meeting."

"If you think so," I said to myself, heard by Julie and Abigail.

"Some are born great and some have it thrust upon them," he continued. "Please hold hands everyone."

I had no qualms about holding the hand of my wife, even though she did about holding mine, but I was repulsed by the touch of Abigail's manly right to my left. I knew she was a biological cousin, but I still searched my memory to uncover any possible information that she was not genetically tied to my wife.

When compared to the rest, Abigail was a mess. She obviously had issues with nutritional self-control. Her hands were warm, rough, sweaty, and smelled of salt and sulfur. The family average was slim and beautiful with smooth perfect skin. And I was certain that, even during the most strenuous of tasks—sports or a family competition—on the hottest of days, I had never seen one of them sweat.

Mr. Douglas began his prayer with, "Bless us our Lord for these gifts that we are about to receive..."

As he continued, I had trouble concentrating on anything but the insufferable woman's greasy palm rubbing against my own. I began to feel nauseous, but managed to fight back the urge to regurgitate all that I had eaten that day. I knew I had already made the wrong impression on the family; spewing partially digested food at them during a prayer would be another large step in the wrong direction.

The ridiculousness of that potential scenario made me chuckle, however, a chuckle that was apparently heard around the table.

"Do I amuse you, Nicholas?" Mr. Douglas asked.

"I wish," I muttered to myself.

At that, Abigail dropped my hand releasing me from her foul grasp.

"Excuse me?" Mr. Douglas asked.

"I'm sorry, Sir," I said, smiling at my freed, but disgustingly tainted left hand.

He paused for a moment before declaring, "Supper begins!"

Julie threw down my hand, knuckles rapping sharply on the armrest of my seat.

"Auhh! What are you doing?" I shouted in protest, massaging my injured hand.

Again, all eyes migrated in my direction.

Julie ignored me and lightly tossed her salad with her fork, distributing the dressing as needed. The rest of the family decided to do the same, ignoring my outburst and my very existence.

The salad was thin, but crunchy, and looked artificially greened, but I assumed it was natural and probably organic. As I ate, I looked around the table at the thirty or so people all bound by love. I fit in in no way. One of the newer members of the family, Emma's current husband of one year, attempted to kiss up to Mr. Douglas by asking about his sailing.

"Excuse me, Captain. How is it that you got into sailing?"

Mr. Douglas masticated then swallowed the salad in his mouth before putting down his fork so he might speak with both his mouth and his hands. "Hmm... who was it that said necessity is the mother of invention?"

"Plato," I muttered under my breath, heard by none.

He continued, not answering his own question. "That is how I got into sailing. I needed a hobby, so I built myself a sailboat."

I turned to Julie and whispered, "That is a lie and it doesn't even make any sense. I doubt he ever built anything in his life. And it was Plato who said 'necessity is the mother of invention.' "

"Do you have something to add, Nicholas?" Mr. Douglas asked, unexpectedly.

Despite the unanimous decision to ignore me, all eyes again rested upon my space at the table.

"Plato," I responded confidently. "It was Plato who said that."

"Said what?" he asked.

" 'Necessity is the mother of invention,' " I clarified.

"We are done talking about that, Nicholas," he said with a dismissive tone.

All the eyes at the table remained fixed on me as the leader of the pack continued with what I knew to be a fraudulent tale (based on my educated assumptions) about his involvement with building a sailboat. None hid their judging looks, eyes raking me up and down.

I whispered to Julie, "Maybe he would have believed me if I told him the burning bush told me."

But all I could pull from Julie was "sshhhh."

"I think your father is afraid of me usurping his throne," I told her quietly.

Again, I was shushed.

Mr. Douglas then included his wife in his fairy tale. "But the issue with my sailing was that I couldn't take with me my beautiful bride." Julie's parents smiled at one another and held hands lovingly while the rest of the table beamed at them.

"I love my wife…" he continued. "Her name is the most beautiful two words put together in our language. Marry-Anne; music to my ears."

"Actually," I whispered to Julie, "it's 'Cellar Door.'"

"What?" she asked me with a tone that did not encourage an answer.

"Have you, yet again, something to add, Nicholas?" Mr. Douglas said, clearly provoked by my interruptions.

"Cellar Door," I said loudly to all. "Tolkien, the writer and philologist, tells us that it's 'Cellar Door.' He was a respected scholar of phonoaesthetics in addition to an author. The word 'cellar' and the word 'door' sound the best together of any two words in the English language. It's a widely accepted fact."

It took me saying 'Cellar Door' out loud to realize that the combination of my discomfort and defensive posture when among Julie's family combined with my need to impress while striving for their acceptance—that I knew was impossible to obtain—turned me into a socially awkward, rude, and inappropriate boor of a guest.

The realization and the resulting increase in discomfort pushed me deep into my seat. I finally saw myself from the point of view of the family and I was quite embarrassed.

Mr. Douglas continued talking about sailing and his boats, the sea and his journeys. In that time, I had vanished into obscurity, but, having truly seen how rudely I had behaved, I wanted to positively add to the conversation as opposed to just sitting back and enjoying the third course.

When Mr. Douglas came to the question and answer portion of his talk, I was eager to contribute.

"Would anyone fancy a glass of port after dinner?" he asked to the table.

Most nodded, some replied with a "yes" or an "okay," but all knew there was more to come; that they were merely setting the man up to deliver a punch line.

"How about a glass of starboard?" he zinged, laughing.

The rest of the table followed suit, but laughed even harder.

"Oh my!" he exclaimed. "I must apologize. Just a bit of nautical humor, you see. How about this, does anyone know where the word 'posh' came from?"

I raised my right hand.

Mr. Douglas then highlighted my misstep. "Nicholas. We don't raise our hands here. We can contribute to the conversation without being called on. I think you've already proven that quite extensively."

My right hand remained in the air as I processed his intention. Then it slowly came down to my chair's armrest. "Sorry," I said.

"Go ahead, Nicholas," Mr. Douglas begrudged, sounding tired from my previous antics.

"Yes. Posh stands for 'port out, starboard home.' Upper-class passengers going on vacation would reserve rooms on ships on the port side when traveling in one direction to avoid the sun and get the breeze through their windows. Then, on their voyage home, they would reserve a room on the starboard side for the same reasons. Their tickets would read 'posh' to indicate the appropriate side of the ship."

"Incorrect!" Mr. Douglas exclaimed joyously. "A common misconception, but the truth is far from your wrong answer. The word 'posh' came from the Romany word 'posh' which meant half, as in 'posh-kooroona' or half-crown. It was a measure of a large sum of money." Mr. Douglas smiled at me victoriously.

"But that's wrong," I muttered quietly to myself.

"Something to add?" Mr. Douglas asked of me.

"No, no, Sir," I said after weighing the pros and cons. I knew that I could have given him either answer and his response would have insisted the other to be true. I had corrected him far too many times for him not to fix the deck in his favor. I determined this stolen victory to be one that I owed him so I sat back, forcefully defeated, waiting for another chance to contribute to the conversation.

The following two courses satiated me substantially. I had not eaten well for days, weeks, longer, but, despite the magnificent food, my level of frustration remained consistently elevated as Julie's father and several other members of the family confidently presented shockingly wrong information or obvious fabrications or exaggerations of the truth as fact numerous times. I had bitten practically through my tongue to silence it. And, somehow, confusing me and adding to the turmoil inside, I noticed that each member of the family older than sixteen ate and drank very generously. I questioned their ability to stay as thin they did after witnessing such a magnificent disappearing act.

Finally, I could take the silent suffering no longer. The bathroom at the far end of the house was determined, by my fogged thinking, to be the perfect sanctuary. I whispered to Julie my intentions, then stood up to be on my way.

"Can we help you?" Mr. Douglas asked me.

"I'm just headed to the bathroom. I didn't think I had to ask for permission. No hand raising, right?" I said jokingly.

He then shooed me off with the back of his right hand.

As I strolled casually in the direction of the bathroom, I began to consider straying off the path, but my fear of being lost for the remainder of the night was too strong to ignore.

My head was directed down for much of the trip, floors catching my eye. Most of the house displayed fine woods of all different shapes, sizes, depths, designs, widths, colors, lengths, and varieties. In addition to what was under my feet, almost every wall was covered on the bottom third with wainscoting, colored to appropriately complement the wall paper, paint, or plaster covering the top two thirds.

Ajar in position, the arch created by the bathroom door displayed the minuscule sink and mirror. Lightbulb's string off in position, I watched myself in miniature as I approached, darkened.

I do look homeless, I thought as I stared myself in the face. *I look like a complete mess.* It was then that I knew things were over, truly over. I had been rude to the Douglas family, all of them, and it had been going on for years. There was no coming back from it, no mending broken ties. And Julie...

The walk back was quicker than the walk away. I thought maybe by approaching fast, the night would end sooner. I thought about how I would be on the port side on this return trip while the rest of the family was on the starboard. The sounds of a happy family increased in volume as I did in proximity. I almost smiled, but their hatred for me, their justified hatred, made certain that a smile never found its way to my lips.

———

Stigmata

The courses that I missed were one next to the other on the table in front of where I sat. They were rather delicious which made me wish later on that I had paid better attention to exactly what they were.

I looked over at Abigail to see her place setting was clean and untouched.

"Not eating tonight?" I asked her.

"I ate earlier," she snapped back defensively. "Worry about yourself."

I ignored her harsh tone as dessert replaced my two empty plates. A waiter placed in front of me a piece of chocolate cake, assorted sliced fresh fruit on the side, and hot syrupy chocolate fudge in a small bowl for personal dipping or pouring.

"Delicious" was thrown back and forth across the large long table. Chocolate cake was something of a Douglas family tradition. I half-expected to be regaled by an embellished, fabricated, or completely fictitious tale about being lost at sea or in the jungle or in the middle of a vast waterless desert then miraculously finding life-saving sustenance in a cocoa tree, but the story never materialized.

Mr. Douglas, just as the rest of the family, was well relaxed and well quenched of thirst by the numerous glasses of wine, bottles of wine, that were consumed.

The children, all of them on their side of the table, were becoming anxious, squirming in their seats, fidgeting with their fingers, itching to jump down and away, dying to play far from their captive places at the table.

Sensing this quiet unrest brewing in his midst, Mr. Douglas made an announcement that made him the favorite old man in the room. "The children may leave the table and play in the southeast living room. Eliot will lead you all there. You are excused."

Children scattered left and right, knocking over chairs and bouncing off the walls. Laughing and nodding, enjoying the power that he wielded, his ability to make more than a dozen children scatter at will, Mr. Douglas swung his arms up joyously then pulled them back down toward the table, right hand on a collision course with his beloved and overused wineglass.

The old man shrieked, startling all who were around him into frozen horror. Then the butlers and waiters rushed to his aid as his red-covered hands, wrists, and arms shook out of fear, dripping and splattering viscous liquid in all directions. From my distant vantage point, it was difficult to determine how much was blood and how much was red wine as it saturated the white tablecloth and the dozen white napkins the servers used to absorb it.

"Oh. Stigmata..." I said to myself as I took a sip from my glass of white wine and laughed over my better judgment.

Despite the fact that six highly qualified waiters and two butlers were fussing over him, Mr. Douglas was dissatisfied and wanted more professional assistance.

"Nicholas! Nicholas! Come, Nicholas! You're a doctor! Help me, Nicholas!"

"Actually, I have a PhD. I'm no more qualified to help you than anyone else here."

"Yes, you're a doctor! Help me!" he shouted back.

Unsure of his motives, I begrudgingly pushed back my chair and stood. Blood up-close made me as uncomfortable as tears so I braced myself for a bout of weakening knees and overall squeamishness. The size of the table became apparent only when I was forced to walk half its length while being watched in anticipation by all.

When I reached Mr. Douglas, I held his hands, rotated them to the palms up position, then pulled away the ruined cloth napkins to find two wine-stained hands and wrists, only one of which had a small surface scratch on it.

"You should be fine," I said, releasing his hands and beginning to turn away.

"Good thinking!" Mr. Douglas exclaimed. "The bathroom, we'll wash out the wounds."

"The bathroom is so far away," I protested. "You could just wash it off later on, no?"

"There is a bathroom right there," he said, pointing awkwardly down the hall as he held his arms and hands at strange angles.

"Oh," I responded.

Mr. Douglas led me twenty feet from where we stood and instructed me to open a door and flip a switch inside, on the wall to the left of the doorway. A magnificent array of pale pink marble covered the walls, the floor, even the sink was made of solid *rosa aurora* marble. The fixtures were all gold, including the toilet which was almost fully gold plated. White monogrammed towels were draped over a heated towel rack with the letters M. B. G. (Marry-Anne Beatrice Douglas) on half and R. W. D. (Robert Webb Douglas) on the others, both in an almost illegible script. Mr. Douglas grabbed one and started wiping off his hands.

"No," I shouted. "You'll stain them."

"Oh, no bother. We'll just get more," he said whimsically. "So what should we do?"

"Rinse off your hands and arms, I suppose," I said, suggesting common sense behaviors after spilling red wine on oneself.

"Good, good," he said as he adjusted the gold faucets to find a comfortable temperature.

Mark, the waiter who had spent the earlier part of dinner providing bread for the table, materialized and asked, "May I help in some manner, Sirs?"

"Get some Band-Aids and some gauze. Ask one of the butlers," I instructed. I felt it necessary to add "stat," but he had already left the room and did not hear.

With a pristine white monogrammed towel that I dampened under the running water, I dabbed the scratch on Mr. Douglas's right hand. Words were not exchanged, but I had hoped the gesture would help mend more than just the physical wound.

After a thorough dab-drying with another white monogrammed towel, Mark, who was standing in the doorway, handed me the gauze I had requested and a box of children's Band-Aids.

"Really? That's the best you can do?" I asked.

"It's all I could find," he said apologetically.

From the box, I pulled out an appropriately sized Band-Aid covered with little cartoon animals frolicking in a forest then stuck it to Mr. Douglas, gauze in between bandage and skin. Then, for good measure, I stuck all sixteen remaining Band-Aids around his hand.

Looking absurdly foolish, Mr. Douglas smiled at his well wrapped right wrist and hand.

"How is that?" I asked, fighting back laughter.

"Fantastic, Nicholas!" he shouted.

Down the hall we then walked, slowly and without words, until he pointed at a picture of two large boats, one white and the other made from brown wood.

"Do you know what these are, Nicholas?" he asked mildly.

"No, Sir; I don't," I responded, waiting for him to tell a long-winded story.

"These are two of my vessels. They cost a fortune, but they bring me such pleasure. Worth the investment, Nicholas."

"Is that right?" I said.

"You know, Nicholas, this reminds me of a story... Captain's Log, 14 hundred 92 years. Christopher Columbus, the first American in America, landed in what they initially assumed to be 'The Indies,' but then learned to refer to as 'The New World' or 'The United States of America.' The indigenous tribes who inhabited those areas—they called themselves 'Indians'—could not see the three huge ships docked just off the shores. It was because the craftsmanship and ingenuity of those ships were far beyond what those primitive people could comprehend; their brains couldn't process something that couldn't exist in their world. It was weeks before they actually saw what was right in front of them."

I knew that Mr. Douglas had consumed many glasses of wine, so I was not as insulted by his contextually degrading story as I would have been had he told it three hours earlier. What did incite a deep frustration within me was the historical inaccuracy of his ramblings.

Columbus was not the first non–Native American or even the first European to make it to the Americas, far from the first. And he was not American; he was Italian, sent by the Spanish Monarchs. And he made four trips from Spain, only reaching South America during the third trip; the third trip during which he was also arrested due to his gross misrepresentation of the riches of the New World and gross mismanagement of the settlements. He was in the Caribbean for the vast majority of his voyages and he never set foot on what is now referred to as The United States of America.

As for the number of his ships, the first trip had three (one of which ran aground and was abandoned), then seventeen, six, and four for the second, third, and fourth trips respectively; some of those ships were also abandoned or sank.

And the indigenous people did not call themselves "Indians." Columbus called them that (more specifically, *Indios*) because he was not willing to admit that he had not made it to the East Indies like he had set out to do.

Additionally, how would Mr. Douglas know if these *primitive people* could or could not see the ships right in front of them? There is no scientific evidence of this whatsoever. In fact, there is evidence to the contrary. During Columbus's first trip, when he landed on the Samaná Península of the Dominican Republic, he was met with the only hostile group of natives of his trip, the Ciguayos. Their use of arrows against Columbus and his men did little to stop them from their *exploration*, but, because of this, Columbus decided to call this place the Bay of Arrows. So, yes, they did see the ships and felt threatened enough to shoot arrows at them.

I decided to bury away the frustration borne from historical inaccuracy and push out a forced smile instead of factually correct information.

"Those are some nice boats, Sir," I responded, hoping to end the conversation and pull us back into the dining room.

"They're yachts, Nicholas. Rather different, yachts and boats. You see…"

He then proceeded to recite his lengthy explanation of the importance of names. The speech was first introduced to me after he had given up attempting to convince Julie not to marry me and had turned his focus instead to convincing me to encourage her to keep her last name. The speech felt much longer when it was first heard; I listened more attentively back then.

"We should get back to the table," I suggested, interrupting his speech.

"Yes, of course," he agreed.

We moved down the hall once again.

"Hooray!" someone cheered when Mr. Douglas entered the dining room.

I could see that the drinks had continued to flow in our absence. Not one member of the family addressed me, but all sent their verbal condolences and well-wishes to Mr. Douglas for his quick recovery. Even his *immense bravery* was highlighted.

The fatigue of the long drive and the exhausting task of anxiously attempting to interact with Julie's family had begun to take their toll on my strained body. Standing behind my chair and in front of the table inhabited on only one side due to the absence of the children, I stretched my arms out displaying my full wingspan. I then leaned backward, cracking my back and dropping my head behind my shoulders, body forming a large T. In the process, I rose two inches by lifting upward onto my toes, stretching my legs, calves, and feet. I wished for a moment that I could float away, then, when I knew the wish would go ungranted, I fell back onto my flat feet and continued my descent toward the chair.

"I'm sorry, are we boring you?" Abigail asked of my stretching.

I chose to ignore her, glancing in the opposite direction to find myself confronted by Julie's somewhat concerned looking face.

"What did he say to you?" Julie asked.

"Nothing, why?"

"He didn't say anything to you?"

"Well, he told me about his boats."

"They're yachts," she said reflexively.

"Yes. He corrected me too. You know, you're just like him."

She scoffed before saying, "Knowing how you feel about him, I'm very insulted, Nick. But, I'll still take that as a compliment."

I turned my nose up at her then focused on His Greatness addressing the group from his seat.

" 'For my house will be a house of worship for all nations,' " he said, quoting scripture, elongating and emphasizing the word "all" while pointing with both hands and nodding toward me.

"Your father is unbelievably insensitive even when he is trying to be nice," I whispered to Julie.

I was ignored.

After hugging and kissing her husband, Mrs. Douglas, shaking with glee, began knocking her knife into a thick glass half filled with water. "Excuse me! Excuse me, everyone! I'd like to make an announcement."

I perked up, hoping she and her husband were ready to suggest a bedtime for the family, one that was sooner rather than later.

"With this recent brush with death, The Captain and I have come to realize that we love these times; this time we spend with all of you, our family. But we know that you, our family, will have to return to your separate lives when this weekend ends. Yes, we will get together again, throughout the year and a year from now, but how many of us will be here; how many not able to make it or just not here…" She trailed off, her words chopped by her choked-up voice.

Mr. Douglas continued where his wife left off. "This is why Marry-Anne and I have just decided to get a kitten!"

This *news* was met with cheers and congratulations.

"Actually," Mrs. Douglas added, "it will be a pedigree kitten."

"Pedigree kitten?" I questioned quietly. "Do those even exist?"

"Yes, Nick!" Julie whisper forcefully, finally addressing one of my comments. "They breed them in a controlled manner; pairing them to emphasize specific characteristics in the offspring. They have certifications and cat shows. They cost a fortune."

I ignored the fact that I had been ignored for most of the night and I ignored the fact that she chose to break her silence toward me to talk about cat shows and responded instead with my immense disbelief.

"That can't be true. You can just find a cat on the street. Why pay for one? And why did they feel it necessary to announce this to the entire family? And when did they even talk about all of this? They've been sitting there for less than a minute after The Captain's 'brush with death.' And don't they have a dog, Scrappy?"

"Scrappy died last month, Nick," Julie growled, apparently assuming that I was making a joke about the dog to which her parents had grown so very close.

Feeling a bit guilty about bringing up their deceased dog, even if it was just to Julie, I thought about how I could somehow add to the celebration of this new addition to the family. I raised my hand quickly and was waiting to be called on to share my idea.

"Yes, Nicholas," Mr. Douglas said, pointing at me.

"You should name it Caboodle," I suggested.

"Caboodle?" Mrs. Douglas questioned.

"Yes, yes," I said.

"Why Caboodle?" someone else asked.

"I don't know; it just sounds right. Kitten Caboodle…"

A laugh was the goal. A smile or nod would have sufficed. An iota of acknowledgment was the least I would accept as a positive outcome, but the topic of conversation changed in an instant without any reaction to my suggestion.

"Let's all find our way to the den, shall we?" Mr. Douglas said as he stood up slowly, a butler rushing to his side to aid his painful ascent.

I remained seated while the rest of the table took their cloth napkins from their laps and placed them on the large table. Small conversations started. Brothers, sisters, cousins, aunts, uncles, nephews, nieces; led by Mr. Douglas, they all squeezed their way down the narrow dark hall.

After the last family member shuffled behind them, an old man to whom I did not pay enough attention to recognize, I stood and yawned, becoming increasingly tired as the day increased in length. Then, somehow, someway, someone turned off all of the lights in the room simultaneously.

"Really?" I questioned aloud. "The lights?"

———

Edward

I followed the dim glow from the hallway out of the dining room to catch up to the older man who moved very slowly, leaning against the wall as he shuffled along. He knocked three paintings askew, all of which I righted behind him. They were magnificent portraits, reminiscent of the *Mona Lisa* in style and size. Clearly commissioned, I pondered their cost while chuckling at their likely value. Until that moment, I had never witnessed a dog, alone on a canvas, smiling and crossing its legs while sitting on a small couch. The same was true for the cat and bird in the second and third paintings respectively.

"Art..." I muttered to myself.

The leader of our two person caravan, moving very slowly, fell off the wall when it opened up into a doorway. From my vantage point, he had disappeared. I entered the dim room, lit only by the spill-off light from the hall, and began searching the walls with my left hand for a light-switch. When I finally found one and flicked it on, I found that the old man was nowhere in sight.

My eyes moved around the space, lined with dark wood paneling, a rich chocolate brown color that was enhanced with streaks of sapwood. One corner housed a very large television with several speakers and light brown couches that looked plush and inviting. There were additional speakers built into every wall and in the ceiling, different in color than the surrounding paneling. The billiards table near another corner was made from the same mahogany as the tall chairs against the wall adjacent to it. The mahogany theme carried over to the bar and the stools on another wall.

"Hello?" I said loudly. "Hello?"

"Oh, hello!" I heard from behind the bar. Then a head popped up, followed by shoulders and a torso.

"Edward Martin?" I said, finally recognizing the man developed in years.

"Yeesss. Who's there?" he slurred, finally standing, but just barely.

"Nicholas. It's Nicholas Thesiger."

Edward, swaying back and forth, came very close to losing his balance then stopped his swaying for a moment by tightly grasping to the bar before releasing his grip to repeat the cycle.

"Edward. What are you doing here?" I asked, as I approached and sat on a stool at the bar cushioned with red velvet.

Equilibrium noticeably off, he swayed while squinting his eyes at me. "Shouldn't you be in the kitchen?"

"Edward. It's Nicholas. Nicholas Thesiger? Julie's husband. I was at your cocktail party last night."

Still swaying and squinting, he attempted to focus on me more closely. "Nicholas! Nicholas! I see you now!" he realized.

"Yes! What are you doing here, old dog?" I asked, laughing.

"What'll it be, Nick?" He wafted his hand in a semi-circular motion, fingers together from up and down and left and right, displaying the variety of liquors, brandies, cognacs, vodkas, and more on the wall behind him. He then added, "Haza!"

"Nothing for me, Sir. Thank you. Taking a bit of a rest from all the people?" I asked. "Is that why you're in here?"

"The Captain said, 'We'll meet in the den.' Did he not?" Edward asked.

"Well, he likely meant another den because we're the only two in here," I told him. "But why not stay and relax? Take a break from everyone with me, huh?" I felt as if I could be honest with a drunk man without fear of our conversation leaving the room. "I'm having a little trouble fitting in with the family," I admitted.

Just as I began to divulge to Edward's inebriated subconscious, he spun around quickly then regained ocular focus on a line of photographs framed on the wall.

"Look at this!" he shouted. "There are my siblings! The Captain, Otis, Thomas, and Jillian."

"They're your siblings?" I asked, confused.

"Yes! Of course. You knew this. We are family, young man. We are family, but it's not spoken about all too often."

"And why is that, Edward?"

"Don't ask me," he answered quickly. Then he went on to describe another picture. "Yes, there we are in front of the old townhouse on the west side. The five of us as children, our parents, and our paternal grandmother." He picked the frame off the wall and held it close.

"So you are Mr. Douglas's brother? No one ever told me this."

"*C'est la vie,* my good man. *C'est la vie!*" Edward then began to spin along with his perception of the room, remaining on his feet to my surprise.

"Edward!" I heard from the doorway. "We've been looking for you!"

Elisabeth, Edward's worried looking wife, hurried in, followed by Julie and Julie's cousins, Abigail and Kathy. Kathy, just as useless as Edward at the moment, plopped headfirst onto the couch while Abigail attempted to help Elisabeth with Edward.

"Come on, dear," Elisabeth said to Edward. "Let's get back to the party, okay?"

"I shall do as I please, m'lady!" he insisted.

"Don't make me carry you, old man," Abigail threatened, but was waved back by Elisabeth who continued to attempt to convince an alcoholic that leaving the bar was a good idea.

"Can't find the answer to a problem in the bottle, huh?" I said to Julie as she approached me, looking ready to spar.

"What are you doing in here with him?"

"Just shootin' the breeze," I said. "Oh, and he told me that he is your father's brother? You never mentioned that."

Julie looked away from me and toward Edward, Elisabeth, and Abigail, then to Kathy, who had decided that the billiards table was a more appropriate location than the couch upon which to drunkenly collapse.

"That may be true, yes," she said candidly. "But we don't talk about it."

"Why not? What happened between them? Why is he here? Why did you keep this from me?" I was full of questions and hoping for at least one answer.

Julie spoke quietly. "Thirty years ago or so he had some drinks before taking a drive and ended up getting into an accident. The other driver died. Edward had to be separated in name from the family to avoid a larger settlement. He lost everything that was in his own name so he's been supported by Elisabeth ever since. That's all, okay? There's nothing more to tell. He's been to a rehabilitation clinic and continues with meetings and he's been doing fine until recently."

"So he's serving drinks?" I said with a sarcastic tone, pointing to him behind the bar. "Julie, the mouse serving the cheese is never a good idea."

"This is serious, Nick. Stop making jokes. He shouldn't have been able to walk away from that accident. The police said that the only reason he survived was that his muscles were relaxed because of the alcohol or something like that. He could have... should have lost his life so we should be thankful that he didn't."

"Ironic..." I said.

Julie looked at me angrily, then began to walk. I held her arm before she got away.

"So what is happening now? Who let him drink? How did this happen?"

Two butlers entered the room to assist in Edward's removal. Julie's voice fell to a whisper. "He takes some drug or something that makes him sick when he drinks."

"Well, he must be planning his relapse by not taking the drug: the fatal flaw of a stupidly self-administered medication to control an alcoholic's own behavior."

"He is not an alcoholic!" Julie whispered harshly to me. "He is a *recovering* alcoholic."

"Julie, 'recovering alcoholic' is a misnomer. Once an alcoholic, always an alcoholic. All an alcoholic can do is try to keep himself from falling down the path of addiction again and the best way to do that is to not drink." I then looked toward Edward and said, "And I believe this man is currently drinking."

Edward's lips were tightly wrapped around a fat short bottle of whiskey, gulping down the ounces as quickly as he could before one of the butlers pulled it away. He then turned to me and shouted, "It's called controlled drinking, my good man." He was smiling and comfortable, no longer burdened with the task of holding himself upright due to the aid of the butlers.

I looked at Julie, tilting my head to the left, smiling, and raising my flat palms and shoulders. "Enough said?" I asked.

Julie then pulled me close to her and whispered, "He decides when to drink. He just had a little too much this time."

"And last night too and how many times before?" I asked quietly. "Once an alcoholic, always an alcoholic."

Then, somewhat unexpectedly, but fully expected, Edward keeled forward and regurgitated much of what he had ingested over the previous three hours. I meant not to inspect the splatter on the tan carpet, but for some unexplainable reason, my eyes could not direct themselves elsewhere. The bread that Mark had given out earlier was in clear large visible chunks mixed in with the wine that John had so generously poured.

"Oh," I said. "He's the devil."

I left the room alone, passing Kathy squirming around the billiards table, struggling to find a comfortable position. I assumed that to be her bed for the night.

I moved swiftly down the hall and back into the dining room where the lights had been turned back on and the table was clear and clean; a result of live-in domestic help aided by the six waiters. I then remained as quiet as possible so I could follow the sound of the family out of the dining room, down a hall, through the large two-story room with a double staircase, then down another hall and into yet another den, which looked suspiciously similar to the one I had just exited, although with a piano replacing the billiards table and no large television.

I stood in the doorway for a moment then took a step out and looked around the hall to see if I could determine if this was the same room as before, just cleaned of vomit and filled with people and a piano. My mind went to the possibility that the family was trying to disorient me for some sinister reason, but watching them interact in their loose liquored-up way put any suspicion of devious plans in motion out of my mind.

One of the cousins that I did not recognize was playing the piano while a number more were singing, arms around one another. Some of the older generation sat on the corresponding light brown couches, smiling and reminiscing.

I moved toward the bar and sat on the same stool that I had sat on only a few minutes earlier. Déjà vu hit me as I swiveled around to face the bar. I quickly found myself looking not Edward, but Mark the bread waiter in the eyes, mine much more pensive than his.

"What'll it be?" he asked ominously.

"Nothing for me, Mark," I responded uncomfortably.

I looked behind him to see if I could spot the framed pictures, but none were present, then I turned to take another look around the room. "What's that under the piano?" I asked, spotting a small red object.

Mark leaned over the bar and lowered his eyes to gain a better angle. "Looks like a red plastic cup," he responded.

"Wonder how that got there," I said.

Mark said, "I wonder why no one has gone to remove it."

"Same reason people try to avoid standing on the letter X drawn on the street," I said.

"Why is that?" he asked.

"They're afraid of a piano falling on their head."

He laughed loudly, whole body tensing while his head was thrown back. I smiled at this unmistakable proof that I was indeed hilarious and it was the family who had no sense of humor. Mark was forced to calm himself quickly when two cousins, Isaac and Joseph, and another whom I did not recognize approached to ask for drinks.

I left the bar and sat on one of the tall chairs against the wall. These chairs had a purpose in the other den, as companions to the billiards table, but their placement in this den seemed suspicious and made me feel uncomfortable; nonetheless there I sat watching the glee in the room bounce from family member to family member to family member.

I awoke to Julie shaking me. I was certain that I had not been asleep, but that I was merely tired and lost focus on the present. However, when I realized that half of the room had emptied and the other half was following suit, I mentally acknowledged my loss of consciousness.

"Everyone is going up to their rooms. Nick, I know that I was the one that rented a room for us so we could spend some time together and alone and away from everything, but maybe we should just spend the night here?" Julie's tone was approaching playful. She had clearly been brought to happiness by her family, but I was the opposite after being startled out of rest.

"Absolutely not!" I said in a starchy, sleepy voice. "I agreed to come this time because last week you told me you rented a room elsewhere. Now elsewhere we shall go!" I fell to my feet from the tall chair and wobbled my way out of the room and down the hall.

"This way," Julie said reluctantly after leaving the room and turning in the opposite direction to my disoriented choice.

I said nothing, but followed slightly behind her.

"Mother! Father!" Julie shouted. "Nick and I are leaving."

When we finally made it to the front door, we were met by Julie's parents. I was a bit cranky from my interrupted nap so my frustration as a result of their presence was magnified that much more. Then Mr. Douglas's hand wrapped in cartoon animals brought a smile to my mind, but not to my face, while Julie slipped her feet into her shoes at the edge of the pile behind the door.

"Why not spend the night at the estate, Julie," Mrs. Douglas insisted. "Nick, you can go to your hotel if you're uncomfortable."

"No, that's fine, thank you," I responded as I focused my attention on the pile of shoes. "The plan we made weeks ago was for us to spend a bit of time away from the hustle and bustle, a bit of a vacation from the city. We'll be leaving together." I, of course, meant "a vacation away from the family."

I searched for my sneakers while Julie whispered with her parents. When finally, after well over two minutes, I found them, I slipped my feet in without mishap or mistaken identity and grabbed the doorknob.

"We're off," I insisted.

I moved through the doorway and toward the car. Julie followed behind.

"You'll call us in the morning, won't you?" Mrs. Douglas called after Julie. "You have the number, don't you, Julie?"

"Still '666'?" I inquired loudly as I passed the granite fountain uselessly circulating water up and down.

"I would never forget it," Julie called back to them.

My door swung up and my momentum pulled me in. Julie's door lifted thirty seconds after, delayed as she and her parents shouted pleasantries to one another. She then slid down into the seat, warm from the day's sun, with experienced skill. I turned on the vehicle and opened the windows before plugging in my phone.

"You know their number or it's stored in your phone?" I asked, still a bit groggy from my nap, finding fault in everything.

Julie responded with many more words than I expected. "I actually remember the number, unlike you. You just ignore the important things and store useless information in your memory like a robot or something."

"What does that have to do with anything?" I asked.

She continued, ignoring my words completely. "What would happen if all the cell phones and computers just died? How would you get anyone's number? What would anyone do? You would all be lost."

"It probably wouldn't matter if I couldn't get a person's number because their phone would be dead," I responded.

She looked away through the window and into the darkness. "I guess you just can't understand me," she muttered under her breath.

"Why do we always fight on vacation?" I asked sarcastically. I then followed the directions from the navigation system to the hotel, fifteen minutes of silence from the estate.

Bed & Breakfast

We turned off a street and then down a long dirt road with no lights at all and pulled up to a small cottage which appeared to have only one light on inside. I was confused when the navigation system announced it to be our destination.

"Are you sure you got the address right?" I asked Julie.

"This is it," she said.

"*This* is our hotel?" I said degradingly, looking at the old, beaten looking, badly maintained, and very small cottage.

"It's a bed and breakfast. I thought it would be nice for us."

"Well, it's not. Let's go somewhere else," I said, beginning to allow my anger to color the tone of my words.

"Nick, we're already here. Let's go inside. It will be nice." She opened her door and picked up only her smallest bag, the one by her feet, as I begrudgingly turned the car off.

"What about the rest of them?" I asked, not wanting to carry them inside, but knowing the responsibility would fall on me whether I started then or later.

"Oh, those are for Emma's oldest girl, Madison. I'll give them to her tomorrow."

Happy to hear that, I picked up my duffel bag and we proceeded up the walkway toward the bed and breakfast then through the creaking screen door into a small entranceway, dimly lit, with a desk at the far end. I rang the bell atop the desk vigorously until someone came slowly down the stairs.

"Yes, we have a reservation. Thesiger," I said quickly, glancing at Julie to confirm that she left the reservation under my last name and hoping the dimwitted looking young man would make the checking-in process as simple as his mental processing abilities.

"Name?" he asked when he reached the desk.

I dropped my duffel bag and threw up my arms in disgust, knowing immediately that this process would indeed be a process, and said, "I'm waiting in the car. Come get me when we have a room."

Before Julie could protest, I was again sitting in the car, leaning back and staring at the ceiling. Ten minutes of that bored me out of the car and back inside the bed and breakfast.

"We done yet?" I asked as I picked up my duffel bag.

"Just finishin' up," the young man responded.

Two minutes later, I was following Julie following him up the extremely narrow steep winding staircase to the third and top floor which was, in reality, the attic. The ceiling, low and sloping toward my head at every turn, seemingly intentionally slapped me on the left side of my head in the dark hallway.

"Here ya go. Bathroom's down the hall and breakfast is served at seven," the young man informed us.

"Seven until when?" I asked.

"Uh, it's at seven," he responded.

"Great," I said slowly, turning to Julie with a sarcastic smile. "Seven…"

Julie opened the door, no lock, and gravity swung it into the bureau on the wall adjacent.

"Good craftsmanship," I said of the lopsided door hanging job.

"Did it myself," the young man proclaimed proudly.

I looked at him, perplexed at how someone could possibly be so dumb and still be alive.

"I think we'll be fine from here. You have a good night," I said politely.

"Sleep good," he said, seemingly just to see me cringe, before he disappeared down the staircase.

The ceiling in the room was low and slanted, also sloping in every direction, threatening my head and thus my comfort and consciousness.

"I figured the room would be bigger than our apartment," I said to Julie.

She ignored me and walked to the full sized bed in the middle of the room. She dropped her bag onto it and took out a pair of shorts and a T-shirt then walked past me, out the door, and down the hall to the bathroom.

"Fantastic," I commented to myself.

I walked to the bed and threw my duffel bag next to Julie's bag. After pulling down the top cover to examine the sheets below, I decided that they appeared clean enough, but that I would surely fall asleep if I tested their comfort, so I nodded to the bed then dropped myself into the love seat in the corner of the room by the windows.

From that vantage point, I passed my eyes over the space. The bed was dead center, an odd choice in most rooms including this one. The triangular windows on the wall to my left mimicked the roof's slope which was only a few feet above them. The wall opposite the windows contained an old clock which read 10:03 p.m. I assumed it to not be correct, but had no intention of checking. Also against that wall was the bureau with the lopsided door, ajar, leaning against it and a jar of marbles atop for no reason I could imagine. Finishing off the room were nightstands squeezed on either side of the bed.

The absent breeze indicated the vents for air-conditioning to be not the most efficient. They blew like an asthmatic wheezing through a straw.

"This is to be my sanctuary for the weekend's journey?" I asked aloud.

I stood up to check the contents of the bureau and smacked my head into the sloping ceiling, landing myself back in the love seat, holding my head and being angry at Julie until she returned.

This time I stood slowly and deliberately, saying nothing and hoping Julie would somehow befall the same idiotic fate. I then grabbed my duffel bag and hiked to the bathroom to ready myself for bed.

It was how one would expect the bathroom in a small run-down bed and breakfast to be. Small, dim, sticky feeling, dreary sounding, frighteningly damp; moist. I saw fear and anger, frustration and anxiety in the mirror, but I ignored them and moved carefully back down the hall.

It was becoming increasingly obvious that the floor was quite a bit uneven. I was unsure if it was a result of the house's foundation settling in after a hundred plus years or if the floors in the attic had been redone by the craftsman who installed the slanted door to our room.

I entered through that slanted doorway to find Julie already under the covers so I closed the door behind me, still no lock. I pushed the bureau over as makeshift protection against intruders then took a marble out of the jar atop the bureau, dropping it to the floor. It rolled toward the other side of the room and settled at a point past the bed but not all the way to the wall with the triangular windows. I repeated this with five additional marbles, each making a slightly different but loud sound on impact with the floor and following the same path to the same destination.

"What are you doing?" Julie asked from the bed.

"Look. If you drop something on the floor, you know where to find it!"

Julie was unimpressed with my trick, evidenced by the shaking of her head as she looked at my face to insure that I interpreted properly her silent response.

Struck by a fleeting moment of sympathy for Julie's clearly depressed state over her terrible bed and breakfast choice, I attempted to say something positive.

"The design on these sheets is nice. And I really like this dust ruffle."

"What's a 'dust ruffle?'" She laughed in a baffled tone.

"I don't know," I said, embarrassed that I knew so much about dust ruffles that I could determine which dust ruffles were better than others.

Then Julie screamed, "A spider!"

I jumped from my place and hit my head on the ceiling again. I cursed in my mind and said in a strained voice, "There's no spider. What are you talking about?"

"It's over there, in the corner!" she insisted.

I looked at all four corners and saw no spider.

"Where?" I asked.

"In that corner." Julie pointed to the corner to the right of the triangular windows, across from the love seat.

"Oh, that?" I said of an extremely small spider. "It's not bothering anyone over there."

"Yes, it is! It's bothering me," she shouted. "It being there is bothering me. If it starts crawling on me, it'll bother me. I can't be comfortable with it in here." She went on huffing and puffing until I shut her up with a loud thud, murdering the spider between my delicate left hand and the slanted, warped, and uneven floor.

"Okay?" I asked.

"No! There could be more. I know I'm going to obsess over this."

I rolled my eyes then searched the room for a thermostat while leading Julie to believe locating additional spiders was my intention. The room's temperature had increased since the door was closed. I saw none, so I moved the bureau, opened the door, and searched the attic. No thermostat.

Down back at the front desk, I rang the bell until I was met by a man older than the first who informed me that the air-conditioning "dunt work; hazzent fur monts."

I did not ask why no one had tried to fix it or why we had not been informed of this before we made our reservation. I just walked back up the narrow steep winding dark staircase.

"Open yur winda. It'll cool 'er right down," he suggested in a shout.

I kept walking up and up then through the unprofessionally hung door and into our room, again moving the bureau to defend against intruders. I looked more closely at the triangular windows to find that they were the unopenable kind that were merely for looking through and, unfortunately, not jumping out of.

I laid on the bed, on top of the cover, and removed my sweatpants and shirt. I was still overheating, but I laid back anyway, trying to get to sleep.

Thirty minutes were spent keeping Julie awake by continuously squirming around, trying to find a comfortable position on the uncomfortable mattress. The heat made it an impossible task.

Another thirty minutes later, I decided that it was the absence of sound that was keeping me awake. The undulating urban hum from the concrete jungle was something I needed. My ears were designed for the city so the dead of the country night did nothing for my slumber. All I could hear was the incessant ticking of the clock hung on the wall against which the bureau was leaning, protecting us from the impending danger of an intruder bursting through the lockless lopsidedly hung door.

Thirty minutes after that, I accepted the inevitable and walked over to the love seat, feeling for the ceiling as I lowered myself down.

My mind brought me to years prior, to before Julie and I had ever come to this forsaken place, to before we wed. She would describe it in the most wonderful ways, ways in which I could not even fully understand or perceive at the time. "If you stand still and look up," she told me, "you can literally see the stars moving around you. It makes you feel like you're the center of the universe, the most important thing in the world. We must go. You'll love it!"

Thirty minutes of staring into the darkness through the unopenable window was broken by Julie's faint voice.

"We used to try so hard to be like my family," she said with a tone of sorrow.

"Who?" I asked. "Your family?"

"No, Nick, us. We used to try to be like them, to fit in, to be happy. Everything was supposed to be different with all of us. We were supposed to be a happy family."

I was unsure where she was attempting to bring the conversation so I said what was on my mind. "Sticking feathers up your butt doesn't make you a bird."

"What?" she asked. "Why would it? Birds don't have feathers in their bottoms…"

I considered her perspective then responded. "My point is, we started out trying to be something that we weren't, my metaphorical bird. But, in the end, we just ended up with feathers up our butts. But, if you ask me, we also ended up close enough to our goal."

"Just forget it, Nick. You can never take anything seriously."

"I thought I made a good point," I insisted, but those were the last words to be exchanged that night.

An hour later, I was still awake, no longer feeling hot, body adjusted, but still awake. I began to grow tired of counting sheep.

"Well," I whispered to myself, "I guess sleep is the cousin of death."

————

Courtland

Another hour later when my fatigued mind began to wander, it rested on my sadly and recently deceased patient Courtland. In the dizzy of a dark conscious dream, there we were, in the office again. Our last session...

—

"Feeling okay?" I asked him.

"Eh, sick and tired of being sick and tired," he responded without conviction.

"Expand on that," I encouraged.

"When you're depressed, everything, anything is fatiguing and it's so incredibly lonely. And no amount of support can convince you that you're not alone. It's as if someone pulled a plug out inside me; things just don't feel right. I can't really feel anything at all except the fatigue. I'm just indifferent to everything, everyone. And no one understands it so they just get frustrated with me, angry. So now I don't even have the support from people that wouldn't be helpful to me anyway. I'm just sick and tired of feeling like this. Sick and tired of being sick and tired.

"Walking from the subway, I crossed against the light. I guess I just wasn't paying attention. Couldn't tell you what I was paying attention to or if I was even paying attention to anything. A taxi; this guy was honking and yelling at me. I just felt nothing. Absolutely nothing."

Then Courtland paused, a pause I did not interrupt with my own words, just waited for his to continue.

He asked me, "Do you think you'll go to some kind of afterlife or on to another life? Anything like that? Something different than this? Something the same? Where do you stand on that kind of thing?"

"I don't know," I told him. "I never wanted to take a stand because I was afraid of being wrong. What do you think?"

"Well, I don't really have any real intention of reaching any kind of heaven, but I know that I'll be leaving hell."

"Ha," I laughed at the play on words. "Promise me you'll take me with you," I joked.

"Sure thing," he responded.

Courtland and I often joked about the topic. Only retrospectively did it appear to be in bad taste.

My hazy mind then placed me standing over him in his apartment, he on the floor, his parents kneeling next to him, crying. And then it was me in his place, helpless, lifeless. Sprawled out there on the ground for an endless duration in my imagination, I still could not determine if it was a poetic way to die or not. The immense emotional pain he felt led to the overdose of painkillers... Or maybe it was just a cliché foolish thing to do.

And then I was standing there staring at myself on the floor. I could not help but think that he deserved better, but was unsure if I did. Or maybe I had been wrong about it all. Maybe that was better.

———

Night into Day

My body jolted to fully awake but saw nothing, just the blackness of the vast outdoors, no light to be glimpsed in any direction. I rubbed my left shoulder and frowned.

"Why did he do it?"' I asked myself.

My wildly wandering mind then stopped on *Hamlet* for an answer. When Hamlet contemplated ending his life, he spoke of how sleep was a terrible alternative, "To sleep: perchance to dream: ay, there's the rub."

My mind was back on my own inability to sleep. Maybe it was a blessing in disguise. Maybe I was saving myself from the agony of my dreams; pointing out my reality or infuriating me with unreachable goals that could never be realized; nightmares.

My wandering, angry, fatigued, confused mind then went toward waking life and all that it held to infuriate me. I was immediately filled with hate for everything worldly including myself, especially myself.

Why do I remember so well? Why can't I forget things? Let me forget things.

My life was a long lucid nightmare from which I would never awaken. My mind connected me with Hamlet. That too was his struggle; he could not forget the problems in his life. They haunted him as I had been haunted by my own past.

I looked straight up and shook my head vigorously. I learned long ago, when I was a young boy, that when my memories were too vivid and intense, this was the only thing that made them go away, but just for a fleeting few minutes. For those few minutes, I was free. This had always helped me, been my true salvation, but I, ashamed at my inability to cope with my life, was immediately angry. Those few minutes of freedom were always spent in anger, tense frustration. Freedom was a fallacy. I would never be free.

Some hours later, after time had calmed me, straightened my brow, I watched the sun come up from the love seat in front of the window.

"And then there was light," I whispered to myself.

As the sun slowly came up, I went down; the night watchman surrendering to his daytime counterpart. I could feel the sliver of yellow slipping through my eyelids, battling with my fatigue, trying to keep me around, yearning for company on its ascent, but, after a lengthy battle, it remained alone on its journey upward as I was gone, downward.

Saturday Morning

As my body shook not under its own power, I slowly awoke from an effectively sleepless night with my mind completely out of focus.

"Wake up," Julie was saying over and over again in what felt like a low droning monotone, but at first I only allowed myself to perceive her as Courtland's parents trying to shake him awake from the previous night's dream, nightmare.

She was greeted by my confused grunts and growls. I moved around slightly, enough to realize I was confined in a love seat; a place only comfortable for the first few minutes of one's stay.

"It's almost seven. Breakfast, Nick. If we don't go, we'll miss it."

She shook me again and I violently pulled my shoulder away from her, eyes still shut, mind still shut. I heard nothing more of her other than the scraping of the bureau on the floor and the slamming of the badly installed door.

I was awake enough to perceive light, but I attempted to shut it out, squeezing my eyelids tighter and turning my head away. My mind tried to get me to the bed, but my body would not comply as I drifted back into a blurry dark daze toward sleep.

Again I was shaken, this time with less force, less strength.

"Breakfast was wonderful, if you were wondering." Julie's voice echoed in my head.

I squirmed around in the confining love seat craving any position, even an uncomfortable one, that would allowed more sleep.

A duration of time, difficult to determine in length, passed before Julie's steady voice and shaking hand woke me again.

"We really need to get to the house, Nick. Get up."

Reluctantly, my eyes opened onto the day, but they closed shortly thereafter.

"I'm going down the hall to take a shower," I heard Julie say. "Please be up by the time I get back, okay?"

The slam of the door startled me awake, eyes flung open to move around the room rapidly in fright. It was just as ugly and cramped in the sunlight as it was by the dim electric lamps illuminating it the night before.

"Not in Kansas anymore," I said to myself before standing up and hitting my head on the ceiling.

I laughed heartily at my own stupidity because it was all I could do. "Fool me once…" I said, shaking my index finger to the sky above.

Holding my bruised head, I explored the space, moving along the uneven floor, around the bed, and past the bureau. On my trip, I noticed a full-length mirror that I swore was not there the previous day. It was warped beyond being useful to gauge much of anything. On my way back toward the love seat, I stopped at the window where I peered out at the expanse of land that surrounded us.

The clock on the wall ticked to 8:15 a.m.

Julie's voice was faint behind my back. "It's a preserve. The land is protected. That's why this was supposed to be a nice place to stay."

120

"I think I would have preferred staying at your parents' house," I snarled without acknowledging the beauty of the untouched land.

I turned to see her sad face, which she quickly hid behind an indifferent façade. She wore a light blue dress that looked comfortably airy; a concept that eluded my lungs because of the duration spent in this closed cramped stuffy room.

"I'm done in the shower, okay? So please go take one."

Without confirmation, I slowly opened my bag on the love seat and pulled out my toothbrush.

"Towels inside?" I asked.

Julie nodded, her face turned away from me. I rolled my eyes and walked through the doorway, closing the door with an unintentionally forceful slam.

It took a very short time to learn that Julie had used all of the hot water the bathroom offered. Repeatedly being bombarded with freezing cold droplets is the worst torture a member of the first world can experience, especially when the expectation is for soothing warmth.

The shock pushed me to the corner of the shower. The realization of its inevitable duration inched me into the line of fire. The experience forced me to hurry through my shower routine. As a result, when the time came for shampooing, I blindly decided to use what was offered on the shower's shelf. Lathering was rapid, but the consistency was that of thick hand-soap and it smelled like the bark of a pine tree. I inspected the bottle to find that it was dog shampoo; the word "dog" was small and on the back while the word "shampoo" was large and on the front. I quickly rinsed it from my head, halted the flow of the hellish freezing water, and toweled off.

Feeling pins and needles all over my body, but simultaneously feeling quite numb, I shivered my way back into the bedroom over the uneven floor and down the dark hallway.

"Did you know the shampoo in there is dog shampoo?" I said accusingly upon entering the room.

"No, I brought my own," she responded as she slowly folded clothes to then be placed in her bag.

I slammed the door in protest, assuming she had something more to do with the canine cleaning product on my head than she actually did.

"Can't we just stay here for the day and head back early?" I asked as I dressed.

"No, of course not! We've spent enough time here already and it's been a waste."

"Why?" I asked.

"We came here to spend time together, Nick. That was the plan. Why can't you understand that?"

"We are spending time together," I responded.

As I inspected myself in the warped full-length mirror, which I still did not believe to have been there the previous night, Julie's dress flowed by in the background and I realized that my khaki pants had a tinge of light blue, matching Julie's dress too closely; likely a result of her inability to separate darks and lights properly. Frustrated at the coincidence, I felt too burdened to change into the other pair in my bag so I accepted and lamented the fact that, for that day, Julie and I would be the matching couple that everybody hates.

Standing in the mirror contemplating, I convinced myself that my white collared shirt broke up any resemblance we bore to one another. I then allowed one more button to remain unbuttoned than was my custom and rolled up my sleeves to below my elbows. Warped as it was, the mirror brought a smile to my mouth which Julie noticed in the reflection, shaking her head in silent response.

I retaliated with, "Maybe you should learn how to do laundry properly…"

Probably not understanding and certainly ignoring my comment, she went back to packing her bag. "We should call Mother to let her know we're coming," she suggested.

"Why? She knows we're coming."

"We should call anyway. Do you have the number?" she asked me.

"I thought you knew it?" I shouted angrily.

"It's in my phone. I left it in the car," she responded.

Given the previous night's discussion about remembering phone numbers, I desired greatly to point out Julie's hypocrisy, but, overcome with rage, I could not find the proper words to effectively convey the message that I felt it was imperative for Julie to receive, so I angrily yelled nonsense sounds for five or six seconds.

"Calm down, Nick. I'll just check the phonebook. I think there's one in the nightstand."

My nonsense yelling had subsided into an angry mumble as I pulled open the nightstand on what should have been my side of the bed.

"Bible," I snarled. "Do phonebooks even exist anymore?"

"Of course they do," she insisted before opening the nightstand on her side. "Bible," she declared.

In an attempt to calm myself, I searched the rest of the room to find nothing but two additional jars of marbles in the bureau and still no explanation for the first, let alone this second and third.

"Let's just stay here and watch TV," I suggested. "We can relax and enjoy being out of the city. And we'll be spending time together like you wanted."

"You can watch TV at the apartment. We hardly ever go anywhere but, when we do, you always just want to sit around watching TV. Why?"

"Because it's relaxing!"

She shook her head at me then asked, "Can you just go downstairs and ask them for the phonebook please?"

"Why don't we just leave and call from the car? We'll get there by the time they find a phonebook."

"Just please go and get one, Nick."

I left the room and followed the dark dim narrow steep winding staircase down to the first floor and the small unmanned front desk.

"Excuse me, excuse me, excuse me," I said rather frantically numerous times while ringing the bell. "Hello, hello, excuse me, hello."

An elderly woman slowly walked toward me from a room behind the desk.

"Excuse me, hello, excuse me." I continued my mantra as she approached frustratingly slowly.

When she finally reached the desk, I stopped ringing the bell.

"For whom does the bell toll?" she asked, further frustrating me.

"Hi, yes. We need a phonebook in our room. There are two Bibles and no phonebook and I darn well know the number for my wife's parents is not in the Bible."

"Sorry. We're fresh out of phonebooks," the woman said with a smile.

"Excuse me? How can you be 'fresh out of phonebooks'?"

"I'm sorry. Can I help you with anything else?"

"You didn't help me with this!" I shouted, startling the elderly woman. "Sorry," I continued. "That will be all."

Then I did realize there was something else she could help me with. "Oh. Did you know there is dog shampoo in the bathroom? That's *shampoo* for *dogs* in the *human bathroom*. My head smells like a pinecone."

"Dog shampoo?" she questioned. "Oh, yes! It's an invigorating blend, don't you think?"

At that, I could do nothing but stare for a dozen seconds, not necessarily at her, but at the stupidity that surrounded me.

"Can I help you with anything else?"

"I think we'll be checking out now," I said slowly.

"Okay then. When would you like to check out?" she asked.

"Right now!" I shouted, thinking maybe she was having trouble hearing me.

"Alrighty then. Let me just find your paperwork," she said as she turned to return to the room behind the desk.

"Seriously? Paperwork? Back there? You? Can you just have it ready when we come down?"

"Yes, of course. When will you come down?" she asked, still walking toward the room.

"Less than five minutes," I told her.

"The paperwork will surely be ready by then," she assured me, but I felt in no way assured.

Back up the dark dim narrow steep winding staircase to the attic, down the uneven floor, and through the open lopsided doorway I went.

"No luck; they're fresh out of phonebooks," I informed Julie.

"Let's just go then," she suggested as if it were a novel idea as opposed to one previously suggested by me and shot down by her.

Wanting nothing more than to leave, I said nothing and shoved all that needed to be shoved back into my duffel bag. I followed close behind Julie down the stairs and continued to the desk when we reached the first floor.

"The lady is getting our paperwork together; we're checking out," I informed Julie. "We'll figure something else out for tonight. I'll wait in the car, okay?"

Not by any measure surprised that I had taken the liberty of beginning the checking-out process a day early, Julie nodded while facing the desk.

I exited through the screen door and walked down the walkway toward the car. A white hare darted by, through the grass, over the path, and then back into the grass, almost tripping me. I was tempted to follow him, but was oddly afraid of falling down a deep strange dark hole.

Was he wearing a top hat? I thought whimsically, bringing a bit of a smile to my face.

I continued to the car and slid in, soft seats comfortable, plush, inviting.

"Should have slept here," I said aloud as I tossed my duffel bag between the seats and plugged in my phone.

After ten seconds of being overwhelmed by my pine tree bark scented head, I opened the windows. It was another fifteen minutes before Julie found her way to the passenger seat.

"What took so long?" I asked with an unintentional tone of both hate and disgust.

"The woman picked up the wrong paperwork then we started talking. She knows—"

"I don't care what or who she knows," I said, interrupting. "How long are we spending there today?"

"Nick, I know you don't like my family, but at least try to treat them with some respect, alright?"

"I do! They're the ones you should be lecturing. And if I'm ever disrespectful, it's just because they're disrespectful to me first!"

" 'Do unto others as you would have them do unto you,' " she recited.

"Exactly! I treat them the way they treat me."

Julie squinted and said, "I wasn't trying to justify your disrespectful behavior. I was trying to suggest that you modify it."

"Oh," I replied, genuinely seeing things from her perspective, one that I had not considered in my quick and frustration fueled responses. "I suppose that makes more sense contextually."

The car felt tight and quick; the steering, throttle, brakes. I had become so accustomed to driving the car short distances after it had been sitting in the cold parking garage underground that I had forgotten how it was designed to feel, how it did feel when the fluids were warm. We moved quickly up to speed and around curves with a strong momentum. Dancing as delightfully as the car, courtesy of the light sea breeze, the dry tall grass was illuminated to a fiery yellow by the flaming sun overhead.

"Take it easy. Why are you in such a hurry?" Julie asked.

I did not respond. I did not obey. Then, around one of the many curves, three deer darted across the road. I hit the brakes hard. Julie's head flew forward, torso held back by the seat belt. The nose of the car stopped mere inches from taking two deer down by the knees.

Having skillfully averted disaster, I smiled. "Lions and tiger and deer, oh my!" I exclaimed as I turned the wheel and accelerated off.

"God commands the land to bring forth living creatures," Julie said cryptically.

"What are you saying? God threw a bunch of deer out in front of my car? For what?"

"Maybe so you would slow down… He also created man and woman in his image and likeness," she said, equally as cryptic as her previous statement.

"Julie, what are you talking about?"

"Oh, not a thing, Nick. Not a thing…"

I ignored Julie's odd words and made no response. We were silent until the car rolled between the front gates of Julie's parents' estate which suddenly filled my mind with an awful taste.

128

"Can I just drop you off today?" I asked.

"No! It's going to be fun. Try to be positive, okay?"

Still, I persisted. "I reaaallly don't want to be here today," I told her.

"Come on. It will be like an adventure!" she exclaimed, glee starting to fill her heart due to the increasing proximity to her family.

I moaned, rolled my eyes, and, remembering the white top hat wearing rabbit, said, "Let's fall down the rabbit hole then…"

The car floated toward the house swiftly as the driveway opened up into a field of cobblestone. I was surprised to see dozens more cars parked there than the previous day.

"What are all these cars doing here?" I asked Julie.

"Mother and Father are having a little gathering today, a party." Julie's response had a tone that suggested that she had informed me of this travesty multiple times before.

Desiring very much to bark back with protest, berate her with my anger, I swallowed the impulse behind a tightly held smile. I kept telling myself that it was only one more day, then we would be back to our normal routine away from her family.

One more day… I thought, over and over.

As we pulled around the driveway to the front of the house, I noticed Mr. Douglas standing in the front doorway, guarding his gates like Saint Peter. I feared him, but I was not afraid. Dissatisfaction was the overwhelming tone of his presence, facial expression displaying his emotions without filter.

I pulled the car onto the grass close to the house, where it had been the previous day, leaving more than enough room for two or three cars door to door to pass.

Phone unplugged in my hand, I closed my eyes tight and said, "There's no place like home…" as I knocked my shoes' heels together on the floorboard.

"What are you doing?" Julie asked.

"Oh, I don't know. I thought maybe I would open my eyes and we'd be in the city… or Kansas, either one would be fine."

She examined my stupidity silently before opening her door up and away.

I looked past her as she stood, toward the doorway previously occupied by her father, but it was empty. My view was then chopped off by the closing door.

I sat back for several seconds, wishing myself away, only to be startled by my door opening without my physical permission.

"Sir," one of the nameless butlers said, gesturing me from the car.

It was difficult not to obey; there really was only one choice. Then, before I could thank him, the man handed me a small green card with the number 93 on it then attempted to slide into the driver's seat.

"Wait!" I shouted, grabbing his arm. "What are you doing?"

"Valet, Sir. We are parking the automobiles in the lot." He pointed down the cobblestone driveway toward the dozens of cars.

"Oh, no," I said, laughing. "We'll be leaving this one here. I'm with the family."

The butler was noticeably uncomfortable with my insistence. His battle to choose just the correct words with which to respectfully respond played out physically, all over his mannerisms.

"Don't worry about it," I said before he could respond, putting my left hand on his right shoulder. "I'll make sure Mr. Douglas knows you put up quite the fight to follow his orders."

Still with a look of slight fright and concern, he composed himself with a smile and a nod, then began making his way back to his station.

"Oh, all the bags I brought, Nick," Julie exclaimed, materializing behind the car when I dispelling my assumption that she had already abandoned me. "Open the trunk so he can take them in."

"Oh, yes," I said. Then toward the butler, "you know women; always packing ten times what they need, eh?"

He smiled politely without agreeing or disagreeing as I reached inside to open the trunk.

"I didn't even think it would all fit!" I said, attempting to create some semblance of banter.

My arms, attempting to help, were shooed away. "No, no, Sir. We can bring them in. Please join the rest of the guests."

"Not this one in here," I informed him, pointing at my old beaten duffel bag between the seats.

"Yes. This I assumed, Sir," he said, remarking indirectly at my choice of luggage.

"Thanks," I said to the butler. Then to Julie, "Shall we?" My arm extended, elbow outward, for her to hold.

"Well," she exclaimed, "you're suddenly quite gallant."

"Just putting on a show for the help," I informed her. "Wouldn't want them talking."

Her surprised smile dropped to a frown at my words. "Can you do me a favor and try to control yourself today?" she scolded. "You've insulted practically everyone in the family. I don't want you making enemies out of family friends too."

"Enemies? Is that how they think of me? Maybe I should be the one who is concerned here…" I turned my head away dramatically.

"Don't make this about you. Just try to control yourself." Julie seemed quite focused and direct. There was a confidence in her that I only saw when she was around her family. I feared it.

As we passed the fountain, arm in arm, I noticed Julie's Cousin Abigail sitting on a bench alone eating from a plate, no utensils.

"What's she doing over there?" I whispered to Julie.

Without responding to me, Julie called out, "Abigail! What are you doing?"

"Oh, hi," Abigail responded, startled. "I was just making a phone call." Her mouth was filled with food so her words were muffled.

"We'll see you inside then?" Julie asked, as I forced her arm to continue our forward motion away from her brash, crass, and intimidatingly manly cousin.

Abigail held up her left index finger, signaling for us to wait while she swallowed. "Everyone is in the back. Go around the side." She pointed across the front of the house to another walkway.

"Great!" Julie said happily.

Begrudgingly, I turned to backtrack then cut across the landscaped trees mingling outside the path to find the other walkway leading to the back of the house.

Before we had gone more than four feet, Abigail found it utterly necessary to call after me, "How's the attitude today, Nick?"

I looked at Julie with bugged out eyes. "Do you see what I have to deal with?" I asked her, almost pleading to be allowed to retaliate appropriately.

"Just control yourself today, Nick. That's all I ask," she whispered back.

"Only time will tell…" I called back to Abigail, still stuffing her face out of the sight of others. As a professional, her behavior alarmed me. I thought about saying something to Julie, possibly offering a clinical theory, but she would have ignored it, assumed I was merely trying to start some kind of trouble rather than offering the true and needed identification of a disorder. As an alienated hated member of the family, her behavior bothered me in no way at all; it wasn't my problem. Sometimes one can only do nothing.

Abigail gave no audible response so we continued on our way. Cutting through the small trees, shrubs, and bushes, Julie and I walked slowly, still arm in arm as the low burble of a car much older than I forced our attention, the sound increasing in volume.

"Richard," Julie sang happily, letting go of my arm and dancing back toward the driveway.

Richard's small, preposterous looking, extremely rare 1950s strawberry colored convertible rolled slowly toward us. Its headlights looked like the eyes on a very surprised cartoon character. I wanted to pencil in a mouth, ears, and a big nose. The windshield was half-sized and, to accentuate that fact, Richard wore Amelia Earhart's goggles, leather helmet, and scarf. The only way he could have looked more like Snoopy going on a Sunday afternoon drive would be if Woodstock, Snoopy's little yellow bird, were tweeting on his shoulder.

"I suppose if someone spends that much money on a car, they reserve the right to look as dumb as they want," I said to Julie, but she was deafened by excitement to see her longtime friend and her onetime beau.

He pulled around and parked in front of my car, threatening my bought manhood, then exited his little classic car with a large cigar, unlit, in his mouth. With a preposterous look of arrogance on his face, Richard walked slowly toward us, moving his head around, looking everywhere but straight ahead or below the level of his nose, as if he had lost something in the sky.

There was something about him that I did not like, but I was having trouble pinpointing just what it was. The only bone I found to be pick-worthy was his vaguely pompous demeanor, but that was to be expected, so I tried to ignore it as I did with all others of his stature.

Julie ran to him and hugged tightly, her feet leaving the ground, to then be spun around a full rotation and a quarter by Richard's sheer strength and cinematic presence.

"Hello, my dear Julie," he said as he lowered her to the ground. He then pushed her arm's-length away and said, "You are a vision of radiance in that dress." His words were slightly muffled from the cylindrical cancer stick that occupied his mouth.

"Oh," she said bashfully as she spun around, allowing her dress to follow her body in a delayed flowing dance.

After Richard finished watching my wife model her dress for him, he turned to me. "Nicholas, my good man. It's great to see you." He extended his left hand to greet mine. Then he felt it necessary to add, "It's a Cuban," referring to the cigar which he then took from his mouth and held between his right index and middle fingers.

"How was the drive?" I asked, shaking his hand about as tightly as he shook mine. "You came from the city in that one?" I said pointing at his shining ancient automobile.

"Oh, no! Of course not!" he exclaimed. "Don't think she would make the trip. Well, she would have, but I don't want to put too many miles on her. You know how the vintage car trade is. They don't want these things driven. I had my driver take me from the city to the facility around here where I keep my cars. They maintain them in the off season and while I'm abroad. They do it for all of Manhattan's vintage car collectors. Costs a fortune, but you know how it is; got to have some toys."

"We do like our toys," I told him, pointing toward my own.

But before Richard had a chance to acknowledge or even see what I was pointing at, Julie chimed in. "Boys like toys, Nick," she said as she wrapped her arm around Richard's waist. "Let's join the party, shall we?" Her words were said to us both, but they seemed more directed to her old flame than to her current husband.

The two of them started off, holding on to one another while I followed behind. I glanced back to Richard's car, rather beautiful in its slender silhouette. At that moment, he too glanced back, noticing me admiring what was his.

"Magnificent, isn't she?" he remarked. "I didn't want to sit in a lawn chair at a classic car show next to anything less. It's the only one on Earth."

"The only one *on Earth*?" I asked, perplexed. "I think you could have just said 'the only one.' If you hadn't said 'on Earth,' I wasn't going to ask, 'The only one? What planet are we talking about here? The only one on Mars, Jupiter...?' "

I smiled at my hilarity, but I was talking to myself by that point as my wife had already taken Richard's attention; I was two steps behind. And the walkway was not wide enough for three shoulder to shoulder anyway, no matter how close in proximity two of those three were.

My discomfort seeing the two of them together like that took up most of my attention until I heard Richard shout, "Fabulous! Wonderful! Outstanding! Marvelous!" Then he laughed.

I assumed he was telling some kind of joke or maybe he was the joke or I was the joke. Julie laughed along with him. I was surprised that fool did not quack.

Party at the Douglas Estate

We emerged from the walkway to see a sea of people, a field of family, children, chairs, photographers, butlers, servers, umbrellas, gazebos, cabanas, an orchestra whining away in the far corner, and an opulent large rectangular pool in the near distance.

"Who are all of these people?" I asked, feeling suddenly very uncomfortable.

"A stranger is a friend you haven't met yet!" Julie chirped nonsensically.

"Well, that is quite possibly the dumbest thing I ever have heard," I said in a grumpy tone. But neither Julie nor Richard heard me because they had continued on, smiling their way into the crowd and away from me.

A little boy, not a day over three years old and wearing a tiny sailor's one-piece ensemble, hobbled up to me, looked up, and asked earnestly, "Can I have a apple juice?"

"Uhh," I stammered. "I don't see why not."

He looked at me, waiting, so I looked back at him, also waiting; both just waiting for the other to do something. He blinked first, then continued on his way, spastically moving his arms around to keep his balance.

As I stood at the edge of the crowd, bits of conversations wafted to my ear. I heard one man say, "I make my living in Manhattan; I live my life in the Hamptons."

At that, I knew the day would be far worse than anticipated.

A quick look around revealed Julie to be nowhere in sight. I thought about calling her phone, but decided instead to find something to eat. It was very likely that no one, other than the three-year-old in the sailor suit, would bother me, so I considered it possible that I could get through the day eating snacks in the shade while Julie socialized.

I walked around the field of strange beautiful faces, many of which were hidden behind massive reflective sunglasses or underneath large colorful Kentucky Derby–ish hats which forced me to dart my head left and right to avoid losing an eye. The female heads not adorned by the massive hats sported miniature, yet equally colorful and ornate ones; having been coerced by Julie to watch all live events of the English Royals in their entirety, I knew these to be called Fascinators. I even noticed several scattered women wearing loosely-woven veils. *Is that in fashion again?* I mused to myself, certain that religious mandates were not a factor.

The men mostly wore tailored blue blazers, some with matching pants, others with khakis, but every ensemble coordinated magnificently with the other accessories, shoes, belts, shirts, watches, and cravats of all kinds including a few ascots. White or tan linen suits of an obviously tailored fit caught my eye, but unlike the previous day, jackets were the most popular choice. I noticed several colorful bow ties and pocket squares jauntily peeking out to match another article of clothing or accessory. Even a few scattered straw hats graced some of the gentlemanly heads present. A quick glance down unveiled their preferred footwear; two-tone wingtip shoes or boat shoes were the near-unanimous choice. Casual but upscale.

A dozen scattered photographers moved from group to group taking candid shots—but never unflattering ones I trusted. When I realized I would be in the background of one, I hoped she would get my good side and arched one brow rakishly.

Servers moved through the masses, politely offering meticulously constructed snacks and taking drink orders.

I approached one and requested, "Might I have a look at your tray?"

He brought it below head level to display several empty glasses and used plates.

"Thanks," I said, sending him on his way.

The patio appeared the most likely place to intercept a server as it boasted kitchen access; I made my way through the crowd in that direction. There, the eldest members of the family and guests from a similar era sat under three large umbrellas on their wicker chairs, sipping on their drinks, nibbling at their snacks, and slipping gradually into senility.

The patio also held the bar at which guests were giving their orders to servers who then politely produced the drinks with a smile. From the patio, slightly higher in elevation to the rest of the back field, I could see the children farther away and closer to the woods playing in the open space.

"The hors d'oeuvres! The hors d'oeuvres! They are magnificent! Everyone must try them!"

I turned my head to see Mrs. Douglas waving her arms and shouting into the crowd.

"Hors d'oeuvre without an 's' is already plural," I said aloud, but no one heard me or at least no one acknowledged that they did.

"It was *I* who invented them!" she modestly proclaimed to all.

"I highly doubt she invented hors d'oeuvre…" I said with a sarcastic tone, but again my words fell upon no acknowledging ears.

Then, to prove how wonderful her creations were, she pulled one from a passing tray and popped it into her mouth. "Wait," she said loudly, food still in her mouth. "It needs something…"

It seemed clear that Mrs. Douglas felt it completely necessary to display to all who were watching that she had full creative control over what she had *invented*.

She pulled the server close and said loudly enough that all could hear, "Add a smidgin of paprika and a dash of fine sea salt to each."

"A 'smidgin' and a 'dash' are not standardized measurements. How is he supposed to know how much to put on there?" For the third time, my words went unheard/ unacknowledged and I decided that I liked it better that way. It allowed me to say whatever I pleased without concern, a Greek chorus of one.

"And where is the cake?" she demanded, still loud enough for all to hear. "It was supposed to come out long ago."

The server apologized and scurried away as quickly as possible without his right hand losing the tray, but it was, unfortunately, not fast enough. Mr. Douglas materialized in the hapless server's path and stopped him with one hand held up.

"Why is that cake taking so long?" Mr. Douglas asked with a calm but terrifying tone. "I told several of you to hurry the progress and bring it out. Now get to it!"

Again unimpeded, the server scurried off to the kitchen, shaking with fright.

"Can't get a baby in one month by impregnating nine women," I said, smiling to myself, but this time my words were heard.

"Excuse me, Nicholas?" Mr. Douglas said.

"Sorry, Sir. I was just kidding around."

He looked me up and down, then focused in on my face. "You trying to grow some facial hair?" he inquired in a harsh judgmental tone.

"Ahh, no, Sir. I just haven't had a chance to shave for the past two or three days."

"Now, Nicholas, we spoke about personal appearances yesterday. Did we not?" His right hand descended upon my left shoulder in the most demeaning of ways prompting me to wince slightly as he applied pressure on the lingering soreness.

"Actually, we talked about clothes yesterday and, as you can see, I changed my clothes."

"Nicholas, don't tell me what we spoke about. I *know* what we spoke about."

"Sorry, Sir," I said looking down, chastised by his authoritarian tone.

"I saw my doctor this morning at church," he said.

"Oh, is that right?" I responded. "Everything alright?"

"Oh, everything is fine... just fine, but he did inform me that whatever idiot wrapped my hand in children's Band-Aids was likely attempting to make a fool out of me."

I wanted to inform Mr. Douglas that it did not take me wrapping his hand in some Band-Aids to make him into a fool, but limited myself to, "I have no formal medical training."

After staring me down for several seconds, Mr. Douglas changed the subject. "I saw you park in the driveway a bit earlier," he said, pausing at the end to allow the presentation of a defense or denial, but I remained silent. "Do you mind moving it so other cars can get through." His question was posed in a way that eliminated "no" as a reasonable response.

I nodded, turned, and began to walk back toward the walkway which would lead me to the front of the house.

"Oh, Nicholas," Mr. Douglas called after me. "Move Richard's car as well. He made the same mistake you did. We already spoke; he left his key in the ignition. Permission was granted."

I turned to see the back of Mr. Douglas's shooing hands hurrying me along. I felt unsure about moving another man's car, but I nodded in acquiescence, hesitant to question Mr. Douglas and eager to be done with the conversation.

As I continued on my way I noted Abigail's absence; she was no longer sitting by the fountain stuffing her face in secret solitude. Again I considered bringing her potentially clinically diagnosable behavior to Julie's attention, but then decided against opening any line of inquiry which would require my ongoing involvement.

Lining the driveway were numerous cars with drivers reading or conversing on cell phones, unobtrusively waiting for the guests they had driven to summon their services for the return trip.

I grabbed my duffel bag from between the seats and opened the trunk, tossing it in. After sliding into the comfortable seat, hands on the wheel, I drove back around the driveway toward the dozens of parked cars. I considered passing them by and continuing out the pearly gates and on back to the city.

"Julie wouldn't understand," I said to myself. Then I replied, "What's there to understand?" as I rotated the wheel into an open space between two Cadillacs in a sea mostly occupied by foreigners.

The walk from the car felt significantly longer than, in reality, it was. Although I had a sense of foreboding, the jaunt was not an unpleasant one. The light breeze was consistent and I detected a waft of sea salt in the air; something that was likely negatively affecting the old unprotected metal of the ancient car I was about to enter.

I opened the small door before straining my legs to step up then over then down and in. So tiny and cramped, these classic cars; people must simply have been smaller back then. I was folded up so much I could not see how Richard was able drive the thing for more than a mile or two.

The keys were as described, so I turned the one in the ignition, depressed the clutch, released the parking brake, then started the engine with a roar that quickly dwindled to a broken uneven growl, complete with clanking like the tenement radiator during the winter months of my youth.

"Classics…" I said aloud, shaking my head.

With the clutch depressed, I found reverse on the archaic knob attached to the tall stick, then attempted to balance the engine speed with the slippage of the old unfamiliar transmission. As the rest of my cramped limbs inched the car slowly backward, my left hand rotated the wheel. For forty degrees in either direction, the loose old steering had no real impact on anything, but it finally began to move the wheels when I put my back into a ninety-degree rotation. Rarely did I have a motivation to be thankful for modern day power steering.

But now that forward motion seemed imminent, I began to enjoy the experience of piloting this relic of an automobile as I pushed the tall stick the twelve inches that separated reverse from first gear and pulled the clutch out while feathering the gas forward.

I saw his arms waving in the side mirror before I heard his voice yelling at me over the deafening engine noise. "What are you doing? What are you doing, man? Stop!"

Obligingly I pulled the knob and stick to center, neutral, and depressed the brake. "Mr. Douglas asked me to move your car. He said it would be fine."

"Get out! What are you doing?" he shouted again. "This is a collector's item! You'll strip the gears like that. Do you even know how to drive a manual?"

I could see that Richard was really quite angry, so I pulled up the parking brake, turned off the engine, and exited the car through the small doorway that he had opened.

"You think you can do whatever you want, don't you?" he asked, aggressively perturbed. "You think you're light-years ahead of me and everyone and you can take whatever you want and thumb your nose at us. Do you think I'm dumb or something, that you could just come out here and take her for a ride without asking? Did you think I wouldn't know?"

It was thoroughly obvious that Richard was far angrier than was appropriate, but my surprise paralyzed my ability to respond appropriately to his distress and instead I said the first thing that came to mind.

"Light-years," I informed him, "are a measure of distance, not time."

"Just get out of here," he shouted as he crammed himself into his relic then started the engine, delicately placing the vehicle exactly where it previously had been.

I watched him maneuver the car so I could apologize, but when he emerged he stormed past me, ignoring my attempt at amends.

The drivers, who had all been watching the altercation, were pointing and laughing, having a grand time at my expense. I could not fault them for it, so I raised my hands above my slightly raised shoulders, palms to the sky, and smiled goofily in their direction. Their grand time was made even jollier by my physical acknowledgment of the ridiculousness of the situation.

The walk back around the house was slowed by my desire not to reach my destination. Looking into the crowd of unfamiliar faces in a place where I did not belong—had never belonged—my situation felt increasingly familiar and inevitable.

Mrs. Douglas was still pushing her hors d'oeuvre, walking from group to group insisting that guests try them. It appeared that all with whom she spoke actually believed that she had had significant creative input in the food's preparation because all politely declined a sample.

Knowing that Mrs. Douglas had not lifted a finger in the kitchen for more than fifty years and driven by my hunger, I stopped a server and took a napkin and two crackers with a fish amalgamation atop.

"Thank you, Sir," I said to the smiling server.

Then I saw Julie talking with four others, none of whom I recognized. I approached her and tapped her on the shoulder.

"Pardon me," she said, excusing herself. As we moved away from the group, her tone changed from charming and elegant to disgusted and antagonistic. "What is it?" she said to me.

"I saw you... just wanted to say hi. That's all."

"What's this about you trying to steal Richard's car?" she accused.

"What? Your father asked me to move it."

"No, he didn't. Richard asked him. Daddy said he didn't know what was going on. What were you doing in his car anyway? What did you think you would find there?"

"Wait! Your father said that? He really said that? I can't believe he's playing dumb! And how did you hear of all of this so quickly?" I was furious, but unsure how to retaliate appropriately. Mrs. Douglas then presented an opportunity.

"Oh, Nicholas," she said, right hand suddenly appearing on my right shoulder, a transparent attempt to quickly and silently control my response to her coming question. "What do you think of my tuna hors d'oeuvres?"

"Oh, let me see," I said, quickly popping one into my mouth, then making a terrible face.

The look of shock and humiliation on Mrs. Douglas's face jolted me into realizing that insulting her cooking, whether it was her own or not, was not only cruel, but an inappropriate retaliatory plan of attack against her husband.

I quickly replaced my sour face with a smile and shouted, "Magnificent!"

To this, Julie and her mother and all who were watching exhaled and smiled in joyous relief.

"It feels like there's a party in my mouth!" I added to Mrs. Douglas's great delight.

She then continued on her way, pushing her merchandise from group to group, finally having received a testimonial to its edibility.

When she was far enough away, I spit the partially masticated hors d'oeuvre into the napkin next to its intact twin.

"Ehhww," I exclaimed. "That party I was just talking about," I said to Julie. "Everyone at it was regurgitating the hors d'oeuvre."

"I appreciate you not saying that in front of my mother, but you don't need to be so mean about it. They taste fine."

"Well, it tastes pretty bad to me," I insisted.

"It tastes fine," she argued.

"Kind of a subjective thing, taste, isn't it? By definition?"

"Nick, it tastes fine. Stop complaining," she said before patting me on the chest then returning to the group of four and resuming her conversation.

I followed her, loitered behind her, then alerted her of my presence with a tug to the back of her dress; she turned, acknowledged me with a slight smile, then turned back to her group.

I walked away, shunned and ignored by the popular pretty people, even the one to whom I was married. Not paying enough attention to where he was going, Brendan, one of the preteen cousins, bumped into my side as he split between two other young cousins, running and playing through the crowd.

"Oh, well hello, Brendan," I said as I put my hand on his shoulder, stopping him in his tracks. "How are you, Cousin?"

"Don't touch me!" he shouted. "Nothing gives you that right." With that, he was gone, but the eyes of all who stood nearby remained on me, judging with their stares until I removed myself from the vicinity.

Wandering around, avoiding the trays held by servers but becoming increasingly hungry in the process, I eventually found myself alone at the sharp edge of a sea of conversations, benched from the game. The stone bench in the shade of the house was cold and hard under my weight. From my seated vantage point, I could see just enough to be satisfied with my lowly position on the team.

My verbal attempts to attract Julie's attention when she passed by my cold stone perch were blatantly ignored, further filling me with the feeling of nothingness. I watched as Julie found her mother who was still harassing guests about her "hors d'oeuvres." The two of them hugged tightly for an extended duration, their mouths moving, whispering as they held one another.

Their embrace brought a smile to my face which was quickly wiped away when Mr. Douglas appeared beside them, right hand on Mrs. Douglas's back, left on Julie's. He looked straight at me as he held them close, proprietarily watching me watch them, as if to challenge or provoke.

When they all pulled away, Mr. Douglas motioned to a man standing nearby. He was small, and seemed even more minuscule because of his skin-tight black pants and black short-sleeved button-down shirt, just as tight as the pants and unbuttoned three too many buttons, exposing most of his chest and a few wispy black hairs.

In contrast to his shrunken clothes his large clunky untied black boots seemed oddly out of place and magnified his tiny proportions. The man's hair, black, was mostly hidden beneath a slightly askew black fedora.

Intrigued and expecting to laugh inside at whatever his story was, I arose from my uncomfortable place of solitude and approached them. I was back in the game.

"Oh, Nicholas," Mr. Douglas said with a very big smile. "Come meet our new interior designer."

I looked deeply and threateningly at Mr. Douglas's smile. Only I knew its true origin was not the joy he felt for his family, but the humiliation I had endured as a result of his machinations.

"Hello," I said, gritting my teeth in anger toward Mr. Douglas. To the tightly wrapped interior designer, I said, "Nick," as I extended my right hand to meet his.

The petite looking man whipped his body around dramatically to face me and, with a firm wrist, flipped his right vertical palm toward his face, then slowly lowered it before speaking in a vague and unidentifiable European accent. "I am Paaaoowwll."

"Paaoowwl," I said trying to parrot his pronunciation. "How do you spell that?"

"P-A-U-L," he replied quickly, slipping somewhat out of his accent.

My inquisitive face was accompanied by my silent thought which was interrupted by Mr. Douglas's powerful voice addressing some passersby.

"Oh, Kipp, Emily, Ethan! Come over and meet our interior designer. After doing the co-op on Park Ave, he is working on a room upstairs."

"Oh, is that right?" Ethan asked as the three relatives, about my age, approached. Having never met him before, I assumed he was Ethan because he was certainly not Emily and I knew Kipp from the previous day when he seemed to truly believe that I was fourteen years old and named Benjamin Button.

"You must go and sample it. Paowl, you must introduce them to your vision," Mr. Douglas insisted.

"Very well then," Paul replied. "Please all, follow Paaaoowwwll."

"Nicholas. Why don't you go as well," Mr. Douglas suggested slyly.

"Oh no, I'm not very interested in interior design. I let Julie handle those matters."

"Looks like you aren't very interested in exterior design either," Mr. Douglas quipped as he looked me up and down.

All those around found themselves greatly amused by his insult and they laughed and laughed. After the hurtful mirth at my expense died down, Mr. Douglas pointed me away toward the house sending me after the group of design *experts*.

———

Paul

The labyrinth that was the Douglases' mansion was explored in an almost endless tour of turns and hallways, into and out of rooms and up and down stairs. After ten disorienting minutes, I began to consider the possibility that Paul was completely lost and we would have to eat each other to survive.

I, lagging back, was unable to hear him speaking, but I did catch a few words. It appeared that he was setting the stage for his design, attempting to ready the audience for what they were about to experience.

At one point in our journey, Kipp dropped back. "Benjamin, right?" he said, extending his right hand to shake mine.

I paused for a moment, then laughed inside. "Yes, that's right... 'Benjamin.' How's tricks, Kipp?"

"Eh, well, you know how it goes..." he said, vaguely.

"And you? You're doing well?" he asked.

"Oh! Couldn't be better. Doing quite well. Feeling very young. No complaints here."

"Alright then..." Kipp responded, still with no idea why my assumed name, Benjamin Button, sounded so familiar.

Finally, we approached two beautiful French doors that rose to the ceiling and were three or four feet wider than standard doors; they made us all feel Paul-sized. The French doors' wood was stained dark while their windows were tinted like those in my car.

"Voila!" he shouted as he swung the huge doors ajar.

The four of us stood in the wide doorway, shocked. Paul entered and strolled around, inspecting seemingly nothing. The blank walls were painted a deep unreflective matte black. The ceiling enclosed the room in the same dark shade, but a more reflective one. An absence of color was uniform through the white wide-plank wooden floors, almost unrecognizable as a natural material due to the extensive bleaching process it likely went through to rid itself of its hue.

The room contained no furniture. No pictures, photographs, paintings, or drawings graced the walls. The one lonely window in the room, looking out over the back patio, the small forest of trees, and to the ocean beyond, was framed in a drab gray. This was the closest to an actual color that could be found, but it was not a color at all.

No one said a word as we started to move slowly into the room, walking around, from wall to wall as if there was something to see. A young girl who was probably lost in the house stomped in and danced around in the hollow room. She wore a white dress and was holding a red balloon. We all watched her bounce around in slow motion.

"Where did she get that balloon?" Emily asked, deliberately choosing to not comment on what we had all journeyed to see.

"Look," Ethan said, pointing at the little girl dancing around in a scene that appeared to be all in black and white except for the bright red balloon. "It's a French film!"

The three of them laughed at the astute observation and walked out of the room followed by *la petite fille*. I avoided eye contact with Paul, but I could see that he was doing the same to me. His shoulders were a bit slumped and his head was a bit hung. I turned away from him to see the red balloon bouncing from wall to wall down the hall.

The bouncing floating weightless balloon brought my rapidly wandering mind to automotive designer Colin Chapman's philosophy for his automobiles: "Simplify, then add lightness." By taking out weight, his vehicles handled better and were more efficient, and quicker than their heavier counterparts.

With Chapman's philosophy in my thoughts, I walked around the room, looking more closely at the walls and the floor, hoping to find something deeper. It became increasingly apparent that Paul's ability to paint a wall was unimpressive. The brushstrokes were painfully visible. This observation brought my mind to something that Julie had once told me when she managed to force me into attending an opening at the gallery.

I was criticizing color choice and composition in each of the paintings displayed, suggesting the artists to be incapable of doing the act of painting properly. The paint was too thin and the white canvas was washing out the color or the color did not complement its corresponding color correctly. I had not wanted to be present so I took my frustration out on the art which made me feel much better at the time.

Correcting my harsh critique, Julie told me that everything I see in a painting is a conscious choice made by the artist. I believed her statement gave artists far too much credit, allowing for mistakes and lack of talent and vision to be interpreted as artistic choice. But what Julie's words did was allow me to see more deeply into the art, to see past what I believed to be mistakes, and to then attempt to find the meaning behind the artists' alleged choices.

I tried applying that technique to Paul's room and took a step back, then one closer, and moved my head side to side to examine the brushstrokes on the walls and ceiling of the dark room. I found that they produced a subtle pattern of diagonal lines juxtaposed in squares, but warped squares, all moving away from the window. The resulting effect, when the viewer paid attention to the lines or when he did not, was a trick of depth perception; a shrunken room and an enlarged window.

I began to move swiftly around the room, running my hands along the walls, feeling the texture that distorted my perception. I questioned the possible meanings or reasons behind it all, forgetting that the artist was standing in the room.

Then it came to me as I took several steps back into the wide doorway, wide enough to hold an audience. The room was more of a real-life moving living breathing picture in a room than a painted room in the usual sense. The magnified window framed perfectly the life that was bustling on the patio and property behind the house, dwindling into the gray waters beyond. The light bouncing off the white wooden floor and reflecting slightly off the ceiling while also being absorbed by the four vertical black walls enhanced the outdoors further, creating a perfect picture of both portrait and landscape.

Paul was watching my realization unfold, but his face displayed nothing. I considered for a moment the possibility that I had over-interpreted. Possibly Paul was a monochromatic colorblind interior designer with constantly varying depth perception who happened to be a terrible painter. But it was more likely that he was merely a deeply hurt highly criticized artist made emotionless by a lifetime of being misunderstood. He was empty inside because of them. I was empty inside because of them.

When I looked up at Paul again, as I crouched in the middle of the room thinking, he looked back at me, face still expressionless. I shook my generous assumption about this room-as-artwork from my mind.

"You know, Paul, I used to think I had a good imagination, but, as it turns out, it was just my imagination…"

He looked at me, down at me, then left the room without a word. I stood slowly, bracing myself the best I could to protect my knees. As I closed the oversized blackened French doors, I took one last look through the room and onto the beauty that lay beyond and smiled.

"It was just my imagination," I repeated, red balloon in my mind.

———

Pastor Duckworth

As I walked down the hall, I remembered that I was completely lost and rather disoriented. Then, two dozen or so steps further on, a staircase that I had not noticed on the roundabout journey to the room appeared.

In a flash, I was standing in the living picture I had witnessed less than a minute before. Smiling guests swirled around, talking and eating, drinking and playing. After a moment of vertigo, I realized quickly that I had not eaten since the previous night's dinner so I looked around for something other than Mrs. Douglas's hors d'oeuvre.

The tardy cake about which Mr. Douglas had previously been shouting had finally made its appearance; I was able to count six separate layers. Only a few yards away servers were filling a table with large slices on plates as they cut into the top level. My first plate was significantly heavier than I had imagined. The cake too defied my imagination.

Upon yet another return from the cake table, I deduced that a server had removed my two empty plates from the uncomfortable stone bench where I had left them to retrieve a third slice of the heavenly confection. If anyone was watching, it did not bother me in the least. As long as the cake kept coming, I would keep eating it.

A woman ran to the front of the cake line and shouted to anyone who would listen, "Is this cake dairy free? My husband can't eat it if it's not dairy free."

"Oh, pish posh," a short portly gentleman said, pushing the woman aside. "I'll eat whatever I please, woman!"

I smiled at their marital banter, exposing a grin full of cake.

Midway through the fourth wedge, my cake disappearing act was interrupted by a tall man wearing black pants and a black long-sleeved dress shirt with what I initially mistook to be a small white bow tie, but then realized was a clerical collar.

"Save some cake for me, cowboy!" he said, laughing.

Mouth full, I tilted my head upward. "Let them eat cake," I mumbled, mashing and masticating.

The man laughed again and sat himself down next to me without invitation. "Robinson Duckworth," he said, extending his right hand. "Nice to make your acquaintance."

"Nick," I pushed out as I attempted to swallow what was still working its way around my mouth. "Nick Thesiger. Nice to meet you as well." I waved my fork in greeting then went back to my pursuit of cake and thought about how his name sounded more like that of a cartoon duck than a human.

"Oh, the famous psychologist, Nicholas Thesiger!" he shouted.

I finished swallowing. "My reputation precedes me?" I questioned, wondering who this man was.

"Oh, pardon me, Nicholas. I am the pastor at the church your wife's family attends. I've known Julie since she was born, you see. Baptized her as a babe."

The man looked hardly old enough to have been a pastor since Julie's birth, so I was immediately suspicious of his story, but I was also enjoying my cake far too much to dispute his claim.

He continued. "I always thought I would perform the wedding ceremony for her in our little church, but then the two of you exercised your youthful indiscretion and eloped!" His voice turned to a jovial chuckle.

"Well, there's still time…" I muttered before shoveling another fork full of cake into my waiting mouth.

"Oh! You are the funny one!" he exclaimed, too enthusiastic to be welcome at my bench.

I nodded and tightly smiled, then quickly looked away, hoping he would take his leave.

"Took an early ride before the sermon this morning," he said, clearly not understanding body language or social norms. "And, when I say early, I mean early. About 4 a.m. It was still dark. Great way to meet people; biking."

"I'm sorry," I said, interrupting. "You mean to tell me that getting on a bicycle at four o'clock in the morning is a good way to meet people?" My expression was that of the annoyed antisocial guy at the party who only showed up for the cake, but was then approached by a talkative pastor who did not fully understand to whom he was talking.

"Yes! Of course," he said much too loudly. "Walking and jogging; they have their benefits; but biking has those and more! When you're on your feet, passing by another jogger, you just pass. Maybe there is a smile or a quick glance in their direction to acknowledge their presence, but that's it, nothing more. When you're up on that bike, much more information needs to be communicated.

"You have to watch out for them. They have to watch out for you. With cross traffic of joggers and bikers, eye contact is a must. You need to not only acknowledge one another, but decisions as to who goes first and who goes second, who goes to the right and who to the left, who is to slow down and who is to speed up; it all needs to be conveyed in that moment when you look deep into that other person's eyes and that moment is an intense one!

"The connection I feel when I've communicated like that with another human being is one of the most powerful I have felt. Someone could probably walk around with their eyes closed and be fine, but that's no way to meet people! You try that. You go try that. Walk around with your eyes closed and see how many people you meet."

As he spoke, I watched the pastor preach about his early morning passion in amazement. I wondered how lonely he must be to have to come up with creatively delusional ways to fictitiously meet people on his bike at 4 a.m. *Oh I just passed that person and had an exceptionally intense moment with them. Now we're friends.*

"Are you suggesting that I wake up at 4 a.m. to then walk around outside with my eyes closed to see how many people I can meet?"

To my surprise, he nodded at my facetious question, so I politely suggested to him the likely outcome.

"Obviously I wouldn't meet anyone unless you count the paramedics from my speedy ambulance trip to the hospital due to the extensive damage from all of the trees and walls and rocks that I would inevitably walk into, let alone the damage done from a long fall off the cliff that my luck would allow me to find while I was following your ridiculous advice."

My intention was to indirectly shoo the man away, but he found my words too rude to possibly be genuine. He laughed and laughed, knocking into me, causing me to almost drop my all-important fourth piece of cake. I sighed at the fact that it was becoming increasingly commonplace for polite people to assume that rude people, such as myself, were merely being facetious.

"You're a funny guy!" he shouted.

Giving in, I smiled and went back to eating, knowing I would soon be again bombarded with a non-sequitur conversation starter.

"You know, Nicholas, on a more serious note, I read something alarming not too long ago. Apparently religious leaders and clergymen, not psychologists or other mental health experts, are the most commonly sought source of help in times of psychological distress. And more than a third of religious leaders suggest mental illness to be spiritual in nature and therefore potentially solved with prayer. Even those afflicted with mental illness so severe that medication is their only medical option are encouraged to cease their dosage and instructed to pray instead. What do you think on the topic?"

I knew well of what the pastor spoke and I knew nothing I could say would rid me of his company, so I responded honestly. "As for non-medically trained individuals advising someone to stop taking a prescribed medication, that just does not make any sense. Why would anyone take advice from someone who does not specialize in what the advice is about? But, I suppose that is the pertinent question, isn't it?"

"Hmm, yes…" he mumbled with his curled right index finger to the tip of his nose, thumb under his chin.

"An eighty-year-old woman comes into my office," I began. "She takes one look at me and walks out. What can she learn from me, she's probably asking herself. I'm a man half her age. How could I help her without having at least as much life experience as she's had. She thinks she's better off without talking to me. It doesn't matter that I've been trained to counsel all kinds of people of all ages; that doesn't matter to her at all.

"That same eighty-year-old woman walks into your church and she feels at ease, feels right, feels as though she will respect each word that comes from your mouth because, to her, your words are gospel. The message, as far as she is concerned, could have come from The Lord Himself and, despite the fact that He was a carpenter, not a psychologist, His is the best advice of all.

"The bottom line is this, people need to respect the person from whom they seek advice and they need to respect that person's opinions. That woman made up her mind about you before she entered your church because you represent the church, something she's known her whole life, something she respects, something far older and more powerful than she.

"What does she know about me? That I went to school for a long time. That I am not the same gender as she is. That I've only lived through half the number of years she has, so, as she sees it, I have half the experience from which to draw wisdom. She would need to get to know me extensively before trusting and respecting me and she would only come to that point if I held the exact same morals as she did. You see, she needs to respect me for the process to work. And what makes it even harder is that, as a psychologist, I am generally not supposed to divulge much of my own self to patients. The church, that *is* her morals and she'll always know more about it than about me. Not to mention that the church gives free advice; mine is expensive. How can I compete with all of that?"

The pastor opened his mouth, about to respond, before I added, "And the church suggests all things happen for a reason; that things will end up right on some overarching level. Psychology doesn't offer that. If something bad happens, it does not necessarily mean that something good will happen. Which ideology, if I can call them both that, would you go to in your time of need or if you wanted some kind of help, reassurance? The one that tells you everything will be alright or the one that tells you everything is probably not going to be alright unless you work hard to make things better and, even then, things probably are not going to be all that much better."

The pastor was nodding his head as I spoke and continued to do so long after I had finished. I forked another morsel of cake into my mouth with the thrust of deliberate intention, and nodded along with him.

He then opened his mouth but was cut off before his thought could come out.

"Pastor Duckworth!" an unfamiliar woman shouted as she waddled up to my bench.

"Jackleen! Is that you?" he asked as he stood and began to walk toward her, meeting her in a friendly embrace feet away from me.

"Look at you," he said of the woman, large in circumference from what I assumed to be the child growing within. "When are you due?"

"Six weeks!" she announced proudly. "Here, touch my stomach."

The pastor quickly slid both hands onto the woman's stomach. "Oh! I can feel the baby kicking!" he shouted happily.

"He must like you!" she exclaimed with an out of place seductive look in her eye.

"Aw, a little boy!" he responded with an odd amount of pride, as if he had some connection to the child beyond that of its pastor or a friend of the family. I thought I may have noticed him mentally counting, doing some kind of mathematical paternity test.

"Oh here," the woman shouted in my direction as I watched the pastor continue to touch her stomach extensively. "Come, touch my stomach!"

"I'm sorry, strange woman. I have no intention of touching your stomach," I said as she approached the bench.

"Oh, poppycock," she said, grabbing my free hand and pulling it onto her bulbous mid-section, then holding it there for an extended period.

"Ohhh... isn't that wonderful," I said out of disgusted discomfort. Then I realized aloud, "I can't feel anything..."

"Hmm, seems like he stopped kicking," she confessed.

The woman walked away with the pastor's left arm around her, leaving me and my cake on my bench of solitude with a feeling of sadness and lonely emptiness.

"We'll resume this conversation in a bit, Nicholas! To be continued..." he called out behind him.

"I can't feel anything," I repeated quietly as I filled the void with the last bit of cake on my plate.

I sat without cake for only a few seconds, pondering the pastor's potential response before deciding there was little, if anything, he could have said that had not already been stated. As far as I was concerned, the conversation was over.

Wasting no time, I arose to seek an additional slice, but was blocked en route by someone I had never expected to see ever again in my life: the waiter from Tuesday night's dinner with the Lowerys.

"Hey!" he said, holding a tray. "It's Troy. I was your waiter a couple days ago in the city, at that restaurant in The Village." He extended his right hand, the one not supporting the tray, in greeting.

I recoiled in shock. My mind was certain that he had followed me out to The Hamptons to exact murderous revenge or to injure me in some other permanent way for the harmless bit of sport I had taken at his expense the other night. How could I know he would submerge his head underwater mid-shift on my "medical" advice, live through the experience, and then get fired for it?

"Hello," I said slowly, ready to run if need be. "What are you doing here?"

"Oh, well they ended up firing me that night. Next day, who's at my door but your wife. She got my address from the restaurant. Apparently she felt bad about me getting fired and all so she set me up with this sweet gig out here."

"Oh..." I said, still unsure whether he was to be trusted.

"Yeah, man. It's a pretty great deal. I'm working for this restaurant out here and they got a huge organic farm. Me and some other guys help with the farming and they let us live in the farmhouse; gives me a chance to save up for goin' back to school."

Frozen in confused fright and unsure about his unexpected and oddly convenient story, I managed to break my neck free of fear's cold grasp and nod along.

"Horticulture," he said with pride, framing the word using his free right hand. "I was here last night serving at dinner but you didn't notice me then. I couldn't say anything 'cause I had to keep up appearances and all. You know how it is. Am I right?" Troy extended his vertical right fist, startling me a bit.

When I saw that it was merely a gesture of solidarity, I met him halfway with my left fist.

"Right on," he said. "Right on... So I'll see you around?"

"Uh, yeah. I'll be here all weekend," I replied, still wary about our newly formed camaraderie and questioning why I had just informed him of my weekend plans.

"Nice," he replied as he walked back into the crowd. "Nice."

Slightly thrown off by the odd reappearance of such a minimal character from the past week, I jokingly said to myself, "Maybe I should ask Pastor Duckworth to explain the significance; get his perspective."

I laughed aloud, regaining my composure, then continued on my way to the cake table.

———

Greatest Weakness

Excited to attempt to fill the seemingly endless void in my stomach with cake, I handed my empty plate to the server behind the table just as I saw Mr. Douglas standing, admiring his world.

"Oh, Mr. Douglas," I said loudly as I approached, cakeless. "I've been looking for you... Turns out Richard did not want me to move his car. Didn't want me to touch it, in fact."

"Oh, is that right?" Mr. Douglas questioned with a slightly sinister smile. "I must tell you, Nicholas, I did not appreciate having my hand wrapped in children's Band-Aids when one would have sufficed."

"So this is your way of getting back at me? Your retaliation?"

He smiled the same slightly sinister smile that had been living on his face since he suggested I move Richard's car and then he said quietly, "Brava, Nicholas. Brava."

Infuriated, I wrenched my neck and clenched my teeth as I corrected him. "*Brava* is for women. *Bravo* is for men." Then I shook his idiotic word choice out of my head and said, "Tell me something,

Bob, how long have you made it a habit to manipulate people into behaving in a manner that hurts others, all for your own amusement?"

"Oh, you think I'm pulling all the strings? That everyone is a mere puppet to me? That I'm the Pinocchio of all situations?"

His line of questioning infuriated me further. "Geppetto was the puppeteer! Pinocchio was the puppet!" I shouted before calming myself and telling him, "I am not someone to be manipulated. I'm not a pawn in your little game."

"Nicholas, I have unlocked the key to this," he responded as he gestured grandiosely and leaned in close to my body. "The game is not little. It's much larger than you think, much larger than you could ever imagine. You and I, we have a little bit of a David and Goliath situation. Do we not? I don't believe this is a battle in which you would like to be involved…" With that and without giving me a chance to properly respond, he slithered away through the crowd, out of sight.

"David won!" I finally shouted, realizing his verbal contradiction. "And you can't *unlock* a *key*; you *unlock* a *lock* with a *key*!"

I then thought deeply, standing there by the table under the partially deconstructed multi-tiered cake; I thought about what the old man deserved and how I would serve his comeuppance to him. Because I find it rather difficult to think and enjoy food simultaneously, the rapidly disappearing mountain of cake nearby motivated my quick decision.

The best course of action was to sacrifice my own comfort, pride, and decorum for the greater goal of shaking Mr. Douglas to his core, not directly, but indirectly, by presenting his son-in-law to his guests as a socially inept, complete and utter buffoon.

My fifth and sixth slices were arguably the most enjoyable, not because the lower layers were tastier than their higher in altitude counterparts, but because I was beginning to taste the sweetness of future victory, before I even began putting my plan into motion.

Scrumptious, I thought at every swallow.

The server, dressed in what must have been a painfully warm uniform, long thick black pants, a long-sleeved thick black collared shirt, and a thick black fabric cap with no rim, smiled politely when I waved off the next round of cake he had prepared for my consumption. It was time for action.

Near to the house and patio, the crowd was tight, fanning out in a rather uniform manner as I moved closer to the trees. I kept a concerned, searching look on my face to repel any would-be conversers; I was on a mission.

The fire within had almost begun to die down by the time I located Mr. Douglas, but, as he filled more and more of my visual field, I became more and more inclined to take him down a level or two. He stood with Julie, Julie's incessantly chattering Cousin Abigail, and four others, two men and two women, a bit younger looking than I.

I approached slowly, emptying my head of any specific plans or scenarios I had thought about creating. The decision was to improvise, play it by ear, bring some jazz into my life. The closer I moved in their direction, the more in focus their faces and characteristics became. I stopped, shocked, when I noticed Julie. She appeared happier than I had seen her in years, happier even than the previous day, smiling and laughing and bubbling with conversation.

A glass of wine resided in her left hand, sipped sporadically, and a plate of magnificent cake in the other. These were the only times that I saw her drink more than a glass or two of wine and continue to smile, while with her family, while happy with her family, feeling safe, secure, comfortable. Without them/with me she was sad, bitter, angry, frustrated; she drank to get away from it. The stark differences between the Julie I knew and the Julie they knew were hard to witness, but I stood watching despite what it was doing to me.

"Why did I get the short end of the stick?" I questioned quietly, truly, completely, and ignorantly ignoring the fact that it was I who had changed her from the amazing person that she was into the depressed and sullen remnant of that former beauty.

"In vino veritas," I said to myself, attributing her joyous demeanor to the wine while conveniently ignoring the phrase's true meaning and relevance.

With each forward step, it became more and more clear to me that these good friendly people and Abigail were about to become casualties in my quest to indirectly attack my father-in-law.

"This cake is outstanding!" one of the men exclaimed. "Much better than the one we had at the Kensington party."

"That was a child's birthday celebration, dear," the woman standing next to him said. "Don't you remember the clown? Although it was rather extravagant. There was even a monkey!"

"Nothing says good times like a monkey! Am I right?" I chimed in as I slipped into their circle between Julie and her father, an arm around each of them.

The pause of an uncomfortable duration that followed was broken by Julie. "Ahh, everyone, this is Nicholas..."

"Her much much better half," I interrupted.

"Yes..." she said slowly.

"Hey, Captain Pops! Where's the crapper? You got some outhouses out here or what? Layes Horderveres, aahh?" I said with a terrible French accent as I patted and pushed out stomach.

"Ha ha…" Julie said uncomfortably, hoping the group would feel humor as opposed to disgust.

But not one member of the group saw the humor in my show so Julie again attempted to break the ice with the appropriate introductions.

"This is Adrianne…" she said, gesturing her wineglass at the smallest of the women holding a plate of cake and wearing a long golden dress with thick straps, her blond hair mostly hidden beneath one of the many preposterously enormous hats bobbing around the party. Hers was a deep purple and matched the shoes on her petite feet and thin belt around her petite waist.

"Adrianne!" I slurred in my best Italian Stallion accent. I looked around for confirmation, nodding my head and smiling. None came. "You're right, you're right," I said. "Too easy. You must get that all the time."

"Ah, yes…" Julie continued with a wavering tone of extreme discomfort. She then rotated clockwise around the circle, skipping Abigail and instead indicating a tall skinny fellow wearing a tan suit with a light blue collared shirt underneath. The jacket was unbuttoned and displayed his thick blue suspenders.

"And this is Justin, Adrianne's husband," Julie said.

"It's Justin!" I shouted, extending my right hand toward him. "Just in time, am I right?"

He looked at me with a perplexed expression.

"What's wrong with you?" Abigail asked loudly, creating an even more awkward atmosphere.

Her question was ignored as Julie continued. "This is Julius," she said, nodding to a man holding a plate filled not with cake but with salad.

"So that's Julius's Caesar Salad? Haha!" I laughed loudly as I pointed at his plate, knowing that no one would join in. I wanted to slap Abigail on the back but she was too far away.

"Nick," Julie said with a large fake smile, "are you going to do this with everyone's name?" Her question was posed in a friendly manner, but there were distinct and specific instructions to cease and desist hidden beneath.

"Sorry, dear," I said smiling at the group, focusing my expression mostly toward Mr. Douglas.

"Hi." The last stranger, a tall woman with light brown hair and a yellow summer dress, stepped forward and extended her right hand. "I'm Julius's wife, Bambi."

"Oh, jeez," I responded sympathetically. "I'm really sorry about your mom. I cried and cried when those hunters shot her." I paused for laughter, eyes wide, but none came. I quickly considered the extremely unlikely possibility that this woman's mother had actually died in a horrible hunting accident, but I shook off the suspicion when I realized that my luck could not possibly be that bad, or good.

"You know," I said. "The movie?"

"I don't follow," she remarked.

"Seriously? I can't believe you've never gotten that before."

Mr. Douglas, after unsuccessfully attempting to make me vanish with a hostile stare, turned toward Justin and asked, "What are you up to these days? Still working on The Street?"

The man's eyes lit up, ready to tell a tale of his success. "Yes, yes! My investments are paying off too fast! I'm up to everything and nothing, enjoying the sweet life of not knowing what to do with myself and yet being able to do whatever I want."

"Well," I said, interrupting. "Justin is charmingly modest, now isn't he?" The question was posed in Mr. Douglas's direction, but directed to the group.

No one said a word for several seconds until Justin stammered, "Ahh, yes…" Confused if I was joking or just a terrible guest, he continued. "That's why I decided on a hobby, a pet really. My little psittacine."

"A parrot?" I interjected as quickly as possible to inform all who were around that I knew what a psittacine was. "Why would you do that?"

"Oh well, it's a beautiful and smart bird," Justin began. "He greets me and follows me around the house. Says silly things…" Justin continued to go on about his bird until I interrupted again.

"How do you feel about this, Adrianne? You feel like you're being replaced by a bird?"

The silence was, this time, short because Julie broke in quickly with a laugh to again attempt to convey the joshing intention of my inappropriate behavior. Taking her cue, the group chuckled quietly.

Justin continued on. "He likes to take long drives with me. We just get into the car and drive for hours, doesn't matter where. He just gets on my shoulder and we go."

"So you're something like a road pirate?" I suggested.

There was no verbal and little physical response so I squinted my right eye, angled my arm, swung my fist, and added, "Arrrr, me matey!"

I was beginning to pride myself on my uncanny ability to shut everyone up in disgust.

"Ahh, Nick," Julie began, attempting to change the conversation. "Julius was asking about your car. They saw it in front of the house when they arrived. Julius is into cars as well."

"Oh! What are you in these days, my good good good man?" I asked with far more enthusiasm than was at all appropriate.

"I drive a Mercedes. It's 'the ultimate driving machine,' " he informed me.

"Are you serious?" I asked. "You're telling me that your *Mercedes* is *the ultimate driving machine*?"

"It's a fine automobile..." he said somewhat defensively.

"Is that right?" I asked. "What model?"

"The finest, top of the line; that's what!" he said, laughing loudly and holding up his wineglass. Then he added, " 'There is no substitute.' "

I thought for a moment before telling him, "I have a strong suspicion that you know close to nothing about cars, but you think you do because you're capable of purchasing a top of the line model. You don't even know the slogan that goes correctly with your car. And I've got a feeling you don't even know what model your own car actually is."

The man, large and wealthy beyond his own capacity, was shrunken by my harsh honesty. He was struck speechless, just as the rest of the group was. All but Abigail.

"You're an idiot, Nicholas," she informed me in her raspy angry tone.

I laughed loudly and punched Julius's arm, pretending it was a joke. Julius began to laugh a forced quiet laugh as he looked down and away. The rest of the group quietly joined in.

"I'm hilarious," I proclaimed, smiling at Mr. Douglas whose facial expression showed a man only beginning to realize that he and only he had brought this upon himself and his guests.

This time it was Adrianne, not Julie, who attempted to break the awkward pause in conversation.

"Nicholas, Julie mentioned that you were a doctor. I had a medical question about a procedure."

"Go ahead," I said, having, at that point, given up explaining the difference between a PhD and an MD.

"I was considering getting my eyes done. Justin and I have been talking about it for years and I think now is the right time. I just wanted to know a little more about the procedure and what to expect."

"To tell you the truth," I began, "I don't think you should bother going through with it. Surgery is invasive and I know *I'm* always a little uncomfortable with sharp tools around my face. I say don't worry about those unsightly dark bags under your eyes. They'll probably go away with some good makeup and maybe some rest. Are you not sleeping well? Maybe you should address that before any cosmetic surgery, although I know a guy who is great, raved about by friends. I can have Julie send you his info."

"I was referring to surgery to correct the focus of my vision," Adrianne informed me quietly, rather embarrassed.

"Oh. My mistake. I would suggest talking to an eye doctor about that." My tone was apologetic, but I knew what she was asking when she first posed the question.

Again, it was Julie's turn to attempt to steer the conversation away from the awkward state in which it was wavering.

"Oh, Justin, how is your little dog from the Fourth of July? Did you bring him?" she asked.

"No, no. He ran away actually," Justin said sadly.

"Yes, the children were devastated," Adrianne added, voice full of emotion.

"Oh, I'm really sorry. Why not get another one?" Bambi asked.

"It's just hard to replace him," Adrianne began, eyes and tone welling up.

I then interrupted. "Same thing happened to my dog when I was a boy. I was doing the laundry and he came in, startling me. I spilled a bottle of spot remover all over him and he was gone. He never did return..."

At that point, everyone knew that my insufferable behavior was no misunderstanding or mistake so it was no longer met with a lenient benefit-of-the-doubt response. Justin and Adrianne rolled their eyes while Julius and Bambi looked away in disgust. Mr. Douglas and Abigail shook their heads at me as they had been doing for some time. And Julie just stared blankly, praying for the moment to be over.

"No dogs allowed..." I sang in a slow booming deep voice. Then I laughed at my out of place Charlie Brown reference.

"Oh, Adrianne. Tell us about your next book," Julie said, memory likely jump-started by my comment.

"Oh, don't get me started," Adrianne said, fully intending on getting herself started.

"Oh, please," Mr. Douglas insisted. "We would love to hear about your process."

In that moment, I recalled reading a book that Julie handed to me several years earlier. Gritting my teeth through it, it was clear that the book had traveled through the author's colon to make its way to my hands.

When I finally completed the atrocious thing, my review was five words, "a crime of mainstream publishing." That was before Julie informed me that it was her friend who wrote the book and she had actually self-published, paying for all publishing costs because no publisher would. I then corrected myself, cutting my review to two words, "a crime."

Not until that moment, waiting for Adrianne to bring us through her journey of writing, did I realize that the Adrianne who wrote the book was the Adrianne standing in front of me. For a brief few seconds, I questioned my mind's ability to recall and recognize Adrianne's face from the large-sized photo she placed on the back cover of her book. It took only those brief few seconds to realize that the photo that I was then mentally holding up next to Adrianne's face had been heavily touched up and altered to favorably enhance the author's appearance. The realization brought a smile to my face as she spoke.

"The process of each writer is a closely guarded secret. So is, very often, the topic of their upcoming work, but I will speak briefly on my inspiration and maybe even my future novel."

At that moment I wished for my eyes to grow ten feet in height so that I could roll them to the appropriate level. Writers write whereas authors happened to have put their name on the front of a book at some point. Adrianne was no writer.

She continued. "Aesthetically distinguishable, but we are all infected with the human condition…"

Everyone nodded with intellectual consensus as if Adrianne had just said something profound as opposed to something badly worded and unclear.

"It was a journey, quite a journey. I adored reading and writing always. It became serious when I majored in creative writing at university."

I interrupted her boring and potentially long recount of the "journey" that had produced her terrible book. "You know what Theodor Geisel said about writing, don't you?" I asked.

"What's that, Nicholas?" Mr. Douglas asked because no one else would.

"Majoring in creative writing is a mistake for anyone. He said it was like 'teaching the mechanics of getting water out of a well that may not exist.' "

My words and I were met with angry and disgusted stares of disdain until Mr. Douglas asked, "And who, pray tell, is Theodor Geisel?" mispronouncing the name.

"He wrote under several pen names and created many very popular and timeless pieces. He is best known as Dr. Seuss," I responded triumphantly.

The group burst into an unexpected roar of laughter as even Mr. Douglas smiled. Their skewed and misdirected perceptions of me changed immediately. Suddenly, I was and had always been funny, just two steps ahead of their comprehension.

Undaunted by this turn of events, I continued to explain in an honest attempt to make them hate me. "If any of you knew anything substantial about literature and the man's countless contributions, your heads would be nodding in agreement, not thrown back in hilarity."

This only made them laugh harder. Justin put his left hand on my shoulder. "You *are* hilarious," he said heartily.

"Agreed," Julius added.

"Well, I should continue on," Mr. Douglas said, informing us of his imminent departure.

Everyone shook hands or hugged, saying "good seeing you" and "nice to meet you" and "we should do e-mail" as I stood limp, confused, and angry watching sly Mr. Douglas slither away.

After the unpleasant pleasantries, I snapped back into the moment and jogged after Mr. Douglas, grabbing his arm when I caught up. He turned and looked at me.

"You *are* hilarious," he said, smiling.

"You'll get yours, old man," I threatened, not fully thinking through what I was saying.

"If I do, it will be long after you get yours. But I must tell you, Nicholas, I have not the slightest idea about what you are speaking."

I merely looked with irritation as I released his arm.

"Nicholas," he began, "when I saw you parking this morning, a lightbulb *literally* went off in my head."

"A lightbulb did not *literally* go off in your head!" I shouted, angered by his idiotic statement. "You don't have *lightbulbs* in your head! When, in this language, did the word 'literally' adopt the meaning of its antonym?" Then I shouted louder, "Figuratively!"

"Nicholas, I'm speechless," he said, feigning some kind of shock.

Anger within me only increasing, I shouted, "You cannot be speechless if you're currently saying aloud that you are speechless. You can *never* speak those words! The statement completely negates itself when expressed aloud!"

"Of course," he said with a bit of a laugh, no longer facing me and moving away. "Nicholas, you have nailed it out of the park."

At that moment—the moment he mixed the expressions *hit the nail on the head* and *knocked it out of the park*—it became clear to me. It all became clear to me. Mr. Douglas had not only identified my weakness, but he was using it to harm me. Mixed metaphor by mixed metaphor, he was chipping away at my psyche. I allowed him to shrink in my visual field as the astonishment of realization dripped from my face. I then turned to locate Julie to inform her of her father's diabolical behavior, to prove to her that it was he who was the instigator.

———

Exploding Car

I caught only a glimmer of her blue dress, but chased after it, weaving through the crowd then entering the house from the patio. I dodged and darted, left and right through the dangers of the many oversized hats and trays scattered throughout as I sought to catch up.

The dress guided me through a large room filled with strangers then through a hallway where I was bombarded with four young cousins. Dressed in khaki shorts and white short-sleeved collared shirts, two wearing blue baseball caps and the others wearing yellow headbands, they each held a tennis racket and plastic containers of bright green tennis balls. Strangely, three of the four had argyle patterned sweaters wrapped loosely around their shoulders. The day seemed far too warm for this, but I reconciled the stupidity as what Pastor Duckworth would call "youthful indiscretion."

They, in their flamboyant tennis attire, were brandishing their equipment recklessly as they shot down the hall in between guests who were holding food and drink. I felt it necessary to slow their pace.

"Children! Keep the racket down, children!" I shouted with a laugh.

They slowed to a stop and looked at me inquisitively.

"You know, 'keep the racket down,' " I said, shaking my fist and affecting a mad old man face. " 'Racket' like noise and 'racquet' like a tennis racquet?"

"Don't you work for us?" fourteen-year-old Cameron inquired condescendingly.

"No, I do not work for you," I snapped back quickly. My level of disgust had rapidly exceeded an acceptable one, so I told the children to "run along" as I shooed them away with the backs of my hands.

"I'm pretty sure he works for *us*," I heard thirteen-year-old Callaway say as they continued on their way.

Forgetting as best I could the outlandishly privileged children's thought process, I continued down to the end of the hall to find an archway that opened into a small sitting room. The end of the hall was all but empty except for Julie's Uncle Tommy wandering and stumbling around, likely lost.

As I approached, the wafting aroma suggested that he was indulging in his whiskey just as generously as he had been the previous day. Tommy's smile was wide and his eyes were shut tight as he wiggled his right index finger vigorously and shuffled side to side to the beat of the imaginary music in his head.

I navigated around the dancing silly man and stood surveilling in the archway before entering.

At one of the two couches in the room, Julie sat quietly with three sad looking, older members of the party; two women on one couch and a man sitting with Julie on the other. The couches met at the farthest corner of the room and Julie's arms reached across that corner as she held one of the women's right hand with both of her own. The woman whose hand was not clutched by Julie's and the man held tea cups with saucers.

Playing on the opposite side of the room were two young children, a boy and a girl, both younger than ten years, and what appeared to be their mother. She was entertaining them, trading her time to mingle for time to draw with her children, crayons of assorted colors and sizes in hand.

As I examined the scene, my eyes went up because I felt as though that was where much of the attention in the room was focused despite some heads being bowed. The vaulted ceiling was made up of exposed white painted beams, crossing and meeting at points, creating countless geometric shapes.

The floor creaked quietly under my feet as I entered with a smile on my face in an attempt to lighten the palpable down mood of the room, a selfless gift I felt that Julie deserved to witness me deliver after all that I had put her through.

The quiet creaks were ignored until they stopped as I stood motionless by the older man leaning back into the couch that also held Julie. He turned and looked up at me, then leaned forward and reached for the coffee table upon which he rested his tea cup and saucer, completely ignoring my presence.

I smiled at his rude gesture and attempted to silently catch up on the conversation through eavesdropping. The topic discussed appeared to be a current event that I vaguely recalled Julie mentioning to me about a week before; a news report about someone being killed in an unfortunate car accident. Why they were discussing it was beyond me, but I just assumed that the conversation was slow so this week-old news report had somehow been brought up.

"How old was he?" Julie asked.

"His fortieth was May four…" answered the woman whose right hand was held by both of Julie's.

"His car just exploded. There was nothing he could do," the other older woman said as she shook her head and pursed her lips.

A newspaper sat on the table in front of them opened to a page with a picture of a car mangled and burned. The picture fully brought back my memory of Julie introducing the story to me days earlier, so I chimed in with my thoughts.

"Someone was in a car accident and the car exploded? That's impossible. Cars don't just explode. Accident or no accident. That's just not the way gasoline works. Maybe in movies, but not in the real world."

"Well, it happened, Nicholas," Julie said after the initial startled look she gave upon realizing that I was in the room.

Both older women seemed quite perturbed by my disagreement. They shook their heads while the older man sitting by Julie just stared over his glasses at me. I took this to be an invitation to continue sharing my thoughts on the matter.

"I remember when Julie mentioned this to me last week. I told her then, but she wouldn't hear it. It's impossible for a car to explode the way they said it did. First of all, it is surprisingly difficult to ignite gasoline and, when it is ignited, it merely burns. It doesn't explode."

As I spoke, Julie stood up and turned to me with a horrified look on her face, still holding the woman's right hand.

I continued. "The news sometimes exaggerates things. That's all I'm saying. I'm sure the car burned, but exploded? I'm not buying what they're selling."

"The story was true and it did happen," Julie insisted.

"Okay, fine," I responded, graciously allowing Julie the victory. I then smiled happily at my ability to choose my battles, taking satisfaction that my capitulation had caused confusion on Julie's side. This contented feeling, however, lasted for a mere ten or twelve seconds before I again began to feel it to be my duty to attempt to lighten the collective mood.

"You know, he was a good man," I said, with a slight smile.

"He was," agreed the man.

"Always spontaneous," I continued. "Very extroverted. Some would say he had an explosive personality..."

Similar looks were shot toward me as less than a minute earlier.

"Sorry, sorry. I was just trying to make light of his explosive past..." Again, I received no positive reaction. The woman coloring with the children started to openly weep.

"He had a bit of a short fuse though..." I persisted as Julie gently put down the woman's hand and forced me to the archway. The other woman at the couch stood to console the crying woman with the children, at which point the children themselves began to weep.

At the edge of the room, Julie angrily barked at me. "You're talking to the man's parents, his aunt, and those two over there"— she pointed to the crying youths—"those are his children and next to them, his widow. He died a week ago. The funeral was yesterday."

At that moment, my mind brought me toward a documentary on comedians that I had watched years before. A poignant part was an interview of a seasoned funnyman. The man was explaining that there is a delicate dynamic in a club between the comedian and the audience. They need to understand one another and adjust their expectations and their performance accordingly.

The man went on to say that it was shockingly easy to destroy this delicate dynamic with the wrong joke at the wrong time and, after telling that joke, there was absolutely no coming back from it. "No one will laugh at anything you say after that point, no matter how funny it is."

I decided, at that moment, that the same was true for recently deceased people. It was very easy for an inappropriate joke or two to land the funnyman in a position from which there is no coming back, much like the recently deceased individual just inappropriately joked about.

I left the room without adding a word. I knew anything I could say would only worsen things.

"What do you have to say for yourself, Nick?" Julie shouted after me.

I then heard her apologize profusely to the family who had lost their father, husband, son, and nephew as I moved further from the archway.

"Well," I muttered to myself, "that was the stupidest tea party that I ever have been to."

Seconds later I felt Julie's uniformly warm thin hand on my arm turning me quickly. There was no sliver of cold from her absent wedding band.

"What were you thinking!" she asked less as a question and more as a verbal punishment.

"I'm sorry, I was just trying to be nice," I responded moronically.

"His father, he's furious in there. I was humiliated to tell him who you were. I wanted to lie. I wanted to tell him I didn't know you. Do you know how that feels?"

"Who is he? He looks familiar," I said, trying to change the conversation.

"Nick, that's irrelevant. Are you even listening to what I'm saying?"

"I'm just curious what he does," I said, attempting to bring down her fury by moving on to a different topic.

"He's a designer, but that has nothing to do with this," Julie shouted.

"What does he design?"

"Nicholas! You just made fun of a dead man in front of his family one day after his funeral."

"Yes, yes... I know. I was just trying to lighten the mood. So what kind of designer is he?"

Julie gave up attempting to explain insensitivity to the insensitive and answered my question. "He designs clothes; hats mostly. I wish you could understand that I'm mad at you... and he is mad at you, very mad at you. How could you say something like that then just walk away?"

"So, what you're telling me is that he's a mad hatter?" I asked with a smile.

"Nick!" she shouted loudly. "Stop making jokes. My patience is going out altogether, like a candle. Do you understand?"

"Sorry, sorry. Just trying to lighten the mood again. Add lightness, you know?" I said, remembering my earlier recollection of Colin Chapman's automotive philosophy.

"Just stop then. Stop trying to lighten the mood."

Julie's father appeared behind me at that moment and, with an intimidating booming voice inquired, "What is happening here?"

I jumped, startled, then Julie answered. "Nick is acting idiotic like usual, Daddy..."

I was suddenly saddened by Julie's accurate explanation. Until then, no matter how badly I had behaved, Julie had never said anything disparaging about me in front of her father, the man who despised my very existence, the man who wanted me out of the family, the man who never stopped opposing our marriage.

"Oh, is that so?" he asked. "What has he done this time?"

"Ah," Julie grunted, frustrated. "Just forget it, Daddy." With that, Julie stomped away, leaving her daddy and me alone.

I turned to see an unexpected sight; Mr. Douglas's face was not frowning from disappointment, but smiling with glee.

"Carry on, Nicholas. Carry on," he said slyly.

"What is that supposed to mean?" I asked.

"Not a thing, young man." Then, Mr. Douglas's nose scrunched up and he covered it with his right hand. "What's that smell?" he asked, disgusted.

"Dog shampoo," I confessed, knowing well to what he was referring and why he had not smelled it earlier, the beautifully brisk sea breeze from the outdoors.

Mr. Douglas just shook his head and walked away, disappearing down a hallway and through a door. Then, appearing as if he had emerged through the wall, Julie's Uncle Tommy bumped quite forcefully into my back.

"Oh, pardon me, young man," he apologized.

"No problem, Uncle Tommy," I said, smiling at his red face.

My lips puckered when I inhaled the stench of whiskey from his exhale. He was holding a box and pushing it toward me.

He spoke enthusiastically. "Would you like to play Trivial Pursuit? I have Trivial Pursuit. Let us play a rousing game of Trivial Pursuit."

I shook my head, smiled, patted him on the back, and informed him that "I am unable to join you for a rousing game of Trivial Pursuit, Uncle Tommy."

As I walked from him, I heard fading behind me, "Would anyone like to play Trivial Pursuit? I have Trivial Pursuit."

The breeze hit my body just as the sun did the same, rejuvenating me, blowing and beaming away any odd unresolved emotions and smells that were mixing around in and on my head from the events of the day.

Again I found my bench and exhaled with a bit of an old man moan as I plopped myself down in hopeful relaxation, but the moment was gone in an instant. Julie's perpetually inebriated Cousin Kathy, excited to find a place to sit, dropped herself onto the bench next to me. She then looked in my direction, steadied herself with her partially rotated arms on either side of her body, palms to the bench, then looked forward.

After nearly a minute of waiting for our inevitable interaction to rapidly degenerate into what it always did between Kathy and myself, a seemingly endless line of insults back and forth, I began to calm, assuming that she was merely there to relax and to pay me no mind.

The calm lasted for only another minute of her rocking back and forth, still steadying herself from the spinning outdoors.

In front of us walked a mother and her daughter, likely thirty and five years of age, respectively. The child was balancing a plate of cake in her right hand while she licked her left. The mother quickly slapped the young girl's hand down, almost making her lose control of the plate in the other.

"Don't put your hands in your mouth!" she scolded.

"That woman there," Kathy slurred. "She's unique. Judge, jury, and executioner, all in one."

"Yup, because those words are rarely placed concurrently in a sentence describing a person…" I responded sarcastically.

"She knows how to raise a child. That's what I'm saying. Not like my husband."

"Ex-husband," I corrected.

"We're gonna work things out!" she snapped back, slurring and flailing her body, limp arms, and fiery red-haired head toward me.

"Sorry," I said laughing at her state, in life and in the present.

"Don't you laugh at me!" she shouted. "Two weeks ago, he told me we would meet here at twelve in the afternoon. He'll be here."

"Twelve is noon, not afternoon," I informed her.

Ignoring my correction, she continued. "Too many parents these days aren't firm enough. Too loosey goosey with 'em." Her head bobbed around on her neck as she said "loosey goosey." "Sometimes kids just need a good beating."

"Is capital punishment an appropriate tool to raise your children?" I asked in an attempt to provoke.

"Of course it is!" she exclaimed, throwing her arms in the air and completely losing her balance, saved from hitting the cobblestone only by my quick reaction, catching her with the back of my left arm.

"Let go of me!" she demanded. "Now what was I saying? Oh yeah, sometimes a kid just needs to be hit." She punched my arm on "hit." "You're a psychologist. You know how screwed up people can get when they don't have rules and consequences and stuff." She lost control of her neck for a moment, allowing her head to drop backward, bouncing off her shoulders and ending back where it began. "And here's another question for ya. Why don't you people just tell us what's wrong with us?"

"Who 'us'?" I asked. "Who do you mean by 'us'?" I was almost enjoying the conversation because I had an advantage given her depressive alcoholic handicap.

"Patients! You make us talk and talk and talk and never say not even a word. Why don't you say anything? Why not?" Her tone began to slip toward whining.

"Well, generally we have a theory about the patient's problem, but we prefer to have the patient think and talk and explore their background and memories, emotions and feelings about their family, friends, interpersonal relationships, and overall lives before we as psychologists say anything that might put an idea in their head that could be incorrect thus leading them down the wrong path."

"So then why don't you tell me after that, after I talk about my childhood? You people never say anything! It's frustrating. I hate you people." Kathy's tone had moved to unmistakably whiny.

"Well, there are a number of different kinds of therapists. I like to run sessions like a conversation, but those who say very little generally want their patients to come to conclusions and realizations on their own. It makes it much more powerful."

She stopped her swaying and straightened her spine in shock. "So what I'm hearing is that you're basically the Wizard of Oz?" she responded.

I paused for a moment of thought. "I suppose, yes."

"Waste of my hard earned money..." she muttered as she pushed herself to an unstable stance and leaned herself away. "Pay no attention to the man behind the curtain…" she shouted before falling into a short hedge.

"That was pretty poignant for someone who won't remember this conversation," I said to myself as I slid to the middle of the bench, hoping my new position would discourage others with tired legs.

I watch Kathy fumble around in the hedge for several dozen seconds before Julie found her way over to help. Julie then looked at me angrily as she brushed off her unfortunate cousin.

I raised my horizontal palms in protest. *What did I do?* I mouthed.

After righting her, Julie sent Kathy on her haphazard way toward the bar. She then approached me, her face changing from angry to frustrated to sad as she drew nearer.

———

A Short Walk

"Please be nice to me, okay?" Julie practically begged.

"Okay," I responded slowly.

"Can we take a walk together?" she asked, sounding oddly friendly. "Just the two of us…" Her left hand hovered, palm down and shaking slightly, waiting for my own to meet it, but I pushed it aside, ignoring my promise made seconds earlier.

"No. Just sit down. Relax," I instructed.

Reluctantly, she sat beside me and continued. "Please, Nick. I need this. We need this…"

"What does that mean? I just want to sit and relax. I don't want to take a walk." I spoke with much more confidence than I actually had at that point in the day.

"We can walk to the beach. It's not far at all. Maybe five minutes." She spoke quietly, looking away.

"I hate the beach. You know that," I barked back quickly.

As a child, my mother once brought me to the Jersey Shore. The water was green and brown. Garbage would wash ashore with every wave. Medical waste and dead wildlife from the sea and from the land littered the dirty polluted sand. Children love digging holes and I was no different, until I dug deep enough to find a human hand attached to a human body, lifeless.

"Please," she whimpered, still looking away. "We can walk and talk."

I rotated my body toward her and leaned forward, to see her face just as a tear began its quick journey down her left cheek.

"What's going on? What's wrong?" I asked, becoming uncomfortable.

"Oh, nothing, nothing. Just allergies," she responded.

"What are you allergic to? Being sad?" I asked rather obnoxiously.

"Just have a heart," she begged.

Knowing the appropriate response was to comply was only half of my decision. The other half was my desire to stop Julie from falling into a public crying fit. Enough eyes had already spent their time focusing on me in ridicule. I could take no more.

Slowly, I stood, then held out my right hand to help her up. "Let's go see if we can find my heart then," I told her.

Her left hand in my right, she stood and we were off over the patio and onto the grass, through the thick crowd and toward the far off forest and the path which led to the beach. She loosened her grip on my hand as we walked, dropping it away as soon as she was able. I looked down at my hand, empty, then at her looking away from me.

The dirt path through the small portion of forest opened up to a tennis court where the four children who had insulted me in the hall were playing doubles.

My mind wandered toward Courtland. During sessions when he did not feel like talking, we walked into Central Park and played some kind of sport, any kind of sport. Kicking a soccer ball, throwing a baseball or football, Frisbee, anything. We even hit a tennis ball back and forth once.

On quiet rainy days, chess was the in-office sport of choice, sometimes played for hours. I would ignore any other work I had because I knew that the most important thing in the day was to give him a companion. He needed it more than any other patient. I needed it more than any other patient.

During one long match, Courtland told me a story about his experience with some Japanese exchange students during junior high school. He was intrigued by their culture and wanted to know their stories, but he did not speak Japanese so there was little chance of him communicating effectively with them because their grasp of the English language was only slightly better than his of Japanese. Luckily, some of the exchange students were looking for someone to play chess with and Courtland was one of the few in the school who played well enough to compete, so he was summoned for a few games.

He told me he learned more by playing chess with them than he would have had he spoken their language. Their defensive tactics in comparison to their offensive ones. How they protected particular pieces while sacrificing others. How, when they took a valuable piece from him or their victory was imminent, they would not gloat or smirk or overtly appear superior in any way.

Courtland said he loved the Olympics because of this, "You can oftentimes learn more about a person and their culture through a game, a sport, or a friendly competition than through a conversation."

As Julie and I walked by the tennis courts and continued down the path, she repeatedly looked down then toward me then down again, opening her mouth slightly, then closing it, as if she needed to say something, but lacked the courage.

"Something on your mind?" I inquired.

She shook her head slowly.

"I thought you wanted to 'walk and talk,' no?" I said.

Again, she shook her head, likely not speaking because her words would sound too tearful to be taken seriously.

I decided that pushing her to talk was not a good choice, assuming that she was going to ask to stay an additional day or week. It would be more prudent to merely avoid the conversation as long as possible. If that was achieved due to her sadness or fear of my reaction, so be it.

So we walked, looking away from one another. I watched the ground turn from dirt to grass to dirt to a sandy dirt to dirty sand to sand to dirt and back to grass as we increased our distance from the mansion down the winding, confusingly indirect path.

We came upon the acres dedicated to the horses which were neatly manicured and lined with an ineffective looking split-rail fence with mortise and tenon joints constructed to about chest height with thin but long irregularly shaped old wood. Julie's parents rode years and years back, but no longer. The horses would shake Mr. and Mrs. Douglas's old bones apart if they attempted. Still they kept six large majestic beautiful horses in their pristine stable.

Without words, Julie led us off the path and toward the fence. The birds began to sing the sounds of annoyance, but I endured. Their irritating song was one of the few sounds that were both in the country and in the city. I thought about how different the two were. Then the summer and the winter. Then crazy and sane. Then me and them. Then Julie and me.

As we walked along the fence, an object perched atop it ahead came into focus. It was a lost looking little girl wearing a light blue dress similar to Julie's and shiny ruby shoes. The little girl looked far too young to be alone and away from adults on a fence watching horses.

"Hello, Alice," Julie said when we became close enough for conversation.

"I'm Dorothy," she responded.

"Oh, I thought your name was Alice," Julie said with confusion.

"No. It's Dorothy," the little girl replied in a little girl voice. "I'm Dorothy Alice Douglas." She counted her names on her fingers as she spoke.

"Well, that's a bit confusing," I said. Neither she nor Julie responded to my observation.

"What are you doing here all alone?" Julie asked.

"We were playing hide and seek. I found horseys!" she shouted, throwing her hands up in excitement. "And now I'm trying to get back home."

"Well, we can take you back home. Would you like to come with us?" Julie asked.

Without words, the young lost girl climbed down from the fence and put her arms vertical, physically requesting to be picked up and brought back to where she belonged.

Julie lifted and we were on our way, numbering three.

"Why are you crying?" Dorothy asked Julie.

"Oh, I'm not crying," Julie responded. "But I was crying earlier because I was sad."

"You're not sad anymore?" Dorothy inquired.

"Hopefully soon," Julie said quietly.

We walked along for five or six minutes before the path branched off into two directions; one, a continuation of the regular path, and the other, a long path of golden cobblestone lined with short trees, branches curving to form a continuous arch leading back to the mansion.

"This should bring us to where we need to go," Julie informed Dorothy and me.

Our new path was quite beautiful and, had it not been on the Douglas estate, the walk would have been rather enjoyable as the sound of the birds was almost absent within the curled tree branches.

"Aunt Julie!" we heard behind us after walking for three minutes. "Aunt Julie!"

A boy, of about ten or twelve years, ran toward us. "All my stuff got stolen!" he shouted.

"What? What happened?" Julie asked, alarmed.

"I was on the beach and I put my money and my cell phone in my shoes. We went in the water, then when we got out, my stuff wasn't there anymore."

"Wow…" I responded sarcastically. "Brilliant plan. Nobody has ever thought of that before. Hiding your money in your shoe? Amazing… How ever could the lowly uneducated crooks have cracked that safe?"

The boy and Julie gave me the same sour look as the rest of the Douglas family had been giving me for years.

"Come along with us, dear," Julie said, putting her free hand on his back.

"No brain in this one's head," I muttered to myself as we continued on.

"I can't hold you anymore, Dorothy," Julie said as she put her down. "You're getting so big! Here, let's all hold hands."

Julie held the boy's right hand in her left and Dorothy's left hand in her right. Then somehow Dorothy's right hand found my left. We walked down the path at a painfully slow pace to allow for Dorothy's tiny legs to keep up. Soon enough, on Dorothy's little suggestion, we were skipping along in a somewhat broken, somewhat syncopated stride on the golden cobblestone path under the twisted trees above our heads.

I expected a frantic search party when we returned to the main house, but nothing had changed since we left. Dozens of people still moved around, mingling, laughing, smiling.

The boy ran off to find his parents. For a quick moment, I hoped they would be lenient with him. He seemed nice enough, just unlearned about the perspective of others. His parents' fault, I was sure. They would probably replace whatever had been stolen with newer and better items anyway; no lesson to be gleaned from the experience from their point of view.

Maybe he should be banished to the dunce stool before receiving his new and improved items, I thought. Some attempt, any attempt at parenting would have sufficed, but I was sure that would not occur.

I followed Julie as she walked around casually until she found Dorothy's parents.

"Oh, there you are, dear," Dorothy's mother rang out, blond and sharing Julie's striking features, a cousin with whom I was somehow unacquainted. "I hope she wasn't too much trouble. She tends to go on these journeys then finds people to entertain her until they bring her back home."

"Oh, no. She was an absolute delight," Julie responded. "No trouble at all."

"That doesn't seem very safe," I said quietly to myself.

They spoke together as I stood there awkwardly waiting to be introduced, but introductions never came. Julie did not acknowledge me and Dorothy's mother never looked at me to initiate anything. I merely stood there, waiting to be dismissed as if I was the help which was likely what Julie's cousin presumed.

There I stood, looking up and away, down and away. My mind went toward the failed journey we had just taken. Only Dorothy got out of it what she desired; to make it back home. I still had no heart; Julie found no courage; and the dim-witted boy was no brighter.

"Why didn't you introduce me?" I asked Julie after the conversation ended and her cousin had gone.

Julie merely responded with "sorry" and nothing more.

She walked away and I followed, assuming she still wanted me around, but she soon found another group with which to stand and talk, smile and laugh. I, left behind to watch and wish, decided my bench needed me, or rather, I needed my bench.

———

The Ducks

After risking the dangers of the women's large hats and the head-height-held trays, I finally reached my bench of solitude, but sadly it had been discovered. Abigail sat with a still wobbly Kathy. I glared at them for several minutes, but they did not notice or they chose not to acknowledge me.

Julie interrupted my unrequited staring contest. "Where did you go?" she asked.

I looked down at her with a slanted eye. "Nowhere."

She took a step back, seeing that I was angry, and said, "I turned around and you were gone. I thought maybe we could talk?"

She was finally confident enough to talk to me, tell me what she wanted to say. I suspected it was to ask to stay an extra day or week, but I had no desire to spend any more time than previously promised. I felt that, if I could push off the conversation until that night or Sunday, I could argue that it was too late to change my plans.

"Let's go in the pool," I said after running through numerous scenarios of distraction in my mind before settling on that one.

"The pool?" she asked, perplexed.

"Yes; in which to swim? You know… the pool. I thought we could take a swim."

"Do you have something to swim in?" she asked, still trying to decipher my suggestion.

I put my index finger up to her, physically requesting a moment, then jogged around to the front of the house, down the driveway to the car, opened the car, grabbed my duffel bag, closed the car, jogged back up the driveway, around the house, and to the starting point where Julie was no longer standing. I looked around to find her occupying my bench with Abigail and Kathy; Kathy looking terribly disheveled, red hair in an uncontrollable poof and dress askew.

"Yes, I do!" I said to her, holding up my duffel bag.

"Yes, you do what?" Julie asked. "Where did you go?"

"I do have something to swim in!" My tone of excitement in addition to my out of breath panting was likely quite off-putting.

"Knock yourself out then," Abigail contributed. "This one is staying with us." She placed her right arm around Julie's shoulder as she spoke, holding her captive.

"Change in the pool house." Kathy shouted, then hiccupped. "And then drown in the pool."

Julie smiled and looked at me with a "what can I do?" look.

The pool house was a small white bungalow. Inside were a handful of children; cousins and nieces and nephews and strangers alike. They played Ping-Pong and billiards and watched TV from the soft looking white couches with black and white striped pillows. I found the bathroom behind a door made of small white angled pieces of wood and changed into a gray T-shirt, my swimming shorts, and a pair of sandals.

The occupants of the pool house looked at me oddly as I passed through on my way out, dressed to swim.

The pool was empty. Previously, it had been filled with children, likely the same children in the pool house, but it was empty when I approached. There was only one three- or four-year-old boy wearing blue arm floats and long red shorts walking around the light tan colored pool patio, surprisingly not baking hot from the sun.

Several adults were near the pool, some sitting under umbrellas lounging, some standing and talking, but none were paying any particular attention to the safety hazard that was this young boy, so I made a mental note to keep an eye on the little one as I dropped my shirt to the ground then jumped into the pool, knees tucked to my chin and arms pulled in: cannon ball.

Water splashed about and out of the pool and the young boy wearing the arm floats laughed and clapped. As I settled to a leisurely buoyant float on my back, I turned my head to check on him, only to see his red shorts around his ankles, his bottom half exposed. He then commenced urinating from the edge of the pool patio into the water.

I was far enough away that only the fact that his behavior was embarrassingly low-class should have bothered me, but, regardless of the impossibility of contamination, I was instantly ready to end my brief swim.

"He's going to the bathroom in the pool!" a woman shouted.

Everyone in earshot turned to look at me. I pointed to the urinating little boy at the other side of the pool and said, "I'm quite sure there is no *bathroom* involved in what he's doing, Ma'am."

It was then, as I stroked my way to the ladder, that I was mercilessly attacked. What felt like a flock of ducks swooped down and began jabbing at me with their beaks and the sharp nails at the tips of their webbed feet.

I started shouting to scare them away, but was silenced when they forced me under. After frantically swallowing countless mouthfuls of water, I came back to the surface, coughing. Still they continued. Between blows, I counted three, but there may have been many more.

I tried to scare them off, waving my right arm around, but still they continued to attack, so I dove down, this time by choice, as deep as I could to try to elude them.

They'll go away; think I'm not here anymore, I thought. But, as I sat there at the bottom of the pool looking up, I could see them diving in after me, only breaking the surface by about a foot before their buoyancy brought them back to the surface.

Without proper preparation, I was only capable of about thirty to forty seconds of submersion. When I surfaced, there they were, swooping down, pecking, biting, scratching.

In an attempt to save myself, I began flailing my arms wildly. Scaring them away did not work so maybe fighting them off would. My right fist came into contact with one, knocking it across the pool, but the other two kept coming as I continued to flail. Again I dove down, but out of breath, I had to surface quickly. A miscalculation landed my rapidly ascending head on the bottom of the metal ladder attached to the pool's side.

The resulting drifting away, out of consciousness, then jolting back, fuzzy but conscious, was painful and confusing. The watery blurry scenery faded to black then suddenly burst into reality then the process was repeated.

On the final fade-out, I saw Troy, the waiter, tearing through the water toward me. When I jolted back in, he was pulling me, carrying me, to the shallow end of the pool. I faded out again only to be jolted back in as Troy performed CPR on me, repeatedly pushing on my chest.

I leaned up and to the side, regurgitating pool water and more cake than I recalled consuming. The second round was more cake and less pool water. I collapsed onto my back when it was over, then leaned over to Troy, grasped the back of his neck, pulled him down, and whispered, "Avenge me..."

He laughed and said loudly, "He's okay!"

I turned my head to smile and maybe wave at the anxious well-wishers and nervous onlookers, but there were none to be seen. I expected mass hysteria, but I found nothing more than the scene that I experienced directly before I was attacked and nearly drowned by a flock of rogue ducks.

Feeling myself get furious from the casual atmosphere, I considered how lucky I was. Most of the individuals who have a near death experience are incapable of appreciating it because it is, for most people, shortly followed by their death.

"You alright, man?" Troy asked. "You got it all out of your system?"

The little boy wearing arm floats and red shorts thankfully around his waist again walked up to us, clapping and laughing.

"Hey, little guy!" Troy said to him. "You liked that? That was funny wasn't it?"

I reached to shoo the little clapping annoyance away before he urinated on my head, but I had not the strength. I could not even scold Troy for encouraging him. I could not even thank him for saving my life. All I could do was watch the puddle of vomit to my right; its size was about the same as my laid out body.

Slowly I regained the ability to move. I sat up carefully, gently, with Troy there to steady my progress. My head weighed more than my body and its pain was far more intense. My neck strained to keep it up, clicking as I rotated it side to side to see the unfazed beautiful faces around.

I was still rather hazy, but it appeared that none were at all interested in the drowning that had just taken place. Snickering and smiling, some even laughing aloud, laughing at a man who almost lost his life in a pool right in front of them.

As my eyes became more focused and my head became less heavy, I heard screaming muffled by a squishy splashing sound, one that was not wholly unfamiliar. Abigail had begun to throw up her lunch, but her vomiting was accompanied by her own screams.

Suddenly her problem struck me. *Abigail has a phobia of throwing up,* I thought.

She controlled her eating; everything from where, to what, to when, to with whom. She ate only what she prepared and at specific times of day, never eating what others prepared, so that she could ensure her food followed the correct path through her body. This was why she did not eat at dinner. This is why Julie and I found her eating alone away from the party. And this was why she was screaming wildly as she regurgitated her perfectly prepared and meticulously executed meal.

I put my head in my hands to hold up its again increasing weight due to my theorizing. It throbbed heavier and heavier.

"Oh, merciful Poseidon," I murmured.

I looked up to see Julie helping Abigail away from the pool patio, likely into the house. She handed Abigail off to two waiters then walked gingerly toward me.

"What did you do to Abigail? She is terrified," Julie said to me without concern for my well-being.

I turned my head toward her angrily, wanting nothing more than to shout her wrongfully accusatory theories out of her head, but my unnecessarily dramatic motion only increased the throbbing. All I could muster was a whispered "shut up."

Feeling as if everyone was suddenly judging me, I fought gravity far sooner than was intelligent and, almost falling back down to the pool patio twice, wobbled myself to a standing position, an effort resembling Kathy's previous attempts. Troy offered his help which I waved off, while Julie merely watched my struggles.

"Safety is no accident, Nicholas," I heard behind me, Mr. Douglas's words bouncing around in my head.

I turned slowly toward him. "It was *you*! It was you, wasn't it, old man? You know a bird trainer or something. You trained those ducks to attack me. Ducks don't just attack people like that!"

"Nicholas!" Julie exclaimed out of confusion and horror that I had just accused her father of training a set of ducks to attack me.

"Stay out of this," I told her. Then I turned back to Mr. Douglas with another theory. "Or, no… no! You put the dog shampoo in the shower this morning. The birds were attracted to the smell! You knew this would happen. You planned everything!"

"Nicholas!" Julie shouted again.

"I told you to stay out of this, Julie!" I shouted back. Then, I turned back to Mr. Douglas again. "What say you?"

"I'm sure I have no idea about what you are talking, young man," he said with the same sly smile as before.

"Ah! Ah! I knew it. You've been planning all of this to make me look crazy! You did it so everyone would hate me, but you come out smelling like roses." I then turned to the crowd that had gathered to watch. "I am *not* crazy!" I shouted to the audience. "This man is gas-lighting me." I pointed to Mr. Douglas. "He's been planning this whole thing, everything, all of it!"

Having gained more strength than composure, I stumbled away into the pool house. A woman picked up the little boy with the red shorts and blue arm floats as I passed him. I heard an onlooker say, "Julie should drop him like a hot potato." Another added, "Now this is some kind of sticky wicket, wouldn't you say?" speaking to his female companion, wife or girlfriend, sister or cousin or whatever.

Children were carrying on playing their billiards and Ping-Pong games, sitting and enjoying their leisure lifestyle in the pool house. I bounced off the wall and into the bathroom then ungracefully slipped my white collared shirt over my wet body and pulled on my shoes. I stormed back out to find the same group waiting for act two.

"This man," I shouted in an oddly dramatic stage-voice while pointing at Mr. Douglas, "is the devil!"

An audible shudder echoed across the crowd.

"Now I think you are taking this a bit far, Nicholas," Mr. Douglas whispered to me, after grasping my arm and turning away from the crowd.

"Keep your hands off me," I said pulling back, almost knocking myself over. "You people, everyone here, you're all fools to listen to this man, to follow him blindly. You're all part of a multi-headed gullible jackass that's the result of idiocy eating too much stupidity then throwing up all over ignorance."

Faces fell toward perplexed, including my own. The contusion was having a serious effect on my mental and verbal abilities. I realized that I was no longer in control of what I was saying; my mind seemed to be pulling ideas from old cartoons and comic strips.

"Julie!" I shouted, turning around wildly, unable to locate her. "Julie, we're leaving right now! Julie, where are you?"

I started to stomp toward the pathway leading to the front of the house. "Julie, get your things and meet me in front of the house! We're leaving right now!" Still I was unable to locate my wife, but I knew my loudly shouted words would find their intended target if only I persisted.

When I reached the front of the house, I swung around in circles several times impatiently as I waited. "Julie!" I shouted more than once.

"Nick, what's going on with you?" I heard before turning to see her walking up to me quickly, holding nothing.

"Where're your things? Where are they? I told you to get them!"

"What things? We're not leaving," she insisted.

"Yes, we are! Yes, we are!"

"Nicholas, calm down. We're not leaving yet. Don't do this."

"Don't you do that! Don't you do that!" I shouted, pointing at the words spelled out in white bubble letters that had just left her mouth. "Nothing is changing my mind. Not pleading or crying.

Nothing! Like rearranging chairs on the *Titanic*... that ship is going down!"

"What are you talking about? You're delirious." There was a detectable amount fear in her voice as she backed away from my frantically flailing arms and body.

"I'm not dealing with your family any longer! They're against me. They're all against me."

Kathy then stumbled over to the two of us, red hair still a mess. "How was your swim?" she asked. Her tone was hard to read, but I took it as an insult.

"If you were a man, I would beat the snot out of you," I snapped back.

"If you were a man, I might actually be worried," she responded before stumbling away.

My frantically shifting eyes then found Mrs. and Mr. Douglas who stood far behind, both watching their infuriated, frantic son-in-law verbally abuse anyone within earshot.

"Get your things!" I shouted again to Julie. "Get them now!"

"No!" Julie shouted. "I can't do this anymore!" She was looking toward the ground and clenching her fists into tight balls, visibly holding her powerful emotions back before exploding, but her explosion was weak and unimpressive when it came. "I can't do this anymore," she said, slowly looking up at me.

"You can't do what?" I asked, still frantic.

She spoke quietly and calmly. "Nick, you're the same immature boy I met all those years ago. Back then, it was attractive. We were different then. I was different then. But I grew up, I changed. And you haven't changed at all. You're the same immature boy."

"I have integrity!" I argued, but secretly agreeing with her. "That's more than I can say for you."

"No, you don't!" she said in a louder, angrier voice than before.

"Look up the word, you fool. I am consistent with my morals. I haven't changed. You said it yourself; I'm the same as when you met me. Yes, you've changed, but for the worse. You used to love me for who I was. Now you despise me for being that same person? For not changing behind your back like you've changed behind mine? For not becoming a different person? I have no desire to change!"

"That's the problem!" she shouted, louder still. "You needed to change. How can you not change? How can someone not change? What's wrong with you?"

Mr. Douglas interrupted. "Just come with us, dear," he said, pointing toward the house. "Don't let him come between us again. We must all hang together, or assuredly we shall all hang separately."

I then shouted back, "Don't listen to King Solomon over there. He'd have us cut something important in half or something of the sort…" I trailed off, hearing myself speak foolishness.

"Actually, that was a Benjamin Franklin quote," Mr. Douglas preached.

I squinted at him in anger. "Yes, I know that." Then I turned to Julie and said, "You're suffering from hysteria if you make the wrong decision here. And I do not mean the modern diagnosis."

And then Julie did something that no one could have expected of her; she stood up for herself forcefully, angrily, and with a confident strength that I had never before seen in her.

"Nick, I *can't* take this anymore! I *won't* take this anymore! You do this kind of thing all the time. You treat me like a patient, deconstructing me to the level of a child in a distant, removed kind of way as though I'm a case study with single letter abbreviations for my first and last name. Then you diagnose me in a condescending tone, or silently to yourself as you nod and smile, showing your enormous arrogance.

"And it forces me to regress, to become the infantile child you manipulate me into. And with this forced perspective, do you think I look up to you, revere you? You're the adult, the authority figure, and I'm the underling, the subordinate in need of your supervision, your direction, guidance, oversight. Well you're wrong! All you've accomplished is alienating me; you've pushed me away and I hate you for it!

"It's over..." she shouted.

"Fine!" I shouted back, calling her bluff by turning to walk away alone toward my car. "None of you matter anyway. You're all nothing. You're less than nothing. You're the supporting cast in this absurd theater of hell."

Mr. Douglas, instead of allowing me to walk away with the last word, added, "You know, Nicholas, you were one of my biggest disappointments."

"What are you talking about, old man?" I shouted back quickly, turning around and walking angrily toward him. "You never had any faith in me. How could I possibly disappoint when expectations couldn't have been lower? Wish you made me in your own image, eh? Sorry I don't measure up."

"I never loved you," Julie confessed unnecessarily.

"Come on... did you need to say that?" I questioned, fully insulted at that point. "What's happening here? Everything is happening so fast. One moment we're fine and the next you're telling me you never loved me? Don't you see what's happening? They brainwashed you. Your family turned you against me."

"No, Nick. *You* turned me against you," Julie responded, seemingly as though she was at the end of some terrible movie.

"Are you joking? You must be joking. That's what you choose to say. Could you have come up with a more childish clichéd response?" My tone was angry and condescending.

Julie threw up her arms and twisted around in disgust. "That's it. I can't do this anymore. We're done."

Instead of sorrow or sadness, anger filled me, quickly mending my wounds. I stomped angrily toward her and grabbed her right arm with my left hand powerfully. "Just get in the car," I said quietly, angrily, then raised my voice to a yell. "We're leaving right now!"

I did not see him before and I did not see him for some time afterward, but I saw him during. My focus started at Richard's face, then followed his right fist, the knuckles specifically, hurtling toward my face, toward my right temple, over and over, in perfect focus all through the journey. Apparently he only hit me once, but I experienced it multiple times.

It was during these few seconds that my mind drifted toward a neuroscience class I had taken in graduate school. When the mind and body are heightened, when in panic mode, our eyes see in many more frames per second than we normally do. We take in far more visual information than normal. This leads to an overload in the processing in our visual cortex and is the reason that, during these times of panic, we experience time as being stretched out or in slow motion.

The ground attacked me, blacking out my memory for an undeterminable duration of reality. I lay there on the driveway before slowly sitting up and tending to my sour parts with attention, only making them worse. I looked around to see Richard holding a crying Julie, Mr. and Mrs. Douglas standing close by. Two servers had joined, Troy and another, and the crowd of guests hovered behind, shaking their heads.

"What's going on with Benjamin?" I heard Kipp ask another party guest.

"Sorry, old chap. A man shouldn't hold a lady like that," Richard felt it necessary to say. It infuriated me that, even in this time of chaos, he was still polite and rather admirable.

"I suppose you don't just go to the gym to watch elderly men shower…" I remarked.

He laughed as he transferred Julie to her father then reached his left hand out to help me up. I thought about taking the hand for a fleeting moment, then slapped it away.

"You can't just sucker punch somebody then try to help them up and be all cordial about it!" I informed him as I pulled myself up by my own power. Then I looked him up and down and continued. "You're not so great. Everyone probably tells you all the time that you are, but you're not! I am the great one!"

His reply only cemented his greatness in the moment. "You know the nineteenth-century humanist writer William Hazlitt once said, 'No really great man ever thought himself so.' "

I squinted angrily at him as I wobbled a bit standing on the ground, steadying myself with my arms raised slightly below shoulder level, hands far from my sides.

Then Richard added, "And integrity is not consistency of morals over time. Time is not a factor with integrity. Your definition and thus your argument is flawed. Sorry again, old chap."

I squinted, then took a real look at Richard, then Julie and her parents, then the servers, and then the audience of guests, family, and drivers. All were against me, all.

"You should all be euthanized!" I shouted before grabbing my duffel bag from the ground and walking away backward. "And I do not mean 'to be made younger...' Do not be confused."

I then swung around and slammed my left knee into the granite fountain, shouting in agony, but thankfully not falling in. That level of slapstick was luckily not present in the real world. I sat for a moment holding my knee which, surprisingly, made it feel slightly better.

"I'm taking some leash so don't choke me," I shouted to Julie as I slowly recovered.

The Douglas family and the servers watched me, bruised and battered, sitting on the fountain, muttering to myself. Julie approached so I shouted, "Don't cry because it's over. Smile because it's happened."

"What?" she questioned. "I'm not crying. I just wanted to ask you—"

I interrupted and proclaimed, "I made you. You're nothing without me."

"You made me?" she said, suddenly swirling with anger, fire in her eyes. "Then make another one." With that, she walked back toward her family.

"Good riddance to bad rubbish," I heard Mr. Douglas say as Julie joined them in their united front against me.

Infuriated, I stumbled the long trip to my car and fell into it, bringing the door down with a thud. The engine revved, exhaust roared, and tires squealed. The rear quarter of the car squatted down, compressing the rear shocks almost enough for the rear bumper to touch the ground as the car appeared to make a legitimate attempt at taking flight, but failed due to the aggressive down force.

I stopped short in front of the house, rolled down the passenger window, and shouted to Julie, "Oh, and thank your parents for a *lovely* weekend."

My dramatic exit was intended to last for a dozen seconds as I left two long patches of rubber behind on their magnificent cobblestone driveway, but the disorientation caused by the many blows to my head in surprisingly high frequency led to a loud thud accompanied by an echoing crash and crunch of broken glass, twisted metal, cracked fiberglass, and bruised ego.

A minute later, Mr. Douglas knocked on the driver's side window, the only one not shattered, as he searched the car for survivors.

"Yes… that was a perfectly reasonable thing to do," he said loudly, over the high hiss of the destroyed front end.

En Route to Manhattan

I found myself comfortably surprised at the deceptively spacious interior of the tiny golf-cart-sized blue estate car; riding in it alone on my way back to the city as a result of Mr. Douglas's extreme generosity in even the most awkward of times. Built not for speed, but for efficiency, the trip back was agonizingly slow in comparison to what I had envisioned before my car became mangled and destroyed. Traffic was, however, not an issue because the minimal width of the estate car allowed for driving between other vehicles when traffic around me slowed to a crawl.

As I began to feel comfortable and almost content in the tiny golf-cart-sized vehicle, I started to consider what I had left behind. My atrociously expensive insurance policy would never cover the accident; totaled by stupidity and bravado, I did not think they allowed claims under that description. And the policy was not big enough anyway, not that I was able to afford the outlandish deductible.

I sat high, but humiliated, eyes fixated on the uncertain road ahead. I glanced aside at street signs as I passed. "DEAD END." "NO OUTLET."

"You've got to be kidding me," I said to no one.

Fellow motorists waved at me as they or I passed. I waved back. I saw several thumbs up; a welcome sight as I had grown so accustomed to a different protrusion from the hands waved at my car. I found it difficult not to crack a smile, but it quickly faded when

I recalled the shambles my own car was in; the shambles my own life was in.

At some point during the embarrassing, humiliating carnage of my exit, I heard discussion of bringing me up on assault charges, even conspiracy to commit murder was passed around. I knew not what to make of it, so I pushed it from my consciousness, tried to forget, but it came back, permeating the tiny blue mode of transport. Again, I pushed it away. I had only hurt myself, had I not?

I felt the dry sarcastic indifference that is the attitude of New York City overtaking me, tensing me up as I crossed the bridge into Manhattan.

The parking attendant in the garage stopped me, assuming I was just another customer.

"What happened to the car?" he asked when he saw that it was me.

"She's dead," I informed him curtly and drove down to our spaces, both of which, to my shock, were empty. I pulled in, taking up about a third of the physical space my car normally did, grabbed my duffel bag, which still had shards of broken windshield on it, then on my way out asked the parking attendant where Julie's car had gone.

"Tow truck came and took it away about an hour ago. The transporter you ordered. He showed us papers." He spoke defensively, as if I was accusing him of something, but he always spoke defensively, *they* always spoke defensively; a result of constantly being accused when someone in my position addressed him in any and every situation.

"Thank you…" I said without emotion.

Exhausted from the day, the nights of very few or no hours of sleep, and from life, I entered the Brownstone defeated and deflated. The steps felt like they had multiplied in my absence. The lock on the apartment door seemed like it had become more complicated in my absence.

As I fiddled slowly with keys in keyholes, I heard an upbeat voice behind me. Alicia, having snuck up on me, spoke softly into the back of my neck.

"The sunset was beautiful."

I jumped, startled at the presence of anyone other than me and then calmed when I realized it was just her.

She then told me, "I was outside watching it earlier in the park. Did you do that all for me?"

"Uh, actually the sun goes down almost every day," I informed her.

Finally the door opened and I slid inside.

"Have a good night then," she said as I closed the door. The last thing I saw of Alicia was her blond hair which always appeared to be blowing in the breeze.

My backside hit the hard wooden chair at the small wooden table before I removed my shoes. The laces had gone untied due to the haste with which the shoes had been placed upon my feet so I was able to ignore the intricacies of untying in a proper manner and just pulled them off, left before right. For some reason, not paying much attention to my actions, I then tied my empty shoes.

Picking myself up from the kitchen table chair, I stumbled around before throwing myself onto the couch. The trip down felt like an eternity; the same eternity I imagined every time I stood close to the window in my office and looked down.

"Guess I shouldn't have agreed to go on vacation this weekend," I said aloud.

I pulled my phone out of my pants pocket then, holding it in front of my face, scrolled to my e-mails and noted the time, much later than I expected. 10:19 p.m. I looked out the window to see that the sky was dark.

"How long was I on the road?" I asked aloud.

Then I spied an e-mail from Julie.

The smile on my face was the result of my assumption that she had come to her senses and was sending me an apology message to inform of her return travel plans. The message opened and I scrolled down to read.

—

Nicholas,

Since I met you, you were always the lens through which I saw my life differently from the path which I feared going down, the one that was set out for me. Through you I saw my future, my family, my life, my world differently. And "different" was what I wanted. Different from what I feared would be a terrible life.

After all these years, I have finally cleaned the distorted lens you created. The focus is sharp and clear now. I see you for what you are and I see our future for what it would become. The bleak outlook is disheartening and I will not be a part of it. I cannot be a part of it. I need to get out. I have to get out. Nicholas, it is over.

-Julie

—

Without thinking, without planning, without filter, I wrote a response.

—

Julie,

Listen, you said what you needed to say. So you'll get what you wish for if that is indeed what you wish for. It's the icing on the cake really. You're empowered. You've changed. And now you're liberated; you're free! Free from what's been hurting you and holding you down. Your life will be a lot better from here on out. I'm sorry so much pain was endured, but you came out the other end a better person, a stronger person, a smarter person, a tougher person.

I don't know what else to say... you're welcome?

-Nick

—

I sent the message without thought, putting it out of my mind. It was immediately part of my past and there was no sense in looking back.

I reached over and dropped the phone on the coffee table. I thought about how I had helped Julie, how I made her life a better one.

"I am a good person," I said to myself.

Had it not been for me, she would still be the same weak, fragile, immature pushover she once was, easily manipulated and easily taken advantage of. I changed her life and she was a better person for it.

"I am a good person," I repeated with my eyes closed. "I am a good person..."

Sunday Morning

Sleep was hardly that at all, not restful in any sense of the word. Throughout the night, my body was in an unconscious state of wakefulness. There was very little room to reflexively toss and turn on the couch which resulted in a feeling of confinement, physical and mental alike.

It was the sun that kissed me awake, made me aware. My hands pushed it away as it flickered through my fingertips, but to no avail. I pulled my eyelids tighter, hoping it would somehow help, but I gave up and slowly squinted them open. The birds were again singing, chirping, bombarding me with their birdsong. The sound made my hair stand on end, sent a tingle down my spine. I heard a phantom quack mixed in, but it was more likely to be part of a scattered nightmare than to have been based in the present reality.

"They're following me," I whispered to myself in a raspy voice.

I lay there for another hour soaking up the rays, trying to relax, but, not to my surprise, the realm of relaxation was difficult to enter.

I thought about what my powerfully emotional patient Kristin once told me when she surprised me at the office one afternoon, trying to convince me to accompany her on a walk through the park. "Sunlight is the best disinfectant." It was a quote from Justice Louis D. Brandeis. Not until then did I have reasonable doubt about the validity of anything she said; I still felt as dirty, as tainted, as saturated with scum as the day before, maybe more so.

My mind went from sun as disinfectant to the words I often reflected upon on Sundays. "God, having completed the heavens and the earth, rests from His work, and blesses and sanctifies the seventh day." This was always my justification for sleeping in on Sundays. It just felt right, but I was only able to lie still for another hour on my back, drifting in and out of consciousness.

Not until that moment, the moment at which I began to move, did I realize that I had been numb. The excruciating pain that my body was in made me crave to re-experience my previously unconscious state of paralysis. As I shifted, my left knee and head began to throb, both expanding in and out with pain; a pain just slightly more intense than that of the rest of my body.

No longer able to remain still because the numb had been all but lost, had tingled away leaving agony in its wake, I dropped my legs off the couch and lifted my torso up against the vertical couch cushion. I reached for my phone, turning it over on the coffee table before shouting out in excruciating pain. 8:13 a.m.

Looking at the phone, I considered spending the day's entirety on that couch, but I felt it would only further depress. I arose and hobbled into the bathroom. A shower, no matter how warm or how long, would not clean off the hate and hurt all over my being, so I decided to try to soothe my body and soul with a bath.

My hand, riddled with wrinkles from being mashed into the couch all night, barely felt the water that fell upon it after adjusting the shower faucet to pour water into the tub. A handful of seconds passed before the temperature was determined to be adequate for the task at hand.

Leaving the tub to fill, I found my way to the bedroom through the hallway where my eyes focused on the frame of the bed. We were told that it had been carved from one enormous trunk of a

Redwood. I had no reason to question the claim then, but, looking back, how could it have been true?

I used to marvel at the detail of the carved-in floral arrangements bunched at every corner, stretched across every beam. We had purchased it shortly after we eloped; a symbol of our unity, our cohesiveness as a married couple; one single piece. But, despite our best efforts, we had been unable to get it into our tiny apartment.

Our only option was to cut the frame in two then reassemble the pieces in the bedroom. I ignored the symbolism at the time; just an unspoken irony. Standing in front of it alone as the bathtub filled, it was hard to ignore the eerie foreshadowing of the bed upon which we had slept for the entirety of our union.

"It was probably never only one piece anyway," I said quietly. "Always a lie."

After a minute of blank thoughts, I noticed that the bedroom was rather empty, then completely empty. Nothing but the bed and nightstands in sight. Not a stray article of clothing or a belt or purse anywhere. I felt motivated to open the closet and there I found only my own clothes.

I opened Julie's nightstand. Empty. I limped over to the bathroom and found it too to be devoid of her belongings. I rushed into the living room to find nothing belonging to her but one dark blue high-heeled shoe with straps. It was the left one, alone, sitting on its side under the coffee table, its identical but inverse twin nowhere to be found.

Aimless at this point, wandering around the apartment, I stepped on some broken glass by the television, glass that should have been cleaned up days before. It was difficult to determine if it hurt me or not; pain was so consistent and persistent at that time that a potential increase was completely undetectable.

I reentered the bedroom to continue the search; the lone shoe's presence was dangerously unnerving. The short but extensive search that followed turned up no match, but unearthed another lone shoe, also the left; black, reflective, high-heeled, and without straps.

A disheartening thought then ran through my mind and led me to leave the door ajar as I followed it down the steps into the basement, musky, dusty, and damp. Quickly, I located our storage area; empty of all boxes; all boxes but one labeled "Nick." I opened it to find my college yearbook and some useless worthless textbooks I was never able to sell after my final academic term.

I closed the box slowly then sat on top of it, head in hands.

"This is chess, not checkers," I said to myself.

Just as she had hastily sent for her car to be picked up from the garage after I left her parents' estate, she must have sent for movers to pick up everything except my belongings from the apartment and the storage area in the basement.

"At least I have those two left high-heeled shoes," I joked to myself, knowing in my own mind that Julie was merely throwing a tantrum. "She'll be back," I said.

Despite the knowledge that I would eventually be the victor, the emotion of feeling outfoxed still lingered for a while until I remembered the running bath several floors above my head. I painfully ran up the steps and then through the open door into the apartment to find the bath only beginning to overflow with a deep dark red liquid.

I determined that Julie had mistakenly left a bottle of shampoo or some kind of body wash in the tub. I emptied it and found the bottle. It read "AUBURN WITH A TINGE OF CHESTNUT. FOR BRUNETTES WITH FLARE!"

The exclamation point bothered me. And why all CAPS? And did they mean to use "flare" rather than "flair"? The bottle found its way to the garbage before I washed the red from my hands and down the drain.

"Out damn spot," I said aloud.

Under the sink, I located and then poured bleach into the tub before filling it with water, watching it this time. I mixed around the bleached water before stopping the flow and adding more bleach.

As I stirred after again adding more bleach to the mix, a strong firm knocking resonated from the door through the apartment. I took my time toweling off my right arm and hands as the knocking continued with a dozen seconds of pause in between bursts. I opened the door without inquiring about the identity of the knocker, visually or verbally.

A man, larger than I, wearing jeans and a black T-shirt stood before me.

"Can I help you?" I asked, feeling rather uncomfortable, threatened.

The man reached into his back pocket while asking, "Nicholas Thesiger?"

"Yes," I responded warily.

His left hand extended to me several papers stapled together, folded, and with a rubber band around them. I took the bundle and looked at it briefly before he said, "You've been served."

By the time I had comprehended his words, he was already halfway down the winding staircase.

"Thanks for that, jackass!" I shouted before slamming the door.

After pulling off the rubber band and tossing it onto the counter, I identified the papers as divorce filings. They had been filled out and signed by Julie weeks before according to the dates.

"Chess, not checkers," I repeated quietly.

My mind moved directly to the postnuptial agreement her father had conned me into signing after we had eloped.

The conversation echoed in my head.

—

"I don't want this family's wealth lost in some silly courtroom to the likes of you," he told me harshly.

"With all due respect, Sir," I said, addressing him respectfully because back then I did respect him. "I have no intention of divorcing your daughter and no intention of taking anything from you."

"Why not make that promise on paper then? You just made it verbally. It is exactly the same thing…"

"Seems like reasonable logic," I said before signing, ignoring the bed's clear warning.

—

"That bastard is probably patting himself on the back right now," I muttered, shaking my head.

As I read through the papers, again there was a knock at the door.

"Who's there?" I demanded, this time not willing to be served without proper notice.

224

"Hello, Nicholas. It's Alicia." She paused for the door to be opened, but was met with only the unmoving stationary separator.

"What can I do for you?" I asked through the door.

Hesitant she responded, "Uh, I just wanted to let you know that the boys' frogs got loose and we can't find them. We're leaving our door open in case they come hopping back. Just wondering if you could keep an eye out."

"Fine, yes, okay," I shouted.

"Great. Thanks. How are you doing? Is Julie in?"

"No!" I shouted back angrily.

"Well, let me know if you need company," she responded.

I looked at my side of the door and shook my head. "Have a good day, Alicia."

Mind on the divorce papers still in my hands, I looked at them in somewhat of a stupor of disbelief. Evidenced by the dates on the papers, she had decided weeks before to leave me, but she must have, shortly thereafter, decided to give me one last chance, give us one last try. It was a last chance I threw away without even the knowledge that the chance had been given.

"Chess, not checkers," I said again.

At that moment, I realized that the movers would have needed our key to get in and, for Julie's car, the transporter would likely need the key as well. Plans were in place, waiting to be executed. She had made certain that all the pieces had been strategically set so, at a moment's notice, she could move that last one into position to advance her victory without me even knowing I was her opponent in the game.

"Checkmate," I said to myself.

Maybe our anniversary was the last straw or maybe it was one of the arguments or maybe all of them. All that was clear at that point was that she had completely given up and it was over. I wished she had told me things between us were so bad. I wished she allowed the courtesy of informing me that I had been given a stay of execution. I would have, could have tried harder. Or maybe I would not have. Maybe she did tell me, but I just was not listening.

I left the papers on the counter next to the rubber band which previously held them together. I decided they were more than capable of waiting until later for my eyes. My stomach growled for food just as my body yearned for pain medication, but I was too disrupted to cook for myself. I sat down on the wooden chair, untied the shoelaces on my footless shoes, slipped my feet in, tied the shoelaces on my foot-filled shoes, then I stood from the wooden chair.

After locking the door behind me, I turned to be confronted by four frogs sitting at various distances from my feet. One croaked at my presence. I guided them, scooting slowly with my shoes, toward Alicia's open door, then knocked on it powerfully.

As I walked toward the stairs, I could not help but smile at the prospect of the boys coming to the door and finding their frogs, assuming the frogs had knocked to alert the boys to their return.

The stairwell felt darker than it did on most Sunday mornings. I began to fall into an almost depressive state of discomfort from which I was startled out of by a voice bouncing down the stairwell.

"Oh, thank you!" Alicia shouted, running down after me to stop one step above the one upon which I halted my pace. "I was just bathing Malcolm. He has lice so he has to use a special shampoo."

Her hair was tied back into a ponytail and she wore latex gloves over her hands.

"Okay, good luck with that then," I said as I continued away.

"Thank you again!" she shouted after me.

Beneath the tree in front of the Brownstone was a small puddle left behind by a presumably light rain the night before. As I walked up the sidewalk, I turned back to notice nothing but my footsteps leading away from our home, evaporating from reality.

I passed by a pile of black garbage bags that smelled bitter with flies buzzing around, all of which appeared to enjoy the stench. Shadows of the morning light covered countless surfaces; trees, roads, cabs, cars, buildings, grass, sidewalk.

I walked a few blocks in a bit of a pain-induced daze and stumbled into a small quaint restaurant. They had only a handful of tables, sold no alcohol, and were open for only breakfast and dinner. They survived because of their outlandish prices and the inexplicable constant stream of people who patronized their establishment.

"New York," I said to myself.

They seated me immediately despite the dozen others who were waiting. A small table in the corner behind a structural beam was suited for a maximum of one chair and I was the sole lonely party of one.

"Lucky to have no one," I said to myself as I walked by the jealous faces.

The waitress attempted to hand me a menu, but I stopped her with my right hand on hers and said, "A glass of orange juice, scrambled eggs, and bacon."

"Sorry, Sir, we don't have any bacon today," she responded with a vaguely Southern accent.

"No bacon?" I questioned.

"Sorry, Sir."

"Why no bacon?" I asked, distraught that bacon would not be gracing my plate adjacent to my eggs.

"The chef didn't like the way it looked this morning. He claimed it was 'diseased,' " she whispered, left hand blocking anyone's view of her lips to maintain the secrecy of her words.

"Do you have ham?" I asked, hoping for a somewhat suitable substitute.

"Sure."

"I'll have that then."

"I'll bring your orange juice over in a second," she said with a smile before moving happily through a doorway into what I assumed to be the kitchen.

So there I sat alone and pondering her decision to tell me that their food was deemed diseased by their chef.

As I allowed my eyes and mind to wander around the room, they passed then returned to rest upon a man who sat at a nearby table with his back to me, his wide figure blocking my view of his company on the other side of his table. He wore shorts, exposing his legs from above his knees to his feet and behind his knees were small boils. I looked away rather disgusted when I noticed the pea sized bubbles.

"Put on some pants," I said quietly, knowing he would not hear, but hoping he would get the message subliminally.

My eyes moved to the table adjacent to his at which a family of six was seated, having their Sunday brunch after church, I presumed. All were dressed quite nicely, Sunday best.

An unintended consequence of our proximity and my inevitable boredom was my inability to ignore their conversation. They ordered a "carafe of freshly squeezed orange juice."

It sounded rather tasty when it came from the mother's mouth in her soft smooth voice, making me question if my orange juice would be freshly squeezed as well. The father at the table then added quickly, "And six glasses of ice."

"Apparently they like their orange juice very cold," I said to myself.

The waitress spun around toward the kitchen to fill six glasses with ice. I could see her through the doorway working with pride, being sure to pack each glass to the top with ice. On her return, holding up a tray with the glasses, she was startled by a loud frantic voice.

"Fire!"

She swiveled around losing her balance momentarily then managed to catch only herself but not the tray. The carnage was unavoidable. I watched it coming; the glasses, the ice flying from the glasses raining down, and the tray. Luckily, only the ice and I came into contact; glasses shattered on the floor while the tray ricocheted off the structural beam before landing on the floor.

A male waiter calmly instructed everyone to leave the restaurant; instructions that very few people would not follow after someone has shouted "fire" in a small enclosed area.

After five minutes of standing in front of the restaurant waiting for something to happen, some visible indication of the "fire" finally became apparent. Black smoke began to billow out below the front door.

Another minute of waiting brought the second bout of excitement. Two men, whose attire suggested their position to be cooks, pulled a man who I assumed to be the owner out by his arms, legs dragging behind. He was drenched with black soot, but appeared not to have any burns. He fought them the entire way.

"You're burning down my life!" he shouted over and over, shaking his fists at the sky. "You're burning down my life!"

The scene could only become more depressing from that point so I turned and walked away. I did not know where I was going. I did not care at that point. I saw a red balloon floating skyward above the park. I squinted and rapidly blinked away the sun's intensity, losing the balloon but finding a kite in its place. Maybe the balloon was never there, never ascending or descending.

"The kite flies highest against the wind," I said to myself, then shook my head before looking back to earth, back to reality.

After two or three blocks, I heard the sirens of a fire truck. They suggested the park to be the most appropriate of destinations so, not yet wanting to return to the apartment, I turned in that direction.

As my mind wandered around, so did I, losing track of the minutes passing before finding myself walking around and around one of the small elevation changes/hills in the park. I considered the possibility that the landscape was flat before I created the divot that formed the resulting hill on my continuous circular journey. It felt like a divot. I laughed at my cartoonish imagination.

"I'm hilarious," I informed myself, shaking my head.

A hotdog vender, pushing his squeaky-wheeled electronically driven cart, offered to give me a hotdog for free as long as I bought the bun. I must have looked lost because he clearly mistook me for a tourist.

"No, thanks," I said, waving him on his way.

As I paid less attention to my circumnavigation of the hill that I had created, I noticed a boy who sat on a bench with his father. They were peering into a brown box with ruffled edges. I found it difficult not to stray from my path and walk by to see what drew their attention. Further investigation revealed that the brown box held bugs, six or seven locusts. I was unimpressed and decided the park was no longer where I wanted my Sunday to be spent.

Walking out I saw a thin man wearing a shirt that read, "We may not have it all together, but together we have it all."

"Moron," I remarked when I was far enough out of audible range.

I walked back the way I had come to see how things stood at the restaurant, but the road was closed. As I stood there, questioning my next move, the father and son who had sat on the bench with the brown box of bugs crossed the road in front of me, diverted by the flashing lights of the police car and barricade.

"Why can't we go down that street, Father?" the boy asked, holding his arm up, right hand in his father's left.

"I think they're doing construction over there," he responded.

"When can we go that way? When will they be done, Father?"

"Son, I don't know if it will ever be complete. They're always doing construction in New York City..." he said, sounding defeated.

"I know, right?" I remarked, but to myself.

Their voices faded away to my right as I continued looking at nothing and contemplating everything.

When I found myself there, the steps in front of the Brownstone felt as they always did, bothersome. The winding ones inside felt dark, even darker than they had on the way down. When I reached my floor, I noticed that it too was dark. I remembered that the light above had gone out days before.

"Someone needs to fix that," I said aloud, making a mental note to e-mail the super.

The lock, however, worked better than it ever had. With shoes still on my feet because I lacked the mental fortitude to remove them, I stepped into the kitchen and noticed the divorce papers still on the counter. I shook my head and set about creating some sustenance for myself. When I attempted to start the fire on the stove, I was met with nothing but the wafting of natural gas. I checked the other burners, but none worked. I tried the light-switch. It too did nothing. The switch in the living room also did nothing. And the one in the bedroom, also nothing.

"Power must be out," I said, stating the obvious to no one.

In the third kitchen drawer I searched, I found matches from a hotel in London. I had never been to London. The burner exploded into flame after I had turned the gas on high and then went through two matches before finally achieving fire. I opened the refrigerator, light remaining off. Bacon in hand, I heard shouts, so the bacon found its way back into the refrigerator before I turned the burner off.

I looked through the peephole in the door and saw the distorted image of medical workers in blue pants and blue tucked-in short-sleeved shirts in front of the Alicia's apartment. I swung my door ajar.

"Can I help you?" I inquired, more interested in what was happening than how I could assist.

Before they could response, a crying Alicia leapt out at them, flowing blond hair following her. The blue clothed medical workers followed her inside.

"What's the problem?" I shouted after them, following.

Alicia jumped at me crying, forcing my arms to hold her up.

"I was bathing Darren and the phone rang. I picked it up. The phone, it was slippery from the shampoo... then my hand hit the light... the fixture broke off... old wiring; the long wires... it took a second, just a second..."

"What are you saying? What happened? Why didn't you get me?" I shouted.

She was crying uncontrollably as she pulled me into the bathroom where her crying somehow increased in volume. The medics were administering CPR on the boy.

"He's not responding at all," one said quietly to the other.

The man made a hand motion, prompting the one working on the boy to pick up his limp body.

"Ma'am," the medic not holding the boy said. "We're going to take your son to the hospital. We're going to need you to come with us."

"I can't leave my other child... My other child, my other child?" She looked around the bathroom frantically before remembering, "He went to take a nap."

I knew what she was about to ask so I responded before she had a chance to. "Yes, of course. Go!"

"Nick, thank you," she said as she grasped her purse and darted out of the apartment, following the medical workers and her son.

After they had gone, I walked down the apartment hall and peered my head into the boys' bedroom to see Malcolm sleeping on his bed. My heart sank seeing him there; a single twin alone.

I walked quietly into the living room and sat on the couch then attempted to turn on the television.

"No power," I reminded myself after several attempts.

I then pulled my phone from my pocket to check my messages. There were four, but, before I could check them, Malcolm walked into the room rubbing his eyes with his tiny fists.

"Where's Mommy?" he asked in an adorably little, heart-wrenching voice.

"Hello, Malcolm. How was your nap?"

"Hi, Doc. Where's Mommy?" he said again.

"Your mother took your brother out for a little while," I told him. "He wasn't feeling well."

"Big brother? Big brother?" Malcolm called loudly as he turned around in circles, cupping his little hands to his little mouth to amplify his little voice.

"I thought you were twins. Malcolm, isn't Darren your twin?" I questioned.

"Darren got born four minutes first," he said, pointing toward their bedroom.

There was a moment of silence filled with a thick awkward pause between the two of us.

"Would you like something to eat?" I asked him, not knowing what to say.

"Food!" he shouted happily. He then ran into the kitchen where he instinctively pushed a chair up to the counter upon which he climbed. The daredevil of a boy then crawled to a stand atop the counter twice his height, walked to the bananas, separated one from the bunch and began to decorticate.

"Well, you seem to be able to pretty much take care of yourself," I commented before sitting back down on the couch and flipping my phone in front of my face. The last message in the inbox was from Julie, a reply to my response to hers from the previous day. I opened it, ready to read her apology and grant her pleas to be taken back.

—

Nicholas,

My parents own the building so you should probably move out. And my mother has been sending us money for years. Good luck keeping up with NYC apartment rent, your office rent, utilities, car payments, loan payments, and everything else on your own. You built that pile of debt, now it's your turn to deal with it.

Also, on our divorce papers, I've cited religious differences. You think that you're God and I vehemently disagree.

-Julie

—

I could only smile and admire her wit. Then my face dropped; it was not until that moment that I had considered the possibility that

Julie's parents actually did own the building we lived in. They must have purchased it after we moved in to save face among their peers. That ridiculous story about renting the apartments to low-income New Yorkers as charity was actually true despite the fact that I was lying. It was just that I was the low-income New Yorker being subsidized. I always wondered why Julie was so willing to maintain the untruth, to continue the deceit, but the only deception had been allowing me not to believe my lies.

"Dr. Thesiger! To what do we owe the pleasure?" I heard behind me. Alicia's husband, Alec, stood with hands on his hips as he addressed me. "Why's the front door open?" he added.

"Daddy!" Malcolm shouted as he climbed down from the counter and ran to his father who grabbed him and threw him up into the air; Malcolm's head grazed the ceiling.

I stood up and slid my phone back into my pocket. "Alec. I'm sorry. Something happened to your son. Alicia brought him to the hospital. She asked me to watch Malcolm."

"What's happened to my son?" he asked frantically, placing Malcolm on the floor. The grown man began to shake out of fright when I did not respond.

Thankfully, before I was forced to speak, his cell phone rang.

"Hello... Yes, Nick just told me... What's going on? What's happening? We'll be right there..."

I stood silent through the conversation and hoped that by "we" he meant himself and his child.

"That was Alicia. We're going to meet her at the hospital. You should come too?" he said with a slight inflection of query at the end of the sentence.

"Oh, no... I would only get in the way," I responded.

236

"Okay then," he said quickly, sounding a bit confused and shocked. "Let's go, Malcolm," he said to his son, picking him up.

"Maybe take some toys?" I suggested. "And clothes, shoes for the boys if needed."

"Yes, yes... good idea," he agreed. He then carried Malcolm into the boys' room. They came out moments later holding various toy cars and with a backpack in hand. We three exited together, door locking behind us. They disappeared down into the stairwell as I disappeared into my apartment then fell back onto the couch, no longer hungry for food or for much of anything.

A sharp knocking at the door tore me from my daze an undetermined, but substantial, duration later. The apartment was dark and I could not see much of anything.

"Who's there?" I shouted from the couch.

"Police," a low muffled voice declared. The voice was so distant that it sounded as though it may have been directed toward Alicia and Alec's door. It was so low and muffled that it almost even felt like a projection from within, my mind was playing a trick on my fatigued, starved consciousness.

The ambiguity forced my non-response until the knocking started up again. "It happened next door, across the hall," I shouted from the couch.

"Please open the door, Sir," the voice called out, but again low in volume and muffled in clarity.

I then sat up and turned in the voice's direction, wincing in pain before shouting clearer, louder, "It happened next door, across the hall! They went to the hospital. You're too late."

"If you don't open the door, we'll be forced to gain entry by other means. This is The Police."

I turned back and laid down, assuming the voice was one of two things: a robber who had entered the building when the medics came in or out or a projection from my mind as I was half awake or maybe even fully asleep and within a dream.

I sat back and closed my eyes. The birds began to sing, louder and louder. The knocking at the door became a banging, a rhythmic thud that went on and on. I shut my eyes tighter, while the banging, the birds became louder and louder.

My mind decided that, if it was merely a dream, I would allow it to continue and progress unencumbered. I had not the strength to combat a foe against which I knew I could not defend. If it was a robber and he was about to knock the door down, I would not fight this either. I would let him end it for me. I simply had not the strength to resist.

The rhythmic banging at the door was lost in the chirping of the birds. I put my hands over my ears, but then all I could hear were the screams of the beautiful widow from the restaurant, the last few gasps from her late husband's mouth; Courtland's last words; then Alicia's cries over her lifeless son's body. My head began to shake. I began to shake.

The door came down with a thud to the floor, audible even through my thick hands, my filled mind. Eyes kept closed tightly, I determined that the intruder hit me hard in the head. I blacked out with a sharp dark pain then drifted into an endless headache.

When my eyes finally opened, I was faced with four gray walls enclosing a small windowless cell, disoriented, confused, shackled, trapped, jailed.

Committed

[Later]

Scientists call it the white coat effect. The uniform; it represents purpose; it commands respect. Those who wear it are perceived differently than those not adorned with such specialized attire. Bill had never looked more professional, more deserving of reverence and approbation. His hair; fuller. His stride; professionally intimidating. Exuding from every pore was a confidence that I had never seen from him, especially not when perched atop a stool and hunched over a bar in a dimly lit restaurant, his habitual post back in the days of our weekly lunchtime libation.

Furious, I attempted to shout his confidence away. "I've been sitting in this freezing cold metal chair for twenty minutes! Where have you been? Why would they take me in here if you weren't going to be here?"

"Sorry about that, Nick." His apology felt insincere, an insincerity that caused my mind to flood with the countless disparaging things I could say to him.

Life as a prisoner had taken its toll, guiding me further and further into living more and more in my own head. But it served me well to not respond in a hostile manner, no matter how blatantly provoked.

Through thought I calmed myself and asked, "Did you read my account of the week? I finished yesterday morning and had it sent to you." I shuffled around on the uncomfortably frigid chair, trying to discover the comfortable parts. Futile.

"I received it. Read through. Quite interesting." Bill responded as he sat, lowering himself effortlessly onto the other metal chair bolted to the floor as though his back had gone back in time to when it was strong, no groaning or moaning during descent.

I asked him, "Is it going to help? Is there anything in there you can use as a defense for the trial? What do we do now?"

I attempted to adjust my arms on the metal table, but my right wrist clanked down, held close to the table by the handcuff with which I had become well acquainted yet somehow failed to identify as a potential obstacle as I strived for some semblance of comfort.

Seemingly ignoring my questions while holding up a small brown box the size of maybe four reams of paper, Bill said, "I brought you something."

"What is it?"

"You'll see soon enough," he said, offering as little information as possible.

"Don't be coy... I'm in prison. I don't have the patience for coy."

"But you certainly have the time..." he interjected.

I looked away out of disdain for his condescending yet correct words. "Looks like paper. You got me paper?" I said as I reached under the table with my uncuffed left hand toward the brown box.

Bill retaliated with his left foot, pushing the box behind and away, under his chair.

"Is that what I wrote?" I asked, having seen some white paper with black writing inside.

"Yes, but before we get into that, how are you doing?"

"Well, I'm sitting in a prison visitation room on a cold metal chair, handcuffed to an equally cold and metal table, and I'm staring at you; the only person with whom I've spoken for a week, a week spent writing about probably the worst week of my life." My words were calm until I could no longer hold in the frustration. "Now, what do you think, Bill?" I exploded.

Startled at the extreme change in volume, Bill did not answer, so I more calmly asked, "What do you have for me? What's the progress on this trial preparation?"

"You seem dissatisfied with the way things turned out for you... in life..." he said.

I looked angrily at him as he slipped comfortably into the therapist's role. His posture was impeccable, his hands neatly folded on the table.

"I'm not your patient, Bill. Just please let me know what's going on with this trial." I tried to keep my words calm despite feeling myself rapidly tiring of Bill's patronizing tone.

"Things haven't quite gone the way you planned?" he asked, raising his eyebrows.

At that, I decided to lean back on the uncomfortable metal chair and allow him his alpha moment, hoping it would pass quickly. "Of course things aren't how I had planned them," I said, perturbed, but calm.

"Tell me, what exactly did you want?"

"What are you asking me? I wanted not to be imprisoned for a crime I didn't commit, awaiting a trial that looks like it will not be going my way."

"No, out of life. What did you want out of life; your dreams, your Utopia?"

"Life…" I responded, elongating the word and looking away in thought. "Dreams, Utopia," I said, just as elongated.

I thought less about what I wanted out of life and more about if I should or should not continue to indulge Bill's role-playing. I decided little harm would come from a short session so I responded with honesty.

"I suppose I wanted what everyone wants. Specifically for me… Have a strong practice. Make good money. Be able to retire early, but choose not to. Maybe play golf a couple times a week. Nice place on the park. Waterfront cottage somewhere in the Hamptons; doesn't need to be the most exclusive part or the biggest house; something modest. Two children in one of the city's private schools on their way to The Ivy League. A loving wife. A wife who loves me… That's where I always saw things going. The direction in which I tried to move things anyway."

"And when did you give up on that?" Bill asked.

"I didn't," I responded honestly, clenching my teeth.

"Do you know what the word 'Utopia' means in Greek?" Bill interjected quickly, twisting the knife harder, deeper.

"No, Bill," I said quickly and without even a search of my mind's filed definitions. I knew, but I had not the mental strength to think.

"It means 'good place.' "

"That makes sense," I responded.

Then he added, "It also means 'no place.' "

He paused for my reaction, but it was nothing more than a blank stare. Bill accepted it and continued. "I chose to use that word because it means both 'good place' and 'no place.' It's supposed to suggest that your Utopia is impossible to attain. Utopia should be strived for, but you need to realize and acknowledge that it is ultimately out of reach."

I leaned my head forward and down and lifted my left hand to it, temple on palm between my thumb and index finger attempting to massage away the mounting frustration.

Seeing my distress, he added, "All I'm trying to do is set the stage for a little reflection."

" 'History is a nightmare from which I am trying to awake,' " I said to the floor.

"James Joyce!" Bill exclaimed.

"That's right," I said as I shook my head.

"I bet I have another question that I guarantee you will not know the answer to." The confidence in Bill's voice was becoming sickening.

"What is it?" I encouraged with a slightly wavering tone, confidence hovering far below his.

"Who is Gödel?" he asked with a definitive tone.

I looked up at him to see the challenge of a confident man, words bouncing above his head. "Who is Gödel?" This time, instead of giving up before the search began, I pushed myself to think, quickly, quietly. After ten seconds had passed and nothing had come up, I closed my eyes to aid the hunt. I looked away and covered my ears; the sound of Bill's breathing was distracting me from the massive processing task. I sped through countless instantly accessible memories, organized in an ambiguous chronology. It took an unknown duration, but my answer was a disappointment.

"I do not know who Gödel is," I conceded.

"I thought that was an appropriate question for you to not know the answer to," Bill responded with a tone that was far past confidence and deeply rooted in conceit. "You see, Kurt Gödel was a mathematician who proved mathematically that no one man can know everything." Bill stopped to condescendingly allow time for me to think about his words.

"Oh, yes," I replied, finally remembering and craving deeply to show Bill that I almost knew the answer to his presumed to be unanswerable question. "I know about him. I never knew the man's name, but I know the theorem. Didn't he also starve himself to death? Obsessive fear of being poisoned, I believe. It was an unfortunate mental illness that eventually did him in."

Bill thought for a short moment before replying, "I don't actually know much of the man's life."

"So what are you getting at here, Bill?" I asked.

"I believe it was Sherlock Holmes who said, 'If you eliminate the impossible, whatever remains, however improbable, must be the truth.' " He smiled confidently at his quote.

"*Sherlock Holmes* is a fictional character, Bill," I replied.

"You quote *characters* from *the bible*," he punched back.

"Disrespectful," I said, pointing at him sternly with my free index finger. "And how is any of this relevant?"

He ignored the question and said, "I have one last question for you; one last topic of conversation."

"What is it?" I asked.

"Dementia Praecox…" he said before leaning back onto his metal chair, a bolt fastened tightly at each point the legs met the floor.

"What's the relevance? I know far too much on that topic to give a short answer."

"You tell me the relevance," he encouraged.

Head again between left thumb and forefinger, this time rubbing my tired eyes, I thought before asking, "Bill, what's going on?" His coy stupidity was wearing on my patience.

"I'd like you to define it for me," he responded.

I picked up my head and rolled my eyes. "You and I both know that you and I both know what Dementia Praecox means, but nevertheless I will indulge you…"

Bill bowed his head slightly accompanied by two circular gestures of genuine gratitude from his slightly cupped right hand.

"Dementia Praecox means split personality, but it was a label originally attached to Schizophrenia. This misnomer unfortunately led to the misunderstanding that individuals with Schizophrenia have a split personality. This is, of course, not the case. A split personality, that is, to have multiple personalities, is a different disorder altogether from Schizophrenia. Having a split personality or many personalities describes Dissociative Identity Disorder, or as it is more commonly called, Multiple Personality Disorder. The 'split' which is described with Schizophrenia is a split from reality, not a split of the personality. Schizophrenics are split or separated from reality. Schizophrenia is Dementia Praecox. Having many personalities is

Dissociative Identity Disorder, or DID." I pronounced the letters with exaggerated articulation: D, I, D.

"Good," he said, more condescending than earlier. "Can you simplify that a bit?"

I sighed and said, "Dementia Praecox is Schizophrenia. Schizophrenia is characterized by hallucinations, delusions, and disorganized thinking. This is different from Dissociative Identity Disorder or what some call Multiple Personality Disorder. Dissociative Identity Disorder is characterized by having several personalities that generally do not know about one another. But, most psychologists don't even think DID exists. There is yet to be a scientifically proven case. Now can you please tell me why it is that I am lecturing to you, Bill?"

"You tell me," he responded just as a psychologist would.

"I don't know. Are you trying to tell me I have DID? Or Schizophrenia?" I asked with sarcasm.

"Yes, I am," Bill responded from the doctor side of the table, without a laugh in his tone.

Despite the flavor of anger in my mouth and mind, I spoke quietly and calmly. "Look around you. I'm in prison. Prison… I don't appreciate these games. I thought you were here to help me with the logistics of this trial. Not to mock me and act like a patronizing idiot."

Bill was silent, smiling, nodding. "Think about it," he finally said.

"Think about what?" I asked before giving myself a chance to follow his directions.

He looked, just looked at me, seemingly through me. Then, Bill's motives, what I assumed to be his thought process, came together in my head.

"You're trying to get me committed, aren't you? So I don't have to stay in prison; so I can go to your hospital? Research on the rare DID patient." The ends of my angry frown began to turn upward. Why had I not thought of that?

Bill leaned back in his chair, looking quite comfortable and content, crossing his arms and smiling.

"That's brilliant!" I shouted. "And DID is perfect! So easy to fake!"

"No," he said, abruptly ending my glee. "I'm not trying to get you committed." He spoke very clearly and loudly, projecting far through me.

"Oh... I get it. Wink, wink, right? We can't say anything out loud." I smiled back at him, then pointed at my left eye. "Winking!" I whispered before grazing the outside of my left nostril with my left index finger.

"I'm not trying to get you committed," Bill insisted as he leaned forward in his chair, hovering over the metal table. "Look at me, Nicholas Thesiger. I am not trying to get you committed."

I looked at his unblinking eyes and found little to go on, then I looked away and thought for a moment about his hidden intentions.

"Oh... yes!" I finally exclaimed. "We need to plan this out because they would probably just send me to solitary confinement or to the prison psychologist who would probably just overmedicate me. We need to make it obvious that my situation is far more valuable to science than upholding the backward judicial system's penalties."

Bill looked back at me and shrugged his shoulders, saying nothing. I took his silence to be a sign of encouragement and continued flushing out the plan.

I shared my thoughts aloud. "So, DID is rare, but that's because it doesn't exist. Any semi-substantial clinician knows that... Every potential case in the past has turned out to be psychopaths who were talented actors and well informed about the alleged disorder. So what we need to do is make this a human interest story. Maybe get the media involved. Somehow connect this fictitious disorder and research on it to helping people better understand the mind; maybe develop some drugs for memory or depression or overcoming trauma or something. Yeah, yeah; that would be great! Get the pharmaceutical companies involved! They have more power and money than anyone!"

"No!" Bill said, cutting off my audible stream of consciousness. He leaned back in his chair, arms crossed, this time sighing with dissatisfaction. His face said "continue thinking" to me, but his posture said "stop thinking like that."

"I shouldn't be talking so loud?" I questioned before leaning in and whispering. "Should I write it all down? You can read it then eat the paper or something?"

"Try again..." he said, his level of dissatisfaction with my thought process increasing.

"I could start cutting myself?" I offered, voice back to a normal volume. "That would lead to hospitalization. And, added bonus, cutting releases endorphins... endorphins relieve pain and create a nice high!"

"That's hardly humorous..." Bill responded.

"You're right, it's not," I agreed. "Sorry. But, you're giving me nothing to work with here." Frustration was replacing my patience because of his short Socratic responses. "What is it that you're trying to guide me toward?"

"What I'm trying to get you to see is that you have already been committed." He spoke loudly with a very clear and over-enunciated tone.

Again, I sat back and thought about his hidden intentions. "Why don't you use some of that paper in the box under you and just write down what you want to say and then *I'll* eat it?"

"Nicholas Thesiger, you have already been committed," he said again.

"Oh!" I responded, realizing what he was telling me. "The paperwork is already going through? It's all done? I'm already committed? So what then, you're here to escort me to the hospital? *Your* hospital, right? I don't want to end up at any old research institution where I'll be treated like a stray at the dog pound."

"No, Nick. You were committed six weeks ago. You *are* in my hospital." Bill's tone went from condescending to very serious, but his words followed no logic.

"Shouldn't the one with the alleged rare psychological disorder be showing signs of dementia, not the doctor?" I asked, laughing.

I did not allow him a chance to respond before saying, "You probably stayed up most of the night reading my account of the week. Maybe you should come back tomorrow after you've had some rest." My words were less of a genuine suggestion and more of an attempt at humor, and I knew Bill would not leave anyway. For those few moments, a small but noticeable shot of hope was coursing through me. This plan, Bill's plan, it might actually work.

He looked back at me, no response at all. His face changed from his stoic expression in no way. I thought for a moment about his intentions when telling me I had been there for six weeks when I had clearly only been there for two. I began to shake my head, realizing he was in the process of making some kind of cruel joke out of my situation as he continued to do over and over again, setting up some punch line that I would find in no way humorous.

In my moment of thought, I stood to stretch my cramping legs and began making my way around the table to Bill's side. He reflexively pushed his chair back and straightened up as if he felt threatened, probably assuming I was going to attack him which was a fair assumption given his jokes and condescension.

"Nick?" he asked, voice wavering with audible terror.

Seeing his wild discomfort, I froze, shocked that he truly believed I would hurt him. His jokes were annoying, but he was still there to help me. "I'm not going to hurt you. Calm down. What's going on with you, Bill? You seem really on edge."

"Can you sit back down, Nick?" he asked, still looking rather frightened.

I decided to follow his directions. I was genuinely beginning to feel somewhat concerned for Bill's well-being as I felt the doctor/patient roles reversing in the room. I returned to my seat, but I felt as though the table had been rotated 180 degrees.

"Nick?" he asked again.

"Everything alright with you or is this all just leading to one of your jokes?" I asked.

"Nick, I need you to acknowledge that you are in my hospital. You've been in the in-patient unit for six weeks now."

Despite my attempts to lend to him my services, Bill continued his disparaging joke at my expense so I gave up and threw my arms up in disgust, patience almost completely drained. "I don't have the strength for these jokes. First of all, I've been here for about two weeks. Second, this is a prison, not a hospital. My wife and her parents conspired to have me arrested. These are the facts. Can we get back to the trial?"

He began to speak with more authority in his tone, seemingly again taking on the therapist role; questioning my definitive declarative sentence to find deeper meaning. "How did they have you arrested?" he asked.

"I don't know. They have connections or something of the sort."

Bill continued to press his agenda. "Yes, but for what? Why are you in a prison?"

Beginning to feel extremely frustrated, I crossed my arms and ankles, looking away and not responding for longer than a minute. Bill sat quietly, presumably allowing time for me to ponder his questions, but the only thing going through my mind was Bill's incessant need to continue to make jokes. They were not cheering me up as he previously suggested they would.

But then it hit me, the key to Bill's behavior finally occurred to me after a week of enduring its foolishness. This was Bill's way of beginning the conversation about his strategy for the trial. His constant idiotic jokes were his way of conveying sensitive information to me in this controlled environment in which the guards could hear everything. They paid no real attention to the jokes because the jokes were not funny, just one old psychologist trying to make fun of another. After this realization, I knew I needed to play along and continue to let Bill make his potentially insulting and non-humorous jokes so that he could convey the messages he had been trying to secretly deliver to me for the entire week and advance the progress of preparing for the pending trial.

"Listen," I started as I leaned in, "we need to get back on topic here. For the sake of argument, I am going to allow you to attempt to convince me that you can successfully get me transported to your hospital so, please, go on." I pointed to my left eye then grazed my left nostril with my left index finger.

———

The Plan

"Okay…" Bill responded slowly. "Here goes. You, Nicholas Thesiger, are afflicted with Dissociative Identity Disorder, or DID, Multiple Personality Disorder. You have, from what I can determine, at least two additional personalities, both of which are unaware of the existence of the other or of you."

I had to interrupt. "Now that I hear you saying it, this sounds outlandish. This is a pretty bad plan and no one is ever going to believe it. I'm a psychologist for crying out loud!"

"No!" Bill said loudly, forcefully. "Nick, you need to listen to me. Just hear me out. Your resistance means you're actually hearing and considering what I'm saying. The past five weeks, you've changed the subject or ignored it or started shouting at me."

"What are you talking about? I've only been here for two weeks," I responded. Then I realized that Bill needed to approach the explanation of his plan in a manner that suggested the disorder's presence and the situation surrounding it to be the reality because the guard very well may have been listening and Bill's presumed joke needed to continue without interruption. "You know what," I said.

"Just continue; explain your plan." Again, I pointed to my left eye then grazed my left nostril with my left index finger.

"Thank you. So, you have two other personalities." He paused and waited for confirmation from me. I shrugged and then nodded to encourage his continuation. "You are the primary you, as far as I can tell."

"Okay," I said, smiling and nodding.

"The other two personalities are people you created who have lives completely separate from yours yet also connected."

"What or who are these other personalities?" I asked.

"Darby, the super in your apartment building...*your* Brownstone," he responded.

I froze with a look of shock on my face.

"Nick? Are you still hearing me?" he asked when I showed no movement.

"Yes," I said slowly. "I don't think that I've ever mentioned that super to you. There are two supers for the building; one who is normally there and the other guy, Darby, who is almost never on; he only works odd hours and covers for the other guy, I think."

As I spoke, I realized that there were simple ways that Bill could have found the super's name, knocking on the door and asking residents or searching the Internet maybe. Simple as they were, I became impressed that he had done his homework.

Bill continued. "The super is, as far as I can tell, the first of your additional personalities to have emerged. I think from a dissatisfaction with your job. Maybe also your inability to rise to the success that you desired for so long."

Bill paused again for my reaction. When I showed him nothing more than a blank stare, he said, "Nick?" seemingly assuming that I was slipping into another one of my alleged personalities.

"Yes, Bill," I responded, rolling my eyes, but knowing he needed to pretend for the sake of his ongoing joke so the guards would ignore it.

"Everything okay?" he asked.

"Of course, Bill. Please continue." Again, I pointed at my left eye before grazing my left nostril.

"The super, Darby, believes that he is in prison because he was framed for stealing something that one of the tenants misplaced. Since he has keys to all the apartments, he's an obvious suspect." Bill spoke as though he was speaking of a real person with a real situation and not just a fictitious additional personality created to get me out of prison and into his hospital.

"Why would they frame him? Did Darby frequently suspect others of being out to get him?" I asked, digging deeper into the fictitious additional personality's psyche, table again turned.

"He believes he overheard a conversation that he shouldn't have and a couple tenants wanted him out. Something along those lines." Bill's explanation lacked sufficient details, but I felt pushing for more would lead us off track so I accepted the ambiguity.

"Alright," I said slowly, thinking as I responded. "What about the other personality? You said I had two."

"At least two," he corrected. "I can't be sure. I've only met the three."

"Three?"

"Yes: you, Darby, and Jack."

"Oh, you're including me. So who is Jack then? He's the third?" I asked, genuinely interested, almost beginning to enjoy the building story.

"He's kind of the bad guy," he responded.

"What do you mean by 'the bad guy'?"

At that moment, I began to consider the possibility that Bill was not suggesting to me a plan to have me moved from the prison to his hospital, but that he was actually crying for help, divulging to me his latent life issues. Perhaps he was speaking of his own dissatisfaction with his job? He must have somehow overheard something that he was not supposed to. Theories multiplied in my mind. I felt that I was, at that point, firmly on the other side of the table and Bill was now lying comfortably on the couch, staring at the ceiling.

"Think about your neighbors," he said. "The mother with the twins…"

"Yes. Sad what happened to her. The boy," I said, remembering the unfortunate accident as I thought about how it could tacitly relate to Bill's life.

"Yes, it is… You know what's interesting?" he asked rhetorically. "I actually found out from Jack what had happened before I read it in your recount of the week."

"Is that right? My bad boy alter ego told you what happened to my neighbors?"

"Yes. He went to the hospital with Alicia's husband, Alec, and the other boy, Malcolm."

"Is that right?" I asked again. "What did he say, exactly?"

"I need *you* to say it, Jack," Bill responded.

"I'm not Jack," I said, assuming Bill had mixed up the names.

"Sorry, Bill," Bill responded to me.

"Bill? Why did you just call me Bill?" I asked.

"Nick?" he asked.

"Yes, it's me!" I shouted, getting more and more frustrated with his theater for the sake of the guard's ears. "Can you stop with this ridiculous name game?"

"Sorry. I'm sorry. You have to understand that this is a hard situation. Sometimes you come in and out of different people, different personalities."

"And one of my personalities is named Bill? Like you?" I asked, voice raised to an angry shout. "Are you suggesting that I manifested a personality that's based on you? Bill, I don't know where you're trying to take this, but it's becoming really self-absorbed. Your name shouldn't come up at all."

"I think we're making a lot of progress here," he responded, table again rotated. "There seems to be some intense fixation on me and it is important that, for our next step, you acknowledge it."

"You narcissistic bastard! You're trying to make this thing about you?"

"Nick, can I finish?"

"No!" I shouted, anger in my voice, in my mind, on my face, all over my body, as I shuffled around uncomfortable on my metal chair. All the pent up anger from the past week dealing with Bill's idiocy began spewing out in an uncontrollable rage. "All this time spent writing, waiting, hoping; it was all wasted because you wanted to make it all about yourself, so you could be the alpha. I need to get out of here." I pointed at the door with my right index finger parallel with my entire right arm, waiting for him to stand and walk himself out.

"No, I'm not leaving. You need to hear me out."

"Just leave!" I shouted, still pointing toward the door.

"Listen to me, Nicholas. You need to hear this."

"Guard!" I shouted, ignoring Bill's condescending commands. I stood up and made an attempt at the door, but was held back by the handcuff on my right wrist. The guard turned and looked in at us through the thick glass window in the thick door.

"I don't want to talk to him anymore. I'd like to leave," I shouted loudly enough to be heard through the transparent inches of safety glass.

The guard looked at Bill as Bill held up his hand. The guard then turned back around.

"Guard!" I yelled again, but he did not turn back toward the room. *Why did he ignore me?* I thought.

"What's the problem, Nick?" Bill asked.

"I'm handcuffed to the table in prison in a windowless visitation room standing across from you and you're frustrating me beyond what my words can describe!"

"Nick?" Bill asked.

I then shouted, frantically distraught at the situation. "Bill, what is going on here? Stop with the stupid acting. Your plan is not going to work. What are you trying to do to me?"

"Nick, I am not acting. Just take your seat. Let me finish," he insisted, pointing at the seat bolted to the floor behind my knees.

259

Reluctantly I sat and looked down at my original side of the table; patient.

"Jack," he began, "has been living with your neighbor, Alicia, when her husband, Alec, is away on business and when you're not working. This is a little delicate, but the twin boys, Nick, they're biologically Jack's sons."

"This is ridiculous! Where did you come up with that? You can't drag my neighbors into this thing. It won't work. They won't go along with it. They would need to testify in court. Bill, they just lost a child!"

"Just let me finish…When the boy died—Darren was his name, right?"

I did not respond. I just looked toward the wall to my right, arms tightly folded across my chest, ankles crossed tightly on the floor.

"Well, the stress of the death of his son got to Jack. The stress of your wife leaving you also got to you, Nick, at the same time. Additionally the stress of being accused of theft and the attempts to have him fired were too much for Darby, the super. This all built up, the hormones in the body and chemicals in the brain involved with stress, all of it in that one body, drove you all to have a breakdown."

"What about you?" I asked out of disgust, still looking away.

"Nick? Are you talking to me or someone else?" Bill asked obtusely.

"I'm obviously talking to you. Do you see anyone else here?" I asked.

"Do you?" he inquired.

"Of course not!" I shouted.

"Sorry, I needed to make sure."

I leaned forward quickly, angrily and pounded on the metal table as I demanded, "Just answer the question! What about you? The me as you? The Bill me? You said one of my personalities was you, didn't you? Where does that self-indulgence fit in or were you just trying to further frustrate me?"

"Well..." he said slowly. "Bill didn't have any stress or problems more than normal, but Bill wasn't actually one of your personalities per se."

"But you just said earlier..." I began.

"Yes, I know what I said, but you may have misinterpreted. And this is where it begins to get somewhat confusing..."

"Oh, because it's not already confusing?" I responded.

———

The New Reality

Bill leaned forward and put his forearms onto the metal table before saying, "Bill was actually a hallucination of one of your personalities. You actually; Nick's hallucination. You appeared to have created Bill so you would have someone to talk to about your problems, but that's a theory based on very little so I won't stand behind it officially. And hallucinations are rarely created for a specific purpose, which makes that theory of the root of your hallucination of Bill even less plausible. But, what I do know is that Bill is one of Nick's hallucinations, one of your hallucinations."

I looked back at Bill as he looked at me with hope in his face that I would agree to go along with his preposterous plan to free me from prison. "So what you're telling me," I began, "is that I, Nick, have an imaginary friend? Named Bill?"

Bill smiled and said, "Yes, in a way. You see, you met this Bill at a bar every day to talk about your problems and let off some stress. And this Bill happens to be based on me."

"Are you trying to tell me that I haven't been talking to you at the restaurant every weekday for the past however many years?" I asked.

"That's right. That was you talking to your 'imaginary friend.' " He used air quotes, curling his index and middle fingers, as he said "imaginary friend." I felt my own fingers curling into fists. "Other than the past seven weeks, I haven't seen you for years."

"Seven weeks? You said six weeks before…" I said, pointing out the inconsistency in his fictitious story. "You said I've been here for six weeks."

"Well, we had coffee together on the Thursday before you were brought in. We ran into each other on the street and we went to a café. It's in your writing. I know you remember this."

I said nothing, thinking about the potential for possible perceived plausibility by a jury, so Bill continued.

"It was a strange situation, running into you like that after not seeing you for all those years. You treated me like we hadn't skipped a beat, like it was college again. It felt strange, you were acting a little strange, but I didn't really question it."

Again, I sat and watched Bill deliver to me his plan with such honesty in his voice, a convincing testimony, but the overall storyline pushed a smile and a laugh to my mouth.

"The college buddy was actually a figment of the protagonist's imagination?" I questioned. "Wasn't there a movie like that? The one that was about the mathematician John Nash? In fact, weren't there a bunch of movies like that? A little cliché, don't you think?"

"Yes," he admitted. "This does sound eerily like a cliché ending of a film."

"Well, then your story is a little confused, now isn't it? John Nash was diagnosed with Schizophrenia, not Dissociative Identity Disorder. But you're telling me that I have multiple personalities which is Dissociative Identity Disorder. But, you're also telling me that I have Schizophrenia, hallucinating something that isn't there and interacting with him, having this 'imaginary friend.'" I relaxed my clenched fists to use air quotes, just as he had.

"Yes, you're absolutely right," Bill responded. "This is different from that movie and every other movie, for that matter. That's why I said that it gets pretty complicated. What I'm saying is that you have both Dissociative Identity Disorder and Schizophrenia."

I looked at Bill with confusion. "You've got to be kidding me... no jury is going to buy that. They won't even understand it. Those are two very separate diagnoses, two very different disorders. Even a court appointed psychologist would call foul on that one. Maybe we should just stick with the DID defense, leave the Schizophrenia out of it. And even that's a stretch."

"Nick, you need to get the idea out of your mind that we're talking about a plan to convince a jury that you're innocent of some crime."

"Oh, yeah, right, wink, wink..." I responded. "Well, convince me how this would work, explain it to me, because you're certainly not doing a good job so far. Here, tell me your little story as if I were the jury."

"There is no jury," he told me.

"Yes, I'm well aware that there is no jury… but just pretend that I am the jury. Explain it to the jury." I sat back again and crossed my arms, waiting for Bill's opening statement.

He rolled his eyes then leaned down and began fishing around in the brown box beneath his chair with his right hand then pulled out four dolls. One doll had a triangular-rounded head with three faces, each looking away from the others. The head was capable of rotating, turning on the axis of the neck to display one face correctly with the direction of the body at a time. The other three dolls appeared to be standard single-faced dolls with two arms and two legs. I began laughing immediately, but stopped when Bill sent me a dissatisfied look.

"This is how I would explain it to a jury…" he began.

"Oh, please go on!" I encouraged.

He put the doll that had three different faces in the middle of the table first. "This is Dissociative Identity Disorder doll; we'll call it the 'DID doll.' This doll has three personalities represented by the three faces. None of these faces can see the others so they are all separate, but they are all within the same physical body. The three personalities do not and cannot communicate and they do not know about one another in any way, but they are all very real.

"Each one can only be present if the other two are not; so only one personality is in control of the body at a time. This is represented by the rotation of the head which stops when any one of the three faces is forward." He rotated the head and showed it to the jury to demonstrate.

264

I stuck out my bottom lip and nodded, acknowledging the helpful visual aids.

Bill then removed the DID doll from the middle of the table and replaced it with the three remaining dolls.

"This is someone who is schizophrenic," he said, holding up one of the dolls. "We'll call it the 'schizophrenic doll.' " He then pointed at the other two dolls. "These two are not real; they're hallucinated by the schizophrenic doll. We'll call them 'hallucination dolls.' Only this schizophrenic doll can see the hallucination dolls. They can all interact and communicate with one another. But, don't forget that these hallucination dolls can only be seen by the schizophrenic doll. They cannot interact with or be seen by anyone else."

Bill then reintroduced the DID doll with three faces and dropped the schizophrenic doll back in the brown box beneath his chair. "This is you," he told me, pointing at the DID doll. "You have three separate personalities: Nick, Darby, and Jack." As he named each of my personalities, he rotated the head of the DID doll to a different face. "Nick happens to be schizophrenic, so when he is the face in front, when Nick is in control of the body, he can see the hallucination dolls that no one else around him can see because they are his hallucinations." Bill then picked up one of the hallucination dolls. "This hallucination doll is Bill. Nick sees him every weekday in the middle of the day at a bar."

I sat back in my uncomfortable chair smiling and began to clap. "Fantastic. Brilliant explanation. Juries love this kind of thing; simplifying complex concepts. And the dolls? Nice touch, but there remains one unanswered question."

"What's that?" Bill asked.

"Where did you get those dolls?" I asked, laughing.

"I had someone make them for me. Thanks for asking," he responded, smiling.

"And you carry them around with you?"

"I was quite certain that you would ask for an explanation so I put them in the box."

Again uncomfortable in my position, I leaned forward to rest my elbows on the table. "I have some issues with this story, Bill."

"Please enlighten me," he said.

"It's obvious that you put a lot of thought into this. You even brought part of your doll collection to help explain…"

"I had them made for this purpose," Bill stressed.

"Right…" I said sarcastically. "So, the theories about DID suggest individuals afflicted with the disorder can have personalities that are very distinct from one other, with different perceptions, memories, abilities, desires, goals, even allergies and eyeglass prescriptions. This is physically possible because many allergies have to do with hormone levels that are controlled by the brain and eyeglass prescriptions often have to do with the muscles around the eyes, also controlled in some part by the brain. So I suppose it is technically plausible for one of the personalities to have Schizophrenia while the others do not, but, on a clinical level, it doesn't really add up."

"How so?" Bill asked.

"Well, if I were the court appointed psychologist to review this case, I would bring up some facts about Schizophrenia because, unlike DID, Schizophrenia is a real disorder that unfortunately millions of people have. Scientists know countless facts about the disorder; facts that can verify or debunk the presence of the disorder in an individual who claims to be afflicted. And, if a jury feels as

266

though one diagnosis is wrong, they're automatically going to assume the whole thing is wrong which destroys the case. So if we're doing this, we are not using Schizophrenia, just DID."

"Like what?" Bill asked. "What facts might prove or disprove?"

I shuffled around on the uncomfortable chair as I poked holes in Bill's testimony. "Well, for one thing, Schizophrenia is a young person's disorder. Symptoms first appear when those afflicted are in their twenties and I'm far from that. There is absolutely no way that I became schizophrenic this late in life; it's statistically implausible. Also, it's summer. When someone does acquire symptoms of Schizophrenia, the onset is almost always during the winter. Likewise, those who develop Schizophrenia are almost exclusively born during the winter months. I was born during the summer."

"Remember back, Nick," Bill interjected. "You told me that directly after undergrad, which would have been when you were in your twenties, was when you first began meeting Bill for drinks, yet I have no recollection of this. You know why? Because I was never there. It was you hallucinating Bill. As for the season of onset, I have no proof either way on that one because it occurred long ago during a time period in which we were not in touch. And I admit that there is a strong correlation between winter birth and a higher than average incidence of Schizophrenia, but that is merely a correlation. Many individuals afflicted were born during seasons other than winter."

"Duly noted..." I said, agreeing with a nod that his story continued to hold water. "What about the fact that the vast majority of clinicians and researchers believe DID to be a made up disorder? Most documented cases have, as I said, proven to be clever psychopaths who find pleasure in outfoxing doctors. There is yet to be a scientifically confirmed case."

"Well, how would one go about proving a case to be legitimate?" he asked somewhat rhetorically.

"I don't know. Institutionalize the person and rigorously test them for the rest of their life. The person would have to be monitored constantly to see if they would slip and reveal their scheme. You have to treat it with the assumption that this person is a fake…" I trailed off because the smile on Bill's face had grown from modest to immense.

"That's right," he proclaimed proudly.

"So your plan is to tell a jury that I have both DID and Schizophrenia and the only way to be sure is to monitor me for the rest of my life at your hospital? No jury, no matter how stupid, will go for that."

"There is no jury," Bill said again. "There was no crime. But you need to hear me out. You are a treasure trove for research. There are but a handful of people with a memory that works the way yours does, with this kind of eidetic memory. You remember everything that happens to you, everything that you read or see. That alone is reason enough to study you. Adding to that the fact that you are probably one of the most lucid, insightful, and aware schizophrenics on record… and the fact that you are an extremely well educated psychologist… Add to all of that the prospect of the first confirmed case of Dissociative Identity Disorder… You can't argue with the fact that you belong in a research institution. You need to be studied!" As he spoke, his smile grew larger and his eyes grew wider.

"Yes…" I responded, rubbing my chin with my right hand in thought. "And a jury might even agree with you as well."

"Sure," he said. "A jury probably would agree with that logic."

"So, just so I can get this straight, let me recap. You want me to pretend to have at least three personalities; three including me, Nick." I pointed at myself. "You want me to create two additional personalities with their own lives and goals and allergies and eyeglass prescriptions and pretend to be them at random. Oh, and I almost forgot, you want me to pretend I, Nick"—I pointed at myself again—"have Schizophrenia and that I hallucinated you every weekday for the past twenty years so I would have someone to talk to and then you coincidentally wind up being my psychologist. Is that it? Did I get everything?"

Keeping his composure while continuing to stubbornly tell me the same thing, Bill said, "I'm not asking you to *pretend* anything. I'm explaining your current situation, your current state."

"Right... so this is real. I got it." I pointed at my right eye with my right hand and winked before adding, "As real as any one of my personalities."

"Was that a joke?" Bill asked.

"I think so..." I said, beginning to question my own humor.

Bill laughed and then extended his left hand. "So I think we're done for the day. I'll see you tomorrow?"

"Wait!" I said with a bit of anger. "Where are you going? We're not done. I'm not fully convinced that this is a good idea. You haven't done a good job of convincing me this will work. You have your dolls and all, but all I have is the bones of the story. We haven't ironed out the details of this thing."

Then Bill said, "How about I go over what we've been talking about? I'll do it in chronological order so you can get the timeline down. And remember, everything is either substantiated by evidence or cannot be disproved."

"I think I understand the plan, but if you think it will help, go ahead," I responded, beginning to have some faith in Bill's outlandish scheme.

"After graduating from college, you, Nick, as a schizophrenic, hallucinated *Bill*. Your hallucination, this *Bill,* was based on your roommate in college, me." Bill pointed to himself. "Sometime thereafter you, Nick, became dissatisfied with your job as a psychologist, never making quite as much money or being quite as successful as you wanted, so you created Darby the super as an alternative personality so that you could escape from your work life."

"Why would a doctor want to be a super of a building?" I pondered aloud.

"It's kind of like working for the common good, helping others, finishing a job. As a psychologist you felt that you rarely actually helped much of anyone and the job was never really done. Patients never really changed and always came back with the same problems, repeating the same patterns… This is not really how I feel, but it was in your writing."

Bill's logic had no holes so I nodded him ahead. "Okay. Logical. Continue."

"Thank you. Next, at some point along the way you became dissatisfied with your marriage, so you created Jack who developed a loving relationship with your next door neighbor, Alicia. That was your escape from your marriage. You had two beautiful children and you were with their loving mother. So what you created with Darby and Jack was the life you wanted, your Utopia."

"I suppose that all makes sense," I said, tapping my chin with right hand. "But why would I, Nick, create these other two personalities and other two lives because of dissatisfaction over my own life if I, Nick, did not even know about them? It doesn't make sense. I can't benefit. I can't enjoy the good times or even know when they're happening."

I could see that Bill was reveling in this back and forth because he had a suitable response for each one of my questions.

"That's a good question," he said. "And here is a good answer to it. Your brain and body were taking a heavy toll from the stress caused by your disdain for your job and your marriage. To maintain itself, as a defense mechanism, your brain created a personality that was proud to do his work and fulfilled by his job, Darby, and also a personality that was happy with his romantic relationship, even though it was extramarital, Jack. These two additional personalities helped relieve the stress and dissatisfaction you, Nick, felt about your job and marriage and overall life. So, even though you knew nothing about those other two personalities, you still benefited from them."

"Well," I interrupted, "that's not exactly true. I, Nick, did not benefit from them. My brain and body did. From what you're telling me, it sounds like my brain and body basically wanted a break from the physical and mental abuse it was getting with Nick so it created two other personalities, two other people that caused pleasure to counteract the pain."

"Yes!" Bill said excitedly. "It's the basic premise behind dissociating during a traumatic event, leading to dissociative amnesia. Your brain and body do this as a defense mechanism, like self-preservation. Let me back up, if I may?" he asked politely, wanting nothing more than to lecture to me.

"Certainly," I allowed.

"What we are learning here is that your brain has control over your mind; your mind which is your personality which is you, Nick. Some people might think what you consciously experience is you and that is all there is, nothing deeper; but they would be wrong. Your brain is in control without your conscious knowledge; many call it the subconscious. When you, Nick, have a problem that is threatening your body and brain, your brain will do something about it. In this case, you were running yourself ragged with the stress caused by your dissatisfaction with your life, so your brain created two other personalities to counteract the effects of the stress on your body."

Again, I sat back, silenced by thought as I tapped my chin with my right hand. "Very good, Bill," I said finally. "Sounds like you're forming a nice little theory about the brain and the body and the mind and the personality."

"I'm just throwing some ideas out there. Just trying to explain your case. You know how it works; we look at the information then come up with a hypothesis to explain what we see, then we test it."

I nodded for a handful of seconds before Julie's involvement came to mind. "But what about Julie? How could she possibly not be aware of this affair with the neighbor? A jury would question that. Maybe the personality is Jack when he goes to Alicia's apartment when Alec is out and maybe the personality is Darby when he's fixing things in other tenants' apartments, but it's still my body. Julie would see that."

Bill frowned a bit and looked away for a moment before responding. "Well, Nick, she did see you, your body that is. Jack in your body would disappear into Alicia's apartment. Or, if Darby was the current personality controlling your body, Julie would notice you disappearing into someone else's apartment. Julie assumed that you were having an affair, well, several affairs. She would frequently find long blond hairs on your clothes. That's why she was so sad all the time, always crying for seemingly no reason. Her tacit hostility also manifested in passive-aggressive acts. And she knew those boys were yours. It killed her to see them. You wrote about all of this, but from a perspective ignorant of the reality."

I nodded at his response, knowing a jury would believe it. Then I posed the next logical question. "And Alicia? She was fine with all of this?"

"As far as she was concerned, she was the other woman and didn't care that she was cheating on her husband. Alicia was a little concerned that you had her call you 'Jack' when you were intimate with her, but she played along, assumed it was some kind of erotic nickname game. And since the boys, her sons, Jack's sons, called you 'Doc,' they also called Jack 'Doc.' Jack just assumed it was a nickname, accepted it as his own, thought it was cute that his boys referred to him like that." Bill's reply suggested he had thought of every possible question he could be asked, that he knew every detail of my fictitious other lives, that he was ready to be cross-examined by a prosecutor.

"How did Jack feel about Julie? Cheating on Julie?" I asked.

"He didn't know anything of Julie or you or really anything outside of Alicia and the boys. Jack is..." Bill paused before continuing. "Of your personalities, he is the most one-dimensional. He doesn't seem to have much of an existence outside of this affair."

"And this is why you call Jack 'the bad guy,' " I mused aloud.

"He's not a bad guy really. It's just easier to label him that way because he is knowingly involved in an affair for his own pleasure. Well, your own pleasure, kind of."

"Did he know? Her husband, Alec?" I asked.

"He had no idea and he still doesn't. I interviewed everyone separately," Bill said casually.

"Wait, what? You interviewed them? You can't say that to a jury without having proof. They'll all have to go to court and testify." I thought for a moment and began to feel doubt, anxiety, anger. "No, this isn't going to work… They would all have to go to court to testify, regardless of whether you say you interviewed them or not."

Flustered and suddenly far beyond frustrated, I began shaking my head in anger and raising my voice. "Ahhh! This is never going to work, any of this. All of them will be forced to testify, Julie, Alicia, Alec, probably Malcolm, and the tenants in the Brownstone… We won't be able to keep it to just you and me. This will never work."

"Calm down, Nick," Bill said.

"I will not calm down!" I shouted. "Your plan will never work. We just wasted all this time. I can't believe I even considered this. I think I should go. I should go."

I then stood up and began pacing around the room, thinking about what I was going to do about the trial, about Bill's inevitable involvement, about a new plan, a workable plan.

Bill began to speak. "You know I think that…"

"Just be quiet, Bill!" I shouted, cutting off his thought as I continued to pace, hands clasped behind my back.

Bill obeyed and silently sat back to watch me struggle with the unfeasibility of his plan and ponder what the next move should be. Frustrated, I gave up and walked to the door, banging hard to get the guard's attention.

I shouted through the glass, "We're done in here. Can you please take me back to my cell?"

The guard looked at me, then looked at Bill. Bill put his hand up and, again, the guard turned his back to the window.

Feeling increasingly uncomfortable, I hit the door as hard as I could with my right hand out of frustration, then went over to Bill and shouted at him angrily, "What are you doing?"

Bill's tone dripped with condescension. "I'm just letting him know everything is okay. They just check in to make sure you aren't going to attack me or hurt yourself, and they wait for the thumbs up from the Principal Investigator."

"Bill, I think we both know what your thumb's up. Now tell me what's going on. Why won't he let me out of here?"

Without waiting for an answer, I went back to the door and began banging with both hands, but the guard ignored my attempts to get his attention.

"Come sit down, Nick," he insisted as he pointed to my side of the table.

"Did you pay him off? Slip him some cash to keep me in here?" I asked frantically.

"No, just sit down and let me explain. The fact that you're resisting shows that you're actually listening, maybe even considering the reality."

Watching Bill throughout my trip, slowly I walked back around the table, sat, and then crossed my arms. I knew not what side he was on and I feared that unknown.

Bill leaned over the table then placed his forearms atop, open hands articulating his words. "Concentrate, Nick. I am going to need you to stay with me here. I am about to ask you a question that may shift you away, but you need to fight it. You need to stay with me and concentrate."

I looked around the room for an explanation, but found none. "Fight what? What question? What are you talking about?"

"Nick, where did your handcuffs go?"

———

Unshackled

I looked down at my right wrist, right hand, my right arm, my right side, then my left; no handcuffs, nothing held me to the table. The jolt of shock that ran quickly through my body pushed my feet against the floor, sliding my chair back; it slid freely, it was not bolted down. I recoiled into myself, shocked, scared. "What's happening?" I asked frantically.

"Nick?" Bill inquired yet again.

"Yes, yes… it's me," I responded, but unsure of the validity of the statement.

Still leaning forward over the table, Bill attempted to explain. "You are in my hospital, the one where I work. You are in the research section of the psych ward. You have been here for six weeks, but you, Nicholas Thesiger, have been here experiencing this for only two weeks. You believed that it was a prison because that is what made the most logical sense to you. You perceived your surroundings and your experience to be consistent with what you believed was your reality. As a psychologist, you know this experience to be a 'hallucination.' Do you understand everything that I'm saying to you?"

My face was blank, wiped of all emotion or reaction. My mind, for the first time in my life, was free of thought, halted in its processes by shock, confusion, a feeling of loss of control, loss of self.

"You still with me, Nick?"

I responded with nothing, no movement, no blinking.

"Darn it…" Bill exclaimed. "Not again."

"No, no," I said finally. "It's still me. It's Nick. I'm just trying to digest this." I leaned down, elbows on knees and head in hands. Again I checked for any semblance of shackle on my wrists, nothing. "Did you give me some drug or something? Something to make me loopy, to make me hallucinate, make me more susceptible to suggestion, so my experience would be more real, so I could testify convincingly to the jury?"

"There is no jury, no trial, and there was no hearing. You are in a hospital in the research section of the psych ward."

There was an extended duration of silence as I thought. Bill shuffled around in his seat and placed the dolls back into his brown box, their purpose served. He looked away, allowing me time to reflect, to consider.

Breaking the echo of his slight movement, I calmly said, "You know. Bill, I hadn't realized this was a tragedy."

"I can see why you would think the worst of this, but I wouldn't call it a 'tragedy,' " Bill said in an attempt to console me.

"No, no. Think back to the philosophy class we took senior year, *the easy A*. Aristotle's definition of a tragedy. 'The moment when the hero comes face-to-face with his true identity is a mechanism transforming not only the hero, but the story itself.' "

"That was decades ago, Nick. How would I remember a detail like that?"

"I suppose that is what separates us…"

"Yes, you do have quite the memory, but please continue," he encouraged.

I took a deep breath and scratched my itching left ear with my left hand before responding. "According to Aristotle, what I'm going through right now would be considered the *Anagnorisis*, which

277

is a Greek concept for 'discovery.' Next will come the *Peripeteia,* which in Greek means 'transition from ignorance to knowledge.' So basically I'll have to accept what you're telling me to be a truth..."

After I trailed off, Bill slowly stood up. My head was down in my hands, but I heard him push his chair back. I put my right hand up to stop his progress toward me. "I went through the training too," I told him. "Your hand on my shoulder won't help me."

He sat just as slowly as he had risen. "Are you going through the Peripeteia phase?" he asked. "Are you realizing what I'm saying to be a truth?"

"I don't know," I told him. "I haven't decided yet. Keep explaining; it may help."

Bill, encouraged he was getting through to me, continued. "I asked you to write about the previous week, the week during which your stress overcame you. I knew that reliving your stress alone, that's Nick's stress without that of Darby and Jack, would not make you break down again. It was the combination of the stresses from the three personalities that did you in six weeks ago.

"During that time, that six-week period while you were here in the hospital, I had each personality spend a week writing about the last week before ending up here. The reliving of the stress was thus spread out as opposed to being experienced all at the same time. And writing forced you to think about what was happening in your own life and this kept your one personality, Nick, around while you wrote. The same was true for the other two personalities during their own time of writing. It took six weeks for all of this because we failed with several different interviewing tactics before I thought of this one."

"You remember what Oscar Wilde said about friends, right?" I asked to Bill.

"No, what?"

" 'A true friend stabs you in the front,' " I replied smiling.

"I don't understand. I'm trying to help, Nick. Are you accusing me of something? I don't see the meaning in that quote."

"And you probably never will. Continue; tell me more," I encouraged.

"Consider this," he began. "You have a fantastic memory. You simply do not forget things that you've experienced; sound, sight, smell, taste, touch, emotions, you remember them all perfectly. But there are also holes in your memory, holes in what you wrote."

"That happens to everyone; attention wanes and memory is affected; no one remembers every minute detail about their life," I argued.

"Yes, but you do and the fact that you slip into and out of a daze then find yourself somewhere else is cause for alarm, or at least cause for a closer look. During these blackouts, your other personalities were active, one at a time. Sometimes, even after you went into your bed to sleep at night, Darby or Jack was active, leaving the bedroom and living their separate lives."

"That's why I woke up in the morning tired so often," I joked.

"That's right," he said, not laughing. "I even think there have been times when you've been in the shower, switched to someone else, left your apartment, then returned, went back into the shower, and went on with your day."

I did not respond to his assertion because I was not yet ready to make it that real.

Then he added, "And the weekends. For the weekend you wrote about, you were in The Hamptons, but you also said you rarely remembered the weekends and what you did because you mostly just sat around the office reading and sleeping? Don't you find that strange?"

"I suppose," I muttered, agreeing because I had no real rebuttal. Then I thought for a while as Bill watched me, sitting silently.

"Who am I?" I finally asked with sincerity, then felt like every clichéd patient I had ever had. "Wow, never thought I would ask you that question," I added.

"You are the real you. Nick, that is. You were the first, you have the richest life with the richest history. At least that's my assumption from what I've seen so far."

"How can you be certain that I was the first?" I asked.

"I am quite certain. You have memories that go back far longer than the other personalities. I do not think Nick is just another personality like Darby and Jack. I believe you are the beginning, you are the first."

" 'To thine own self be true...' " I muttered.

"Hamlet," he declared before explaining his method further. "For this one-week period of your writing about the week leading up to this situation, I allowed you to believe that the world you had created was indeed the reality; that is, I allowed you to think that you were in prison. I never said the words or even agreed with your own assertions about being prosecuted for some unknown reason and never contradicted this story about me working with the lawyers. I merely allowed you to freely create the environment and elaborate on its details. You needed to have that tacit reinforcement about your imagined situation. The reinforcement in this case was that I did not dispute your fabricated legal troubles and prison environment."

Feeling unsure of the validity of my existence, I asked Bill, "Is that what you said to Darby and Jack? Told them each they were the primary personality? That you don't think they're just a personality created by the real person? Or did you inform them that you had been playing into their neuroses by not denying their imagined environment, even though, in the end, they were not real?"

"Neither Darby nor Jack imagined their environment to be anything different than it was," Bill clarified. "They are not the ones with the neuroses. They knew where they were and why. It was you who mentally created a reality that was consistent with what you believed to be the appropriate situation for your life; the only thing that made sense to you, prison for a crime you didn't commit."

"You didn't answer my question," I informed Bill. "Did you lie to them and tell each that they were the primary personality and that Nick was merely one of their many alternate personalities? Or did you not tell them about me at all? What did you tell them?" I paused and thought deeply for a moment before continuing. "What I'm getting at is if you're playing the same game right now as the one you just described. Are you allowing me to think that I am the primary personality and that this environment of The Institute's psych ward is the reality when the real world situation is different in some way? Am I just someone else's alternative personality that they manifested and now you are just pacifying me, Nick, so your experiment can progress? You can understand why I would take everything you say, everything you allow me to believe, with a grain of salt."

He spent some time blinking and thinking before smiling and saying, "I guess you won't ever really know for sure."

I acknowledged with a frown. "How did you break it to them? Did they take it badly?" I asked.

Again, Bill spent some time thinking before responding. "Hypothetically, if I were to tell you that you were not the primary personality, would you react badly?"

I did not need to think before responding. "If you told me that my entire existence is completely made up, definitively derived from a neurosis, literally a figment of someone else's imagination... Yes. I think I would take that badly."

Bill made a face and said, "Good to know, but we'll explore that later."

"What does that mean?" I asked.

"We'll get into it later," was all he offered in response.

I decided not to push on the topic because I was beginning to become afraid of what Bill could be hiding from me. It may have been nothing or it may have meant the literal absence of my own existence in the real world.

Not wanting to think about the possibilities, my mind moved to a contrary thought from earlier. "What you said before about the personalities makes sense, but, if we all, my personalities, think separately and behave separately and have separate lives, aren't we all then just as equally and validly human? *Cogito ergo sum?* No?"

"Yes... 'I think therefore I am...'" Bill translated aloud to prove he too had an impressive body of knowledge at his mental disposal. "I suppose one could take that stance, but one could also argue that, because you are one physical person, there is only one true personality. The rest are not real. For each one person, there is one brain and one mind, and thus one personality within."

"That is what science would tell us," I responded. "But you're assuming that scientific assumption is correct. Also, that scientific assumption contradicts your theory about the brain and mind and personalities. It pains me to agree with *your* theory, but, because there is more than one personality in my case, science is wrong, very wrong, and your theory is thus more likely to be correct."

"Duly noted," he said, both conceding and agreeing at the same time; the beauty of contradicting one's self in conversation.

I found the strength to smile, but felt it quickly fade into nothingness. "There's one thing you're missing though," I began. "The most important thing you need for a comprehensive diagnosis."

"What's that?" Bill asked.

"To commit someone and diagnose them with a disorder such as Schizophrenia and, I'm assuming, Dissociative Identity Disorder, the individual needs to be incapable of functioning in society. I've functioned for my entire life. In fact, according to you, my disorders help me function. You can't hold me here, Bill."

"I'm not holding you here, Nick. You're here voluntarily."

His words echoed in my head as I searched my memory to confirm his assertion. Nothing.

"You brought yourself in; well, actually, it was Darby. He said he was having serious issues with stress and his memory was fuzzy so he wanted to talk to a psychologist. It was just luck that he happened to walk into this hospital and luck that I happened to walk in when he was sitting in the waiting room. I approached and he didn't recognize me at all. Then I started to talk to him, or tried to talk to Nick, and I started to realize something was very wrong. He agreed to stay so I got him a room and opened a file. That file grew quite quickly. Now it includes the three of you, Jack too. This was the Sunday that ended abruptly for you, when you regained consciousness in 'a small windowless cell.'"

I stared off and thought, lengthening the moment of silence. "You know, I almost just asked you, 'Why me?' " I said.

He laughed. "I'm sure you could come up with some theories. Childhood trauma possibly? Your father was an alcoholic and—"

"I don't want to relive my childhood," I interrupted him. "Give me some time before we go into all that."

"Fair enough, but do consider the possibility of this coming from a combination of genetics and the environment. Maybe your father drank so heavily to escape from his psychological issues and his harsh treatment of you pushed your inherited genotype of being at risk for psychological issues into the phenotype of reality."

"Thanks for completely disregarding my request…" I muttered.

"Sorry about that, I'm just really glad I have you. This is a huge step we're going through. I didn't think we'd get here for months, if not years." Bill's excitement was clearly affecting his behavior, pulling him from his training.

"So you interviewed my neighbors. You didn't tell them anything, did you?"

"No, just that I was a friend and I needed some information. I showed them our college yearbook and some pictures I took a couple weeks ago with the two of us. Well, of Darby and me anyway. Also Jack signed your name on a release form asking that they provide some information. I figured it wouldn't be a big deal for him to forge your name, for obvious reasons."

"Very ethical," I told Bill.

He laughed. "I also used the same letter for the manager and the waitresses at the restaurant you went to every weekday for drinks."

"Oh, yes. I hadn't considered that aspect of it. How did that go?"

"It's funny. Part of me expected them to recognize me when I walked in," he joked.

"Did they?"

"Nope, apparently you're the crazy one!"

I could not help but laugh at his casual attitude despite the situation. Bill almost reminded me of myself, but the thought confused me so I put it out of my mind.

He continued. "They said you spend an hour there in the middle of every weekday and have done so since the current owner started. He bought the place from the previous owner who has since passed away so I only have confirmation for the past two and a half years. They said you always ordered twice as many beers as you drank. And that you talked to yourself and would start laughing for no reason. They also mentioned that you only paid every other day, but they were happy to run a tab because you always paid it off. Everything was consistent with what you wrote."

"And they tolerated a lunatic like that? Talking to myself and laughing wildly at random?" I questioned.

"They never had any problems with you; you were a consistent paying customer who never bothered anybody. You sat alone at the bar away from the other tables and very rarely engaged anybody except the bartender. Oh, and the new bartender said that she was briefed by her boss about you."

"Only in New York City…" I said proudly. Then, still slightly skeptical, an inconsistency came to the front of my mind. "Wait a second here… if you weren't real, if Bill wasn't real, how did he order drinks? How did he attempt to save the man on that Wednesday? How did he go into and out of the bar, opening and closing the door."

"Well, think back. Think about what you know about hallucinations. You hallucinated *Bill* drinking next to you. The drinks may have been real, put there by the very real bartender, but *Bill's* drinking was hallucinated. Also, from what I could determine from your writing, *Bill* never touched the door to enter or exit. And he never talked directly to anyone but, when he did, he was completely ignored and never acknowledged."

I pondered for a moment then responded, debunking his defense. "You spoke to that girl on Tuesday when you were trying to get her number."

"Not me," he corrected. "You mean *Bill,* and yes. That's right. She was also a hallucination. You seem to have one main hallucination, *Bill,* but sometimes you hallucinated others to interact with him. That, however, appeared to occur only on very rare occasions."

"You can't just all of a sudden tell me that whatever inconsistency that there is in the story happens to be explained away as a hallucination to convince me that this all makes sense. That's a little pathetic," I joked about his explanations. "I think you can do better than that. Come on."

"I assure you that this is the situation," Bill responded, laughing. "Don't you remember that the woman 'appeared as if by magic'? I think those are the words you used."

I thought back in time. "Good point." Then I leaned back and crossed my consciously unshackled arms and thought for a moment before beginning to laugh.

"What's so funny?" Bill asked.

"You're Mr. Snuffleupagus!" I said.

"What?"

"Snuffleupagus… the *Sesame Street* character…" I informed him.

"I don't know what you're talking about," he confessed.

"Really? The character who looks like a wooly mammoth without the tusks or the big ears… How can you not know this? You tried referencing *Sesame Street* last time we met. Now I'm referencing it."

"I know *Sesame Street*. I just don't follow your train of thought," Bill said.

"You really don't know what I'm referring to?" I asked.

"No. Please explain."

I stretched my face in disbelief before responding. "Aloysius Snuffleupagus was Big Bird's friend on *Sesame Street*. Mr. Snuffleupagus, or Snuffy, as he was commonly referred to, would show up and spend time with Big Bird when nobody else was around then he would disappear when another character came into frame. It frustrated Big Bird because nobody believed that Snuffleupagus existed much less lived on Sesame Street. Then the other characters would get angry at Big Bird when Big Bird blamed things on Snuffleupagus even though Snuffy actually was the one at fault, he was always breaking something or knocking something over.

"In the storyline, it remained ambiguous if Snuffleupagus was real or imaginary until the writers decided to have the other characters meet him. It's said that the *Sesame Street* writers decided to change course with Snuffleupagus because they felt that they were giving the wrong message to children. A message that, if something unbelievable happens, but adults don't see it for themselves, then the adults won't believe it happened when the child tells them about it. The writers' main concern was children not coming forward with experiences of abuse because of fears of getting in trouble for making something up, just like Big Bird getting into trouble for telling the adults about what Snuffleupagus did. The writers didn't want to send the wrong message so they had Snuffy meet the rest of the cast in an episode.

"Anyway, that's why I called you Snuffleupagus."

Bill thought for a while before saying, "I still don't fully understand why you called me Snuffleupagus."

"Forget it…"

There was a short silence during which I thought deeper about everything. Then Bill spoke, pulling me from my mind. "A couple more things," he said, having pulled a small notepad from the brown box beneath his chair.

He then threw the notebook at me, right at my face. I caught it with my left hand.

"What are you doing?" I shouted, quietly proud of my cat-like reflexes.

"Do you find it strange that you caught that with your left hand?"

"No. You threw it at me; I caught it," I proclaimed proudly.

"Well, are you a lefty or a righty?" Bill asked.

"I suppose I use both hands," I said slowly, wondering what he was going to say next. "You knew that."

"Unlike non-schizophrenics, almost all schizophrenics show no preference of one hand over the other. The theory is that cerebral lateralization is decreased in those who suffer from Schizophrenia and cerebral lateralization is what leads to handedness. I noticed that, in your writing, you did not note using either hand with more frequency than the other."

"Well, that sounds scientifically sound," I said sarcastically.

Ignoring my comment, Bill added, "Additionally, you made up a few words in your writing. That is also a symptom of Schizophrenia."

"Neologisms?" I questioned. "We're smart people! *We* are allowed to do that!"

There was a short pause during which the two of us looked at one another, pondering the validity of my point. We then laughed pompously for an indulgent moment.

"What about the birds?" he asked, still with a bit of a chuckle in his tone.

"What about them?"

"I thought it was interesting that you heard birds chirping pretty frequently and saw birds just about everywhere you went."

"So?" I responded. "There are birds all over the city. What of it?"

"Well, do you think that maybe you were getting messages from the birds? They were telling you what to do perhaps?"

I shook my head at him. "You're really going out on a limb with this one. Dial it back, old buddy. "

"Too far; I got it. A little too much on that one," he admitted.

"Oh, here's a question," I began. "How do I know you're real? Couldn't you just be a hallucination?"

Bill leaned over the table and pinched my left arm between his right index finger and thumb.

"Ow," I said in a monotone. "That was mildly uncomfortable. Not as strong as you once were, eh?" I said, joking.

"Well, now you know I'm real."

"That could just be a physical hallucination. You know as well as I do that pinching someone isn't a foolproof way to determine if you are a hallucination or not."

"Oh really? Please enlighten me," Bill said.

I took some time to try to detect sarcasm, but determined there to be none. "People usually say 'pinch me so I know it's real' but that only works for people who do not frequently hallucinate. For them, hallucinations are like watching a movie or listening to music. Nothing approaches them or interacts with them and the hallucination can't be felt. That's why feeling a pinch would prove that it was not a hallucination and thus real. But for someone who hallucinates because of a psychological disorder, pinching doesn't prove anything. Those people have psychotic hallucinations in which the hallucination can approach them, talk to them, and it can even be tactile, which means their hallucinations can pinch them and it will indeed hurt."

"Yes," Bill agreed. "And it's quite interesting to hook someone to the brain scanner who is afflicted with one of these hallucination-inducing psychological disorders while they are having a hallucination of a person. Because it incorporates all the senses, we see specific activity in specialized lobes and regions of the brain. For example, hyperactivity in the fusiform gyrus, the area that helps you recognize faces, is correlated with hallucinating faces or hallucinating people."

"But it works the same way if someone were to concentrate and imagine a face; same activation, right? Or even if someone thinks they see a face when it is not actually there, pareidolia. That's not a hallucination, just perception. I'd like to see if you can determine the difference on the brain scanner."

"Does this mean you'll stay and let us study you?" Bill asked.

I thought for a moment before extending my left hand. "I don't see why not. Plus I'm sure you had one of my other personalities forge my name on the paperwork anyway. And maybe I can teach you a thing or two about neuroscience."

Bill extended his left hand to shake mine. "Challenge accepted," he said as he stood up.

"So you're the Principal Investigator?" I asked as I handed his small pad back to him.

He nodded. "I am indeed the Principal Investigator on this one. And I think this will be very meaningful work."

I smiled and said, "This is what you've always wanted, isn't it? What you've always dreamed of for yourself? I suppose this would be your Utopia…"

"I suppose it is," he responded.

"You're welcome," I said, still smiling.

He nodded and smiled back.

Moving Forward

"So what now?" I asked. "Where do I go from here?"

"You're a resident of the ward. You have your own room, TV, Internet. You can go take in a show or take a walk in the park as long as you are accompanied by an intern or someone to monitor you. And everything is on us. You won't have to pay for anything."

"What about my apartment, all my belongings?" I asked, suddenly remembering my previous reality.

"Since you haven't been paying rent, you lost the apartment and your office. And you haven't been making the payments on the office furniture either so that's gone. You've only been in here for six weeks, but they move pretty quickly. And all you had were some pictures, an unused coffee maker, and the items on your desk. All are in your room. In fact, you were using your office computer to write."

"Is that right?" I asked. "Jesus… I haven't been taking my calls on a banana, have I?"

Bill laughed. "Amazing, isn't it? How our perception can make our reality what we need it to be," he responded. "Also, Julie had movers come and take everything out of the apartment; couch, television, bed. She gave it all to charity apparently. All that was left was one box in the basement storage and your clothes, which are also in your room here. I sent an intern to get everything from your office and your apartment before your items were disposed of."

"Oh. Well, sounds like everything is taken care of then. Starting a new beginning here," I said with an undertone of sadness.

"Yes!" Bill exclaimed. "You can be like the phoenix; when it's ready to die it burns up and then it is reborn from its ashes."

"This isn't a Greek play, it's my life..." I informed him.

"I'm just joking around."

Bill's jokes had a constant presence during all of our meetings despite my repeated pleas to leave them at the door. For too long he was holding over me his position as, earlier, not imprisoned and, now, not a resident of the ward. I felt that it was time to show him that maybe he did not have as much control as he believed he did.

I smiled and said, "You know, this could all be made up. I could be just like every other psychopath who just grew bored and decided to take advantage of some people for my own gain, kicks and giggles deceiving the doctors. Are you ready to put your professional life on the line for that?"

"And what do you gain by destroying your life?" Bill asked, rather rudely.

"I gain the luxury of having no responsibilities. Everything is provided for me here. Food, drink, recreation, entertainment, a comfortable bed. I can see plays and operas, visit museums and take walks in the park. I can even go on vacations probably anywhere I want. It's all paid for with grant money."

"Well, that would have been a gross miscalculation of the cost to benefit ratio; ruining all you've created for yourself in one fell swoop."

"Would it?" I asked, forcing him to think, truly think about it. "And doesn't it seem like quite the coincidence that I stumbled into the best funded research facility in the world? The one at which my old college buddy happens to work?"

Bill winced slightly, the look of shock taking a bit of color from his face as he considered the possibility.

"Carl Sagan," I said. "Do you know who he is?"

"Uh, yes. I think I do…" Bill stammered, growing discomfort mixed with anger and shame, the feelings one experiences when they realize they have been manipulated by a con man.

"He was an astronomer, a great scientist," I explained. "He once said something relevant to this. He said, 'If you wish to make an apple pie from scratch, you must first invent the universe.' "

Bill's long stare was loosening all the muscles in his face as his jaw, cheeks, forehead, and chin slowly succumbed to gravity.

"How about George Orwell," I offered. " 'To see what is in front of one's nose needs a constant struggle.' Has there been much of a struggle on your end or have things just fallen right into your lap?"

Bill looked frozen except for the deteriorating expression on his face.

I continued. "I think Oscar Wilde summed it up perfectly. 'The pure and simple truth is rarely pure and never simple.' "

A look of humiliation was dawning as he shuffled nervously in his seat, so I continued to push. "Is there really nothing that happened during this week that led you to believe that it wasn't real? A certain wonderful Wizard, maybe? A Wonderland, possibly that of Alice? Genesis in the days' beginnings? Sunday… Exodus' Book? Red Balloons? The abundant amounts of alliterative amalgamation?"

Bill's shocked sounding slightly shaky struggling stammer grasped at the only reality that would suggest my innocence. "Nick? Is that you? Are you still with me?"

294

His voice was wavering, worried but hoping that he lost me, that I had slipped into some other personality and that the more plausible explanation was not the reality, that I was no different from any other manipulating psychopath.

"Darby?" Bill asked, venturing a guess.

I laughed heartily to encourage the color to return to his face. "No. It's still me, Nick. Just messing around with you."

Bill, still tense and looking rather uncomfortable, exhaled in relief. "You had me going there for a moment, buddy," he confessed. "You know, disorganized speech is another sign of Schizophrenia?" He laughed, mostly out of relief.

"Don't worry, *friend*. I'm not a psychopath. As we learned in school, the psychopaths are easy to spot for professionals with the training to do so. It's never enough for them to plan meticulously for years, execute a scheme with undying commitment, and then get away with it. All psychopaths, all geniuses, all masterminds always build into their plan a way to be caught, a fatal flaw, just to tickle them further. That one little thing, that bit of evidence that would implicate their guilt, expose their lies, it's right there staring everyone in the face, but no one sees it because their focus is somewhere else, misdirection. This is the slow, gradual, and consistent unloading of the burden of brilliance that plagues we who are intellectually endowed."

Bill, still assuming everything to be copasetic said, "Sounds like you have a little too much admiration for psychopaths, friend; calling them geniuses, masterminds, intellectually endowed?" Bill laughed. Then he continued to convince himself that it was real, that it was all real. "And the speed with which you wrote speaks to the authenticity. Not even the best of fiction writers, the most prolific fiction writers, could accomplish such a feat in just a week. You were clearly writing straight from memory."

I smiled large, raised my left hand, and told him, "It's the truth; I swear it." I then leaned in and whispered, "Even if it didn't happen."

The inquisitive smile on Bill's face was met with more confusion when I told him, "The difference between fiction and real life is that fiction has to be realistic, has to make sense. Real life can be more unrealistic than you can imagine."

Confusion was beginning to furrow Bill's brow beyond recognition, so again I brought laughter back into the equation with my own genuine variety which was quickly followed by his.

"I think we got a good amount done today, Nick, old friend."

"So, what will you have me do? What's my homework for tomorrow?" I asked, as if it was my first session with a new psychologist, which it basically was.

"Keep writing," he insisted.

"What do you mean 'keep writing'? I'm done. What else is there to write about?"

"Well, I want to keep you around for a while so we can continue to work on things. Thinking and writing about yourself ensures that you'll be here tomorrow."

"Sounds like a good logical idea," I said smiling. "What should I write about?"

"About this. Now," he answered, pointing around the room.

"This? Our conversation right now?" I asked.

"Yes. I think it will be therapeutic." Bill's words felt more condescending than he had intended. Then he added, "Oh, and you can start with a quote. 'The test of a first rate intelligence is the ability to hold two opposed ideas in the mind at the same time, and still retain the ability to function.' It's F. Scott Fitzgerald." Those words felt even more condescending.

I shook my head at his quotation suggestion. "Can I at least write in the present tense now? It's so much easier and gives the story a sense of urgency; makes it more fun, more interesting."

"That will just make things confusing," he replied. "Just keep it how you've been writing."

I grunted in defiance before another thought came to my mind. "Can I read Darby's and Jack's reports or is there some kind of doctor-patient confidentiality with that? And whose name is on the front of this report? And theirs? I assume my name would be on mine, but what about theirs?"

Bill looked away for a moment in thought before responding. "I'll have to consider and discuss the legitimacy of the doctor-patient confidentiality in this specific situation with a few colleagues before responding. And, as for the name on the front, what do you think?"

I answered quickly. "It's always bothered me that a large portion of famous writers, celebrities who author books, even musicians who claim to write their own lyrics and music, actually have ghostwriters do it for them. I think it's despicable and disingenuous; passing off someone else's work as their own, lying to all their readers, followers, and fans. This is a pretty similar situation, isn't it?"

"No, I don't think it is," Bill interjected, but I would not allow him additional words of defiance.

"I'm basically Darby's and Jack's ghostwriter since I'm the real person; I technically wrote their reports, my brain did the mental work and my body did the physical. I think my name should go on all of them. The one real person out of my personalities, however many they might be, should have his name in the byline."

Bill smiled a seemingly sly smile before saying, "I can promise you that I will make sure that the one real and actual person out of the many personalities in your brain and controlling your body has their name in the byline."

"Oh, okay," I responded, rather surprised that Bill complied so quickly after initially disagreeing with my analogy. We both nodded, Bill smiling the same sly smile as before.

Bill prophesied, "I think this will lead somewhere great for the field. We're really going to do great things with this."

I thought about his intentions and wondered if I would benefit in any way before quoting Shakespeare. " 'Be not so long to speak; I long to die, If what thou speak'st speak not of remedy.' "

Bill responded without much thought into the relevant meaning. "If you're asking about a cure, well, we don't know yet. Maybe one day, but the only way to find it is to keep you here and monitor you. There is likely some light at the end of the tunnel, Nick."

"As encouraging as that sounds, that light at the end of the tunnel you just mentioned could easily be that of a train speeding toward me," I responded.

"You just said yourself, this place has a lot to offer a lucid well educated cultured man like yourself. You're basically retiring early in an all-expenses paid resort in New York City and you're contributing to your field in the process. 'Be able to retire early, but choose not to.' Those were your words, weren't they? That's what you wanted for yourself and that's basically what you will be doing. "

I pondered his words, my words. "How about this for a quotation?" I began. " 'I have nothing to fear; and here my story ends. My troubles are all over, and I am at home.' "

Bill smiled, knowing that this was my way of agreeing with it, all of it, simply everything. "*Black Beauty* by Anna Sewell," he then felt it necessary to add.

I rolled my eyes and then, mind working, furrowed my brow and asked, "Oh, whatever happened to my car and the insurance? Is it still at Julie's parents'?"

"Insurance wouldn't cover it and it was totaled. And, because you stopped making payments on your car and every other loan you had, it's all gone and your credit is destroyed. But you won't need a good credit score here. And what does any of that stuff matter anyway?"

"I suppose you're right," I responded. "Expensive car, office overlooking the park. People spend their lives craving designer suits and shoes, diamonds in their jewelry and watches. The latest and greatest. All of that doesn't mean anything in here."

"What did any of it really mean out there either?" Bill asked. "Where did it get you? Where does it ever get anyone?"

"Good question. When you're suddenly forced to look at your life and the traps of society that you've somehow fallen into, it makes you think about why you spent so much of your time and energy on such superficial things."

Then Bill, likely feeling a little preachy, responded smiling, "Yes, but you have to admit, some of those things are pretty darn enjoyable."

"Can't disagree with that," I said, shaking my head, but agreeing fully.

I followed Bill as he began to walk toward the door before he stopped and said, "Oh, and I had some short notes about two of your patients."

"Didn't think you could tell me anything about them. You know, doctor-patient confidentiality," I said.

"Well, they were your patients," he responded.

"Good point," I commended before suddenly feeling the same disgust I felt while writing. "I don't even know if I want to hear anything about my patients. I never actually looked back at a week in my life before, but, now that have, I see that I don't really respect psychology, therapy as a profession. That's part of the reason I was so unhappy in life. It seems like kind of a waste of time, the whole thing. How much do we really help anyone?" I trailed off, shaking my head out of disgust.

"Don't be confused, Nick," Bill said, sounding somewhat insulted, shaking his head as well. "You do not, by any measure, represent us all. This is your perspective, your experience, one man, and that's fine, but to judge the entire profession based on this week in your life is foolish, outlandish. Psychology or therapy as a profession is extremely helpful to those in need. We might not be curing cancer, as they say, but we are helping people live their lives fuller and happier and many lives have been saved because of our services."

I stopped Bill's inevitably lengthy speech about the merits of psychology with my right hand held to head level. "I was just venting a bit of pent up frustration. I don't actually think psychology is useless. Sorry to offend. Now, please, tell me about my patients."

"They're all doing fine," he said, smoothing his white coat to reassert his love for the profession. "There really is not much to tell.

They've all adjusted well to the change in psychologist. But my question is about Harry."

"Yes, good man, Harry," I said. "Oh, he was diagnosed with Schizophrenia too. No wonder he trusted me."

"I was never able to find him. He may have been one of your hallucinations. I can't be sure yet."

"Oh, is that so?" I asked, but at that point nothing Bill could say would shock or even faze me.

"There is another possibility," Bill began. His voice was rather slower than before. "Maybe we can consider that Harry was one of your personalities."

I did not allow for a second of silence to pass before responding, challenging with a quick paced retort. "You were pretty specific before about how the personalities can't interact with one another. Remember? The DID doll's head rotating?"

"That does seem to be the case for the most part," Bill said, again slowly. "The personalities that we've discussed *so far* don't communicate or have knowledge of the others, but I still think it's worth considering the possibility that you may potentially have additional personalities with whom you, Nick, may have regularly interacted."

Bill paused for a moment of thought before continuing. "You could have assumed he was your patient so you conducted regular sessions with him, but he may also have been one of your personalities. This is a bit complicated because you would have hallucinated him because he wasn't actually there, but the difference between this and your other hallucinations is that you would have also acted out his side of the conversation; you would have actually *been* him and your body would have continued on in his life sometimes. So it's similar to Darby and Jack, but a little different; it's like if Darby or Jack was one of your patients."

As Bill allowed his explanation to linger, I considered my immediate botheration with the logistics of his hypothesis, but quickly began to focus on Bill's incessant altering of his definitions of the disorders and my situation. However, at that point, drained of all that I believed to be me, I started to seriously consider the merits of arguing, but then decided to give him the benefit of the doubt and leave it for another time. After all, he was walking on untouched ground so it was understandable for hypotheses to adjust as more information became available.

Mentally defeated, I told him dryly, "I'll keep that thought in mind while I attempt to come to grips with this constantly changing reality that I'm forced to accept as my life."

He smiled and nodded at my compliance. "Don't think too much about Harry. The concept is just a general thought that I want you to have in your head for a future conversation." He spoke with a sly knowing tone that I mostly ignored after a brief consideration of *if not Harry, which of my patients could you want me to apply this hypothesis to?* But I said nothing.

"And the second thing I wanted to let you know about one of your patients..." Bill trailed off dramatically.

"Yes, go ahead."

"Kristin, she appears to, as you noted last week, fall into a strong erotic transference; she projects her romantic emotions about others onto the therapist..." Bill trailed off again.

"Okay."

Bill then spoke slowly, deliberately, but paused with discomfort at his own words. "What I am saying is that anything you may have felt for her, the emotions you wrote about, those feelings were likely reverse transference; the response within the therapist to what she was feeling toward you which was itself not real... She showed attraction toward you because she associated you with the strong emotions she felt while speaking to you about other people in her life. What you felt in response to that... What I'm trying to say is that your emotions for Kristin weren't real, Nick. I'm sorry."

"I know what reverse transference is, Bill," I said shortly, stiffly.

"Sorry. It's something that we should maybe talk about one of these days," he said, almost putting a hand on my shoulder, then pulling it back to his side.

"What are you? My psychologist?" I asked jokingly.

"I guess I am."

Then I conceded, "Well, I suppose it is quite easy, even for a man educated to the highest degree in his field, to falter and let emotions and his own desires, his own dreams, mentally distort the truth and thus allow clear and obvious fiction to seamlessly pass through the filter of doubt and emerge as unquestioned fact."

"In your defense," Bill told me, "she is powerfully and beautifully emotional."

"Aren't we all?" I proclaimed rhetorically. Then I inquired, "What would you say is the difference between misperception and perception?"

Bill thought for a moment before saying, "I guess there isn't technically any difference."

"Exactly," I responded, smiling.

"I don't follow the connection."

"Oh, I'm just talking," I said quietly.

Bill thought for another few seconds before saying, "We've done so well today, I'm wondering if I should push to the next step." He thought silently again for a dozen seconds before asking, "Maybe we can talk about your stomach?"

"What do you mean?"

Bill continued. "You mentioned that you had been vomiting for two days one week before the week in focus; bad sushi, if I recall correctly. I don't want to shift you away, but start to think about how vomiting may potentially be a response not to bad sushi but to ingesting a large quantity of pain medication."

"What? Like Courtland?" I asked, surprised. "Are you saying he didn't die? But I saw him there…"

Bill interrupted my audible thought process. "Yes, when you found him, there on the floor in his apartment, wasn't that the same time that you were sick with an ailment that could be explained by the same action that he allegedly took himself, overdosing on pain medication? You said that in college he had wanted to become a psychologist, didn't you?"

"Let's get into it next time," I told him, not wanting to rehash difficult memories as I was still attempting to understand my current problems.

Bill smiled. "Next time," he said before leaving the room.

I followed not far behind him as he exited. The guard standing there was half the size I had perceived him to be when I had entered. I shook his right hand with my own and he smiled at Bill, then at me. It was clear that he was nothing more than a college-aged intern.

As we moved down the hall, Julie came to my mind.

"What became of Julie? How is she doing?"

"Oh, she's doing fine. Has a place in the West Village. Still working at the gallery. She's happy."

"Good to hear," I responded, then repeated those three words, surprised that I actually meant them: "Good to hear."

"There's something I should probably mention about Julie," Bill began, slowing his pace as we moved down the long hall of The Institute.

"If you're going to tell me that she was a hallucination, please let's just leave that until next time. I can't take that kind of news right now."

"No no." Bill laughed. "Julie, she told me some things when I met with her for an interview a few weeks ago. As I mentioned before, she had seen you, or Darby rather, going into other people's apartments and she had seen Jack going into Alicia's apartment. Rightfully so, at some point Julie began to suspect that you were having several affairs so she began to follow you when you left the Brownstone.

"Not only did she follow you to the office, but she waited outside and, come noon, she followed you to the bar. She would see you there, drinking alone in the middle of every weekday. And, given your genealogical predisposition, she thought you may have been a closeted alcoholic and that scared her, terrified her.

"Her family had been affected negatively by alcoholism with her Uncle Tommy and Cousin Kathy and most importantly Edward, not to mention a few more. She dreaded what was to come, the future with you if you continued or increased your drinking."

"But I'm not a big drinker," I argued. "I hardly ever drink. It was just at the bar with..." I trailed off.

"That's right. All she could see, all anyone could see was you drinking alone every day at noon in a bar so it's a fair assumption that you were a closeted alcoholic. When you went to that cocktail party and Edward became incoherently inebriated and Elisabeth was trying to take care of him, Julie felt that she was looking directly at your collective future. It was part of why she was certain to keep the familial connection between Edward and her father from you. Her thought process wasn't necessarily logical, but she felt that maybe you would drink more and stop working; really she was afraid of the analogy somehow becoming the reality.

"Julie was already paying for everything for you because you couldn't make the payments on your loans and rent from just your income and the two of you were already living in a building that her family owned, albeit in more modest circumstances. For Julie, it was all too similar to Edward and Elisabeth. She was just waiting for the day you got drunk and then crashed your car into someone. She even thought about planning some kind of intervention, but she simply did not know how to precede, who to include, or even how it would go, maybe backfiring and pushing you into a full blown alcoholic binge."

"Why are you telling me all of this, Bill?" I asked, phoenix-like feelings almost completely extinguished.

"I just think it's important for you to know what Julie was going through, what was happening in her head. I want you to be able to see the full picture."

I thought for a few seconds and then a few more. "Fair enough," I said to him. "Fair enough."

When we reached the end of the hall, Bill looked at me and realized that I had no direction.

"I have a bunch of things I have to get done," he began, "and I want to finish up early today so I can get home and get some sleep.

I stayed up most of last night reading. Looks like you'll have to decide what you're going to do for the rest of the day. You've been locking yourself in your room all day for the past two weeks because you thought it was a prison. Now you have some freedom. And your room, it's a great room. Since you're not a danger to yourself or others, I was able to give you the best one we have, with a separate bedroom and living room, private kitchenette and bathroom, even some of the only windows around here that open wide without a bundle of bars blocking the view."

"Bill, everyone is potentially a danger to themselves and others."

Bill merely laughed off my assertion, not ready to accept it as fact.

I thought for a moment and smiled. "New beginning, I suppose that holds some potential."

"You know what Shakespeare said about potential?" Bill asked, waiting for me to fill in the quote.

"What's that?" I said, allowing him the chance to flex his literary muscle.

" 'We know what we are, but know not what we may be.' " Bill's posture and smile showed how proud he was that he could recall *Hamlet* at will.

"I suppose that's true," I agreed.

"Any idea of what you'll do for the remainder of the day?" he asked.

"Oh, well. Maybe I'll take a walk," I said, unable to think of anything else.

"To where?"

"You know, Bill," I began. "It is possible for there to be a journey with no destination."

He smiled and waved his way away.

"Excuse me while I disappear," I whispered after he had gone.

———

In the Moment

I find my way back to my room, then sit up straight on the soft couch. The room is remarkably similar to the apartment that Julie and I shared two weeks earlier, or six, same layout. It also bears a passing resemblance to my office, despite the floor plan dissimilarities. Even the bar is brought to mind as I allow my eyes to wander around the room.

After removing my shoes, left before right, and placing them neatly together on the floor, I consider checking my e-mail on my computer which sits atop the desk, but I realize that there would be none.

I walk into my bedroom and open the closet. It is filled with my clothes from the apartment. I open the bureau, also filled with my belongings.

"Who touched my underwear?" I ask aloud.

I think about ordering food from a restaurant then consider the possibility of just walking to a restaurant, to any restaurant, and eating comfortably, freely, slowly, alone. To not have to be somewhere… To not have anywhere to be… To not have anything to do…

I think about going to a museum after the restaurant or doing any one of the countless things the city offers, but that I have always been too busy or bogged down to do before this moment, this moment right now.

I lean back on the couch and look out the window, admiring the city for a moment of reflection. A digital clock on the wall reads 1:17 p.m. I smile at its irrelevance.

"What does the time matter anymore?" I ask aloud, then laugh. I realize I do not even need a phone.

I stand and walk into my private bathroom to wash my hands of all that's past, all. Water held in my now clean hands, cupped, finds its way to my face as I bend to lower my head. I see myself in the mirror, literally in a moment of reflection, and laugh.

"What does this matter anymore either?" I again ask aloud, then laugh again. "What does anything matter? What is left?"

There I stand, losing track of time, of myself. I stare at the stranger staring back. We smile. We nod. We laugh as we move back toward the window, again admiring the city.

Courtland is in the reflection, but he was there all along, something I tried to get him to see. I know what Bill is getting at, what he wants *me* to see and, I suppose, I knew it all along, just never wanted to accept the reality that *my* reality may not be *the* reality.

Bill plays along with this whole thing for my sake, for Nick's sake, for Darby's sake, for Jack's sake, and, I suppose, for Courtland's sake. But what is real and what is not? Who is real and who is not? None and all, I suppose, or maybe all and none.

His presence, Courtland's presence, brings me back to my office, Nick's office, standing by the windows, looking through him, through me. Why, when people are on a floor above the third, do they have the overwhelming desire to drop or throw something?

Just as I always have when I am in this position, I wonder what the world beyond is like, how the journey is before the destination is reached. Frightening? Or freeing? The glorious wind flowing through my clothes, between my fingers, by my ears, through my hair.

Content. I smile.